COMANCHE MOON FALLING

Book 2 of the Lone Star Reloaded Series

A tale of alternative history

By Drew McGunn

Newsletter Sign Up/Website address:
https://drewmcgunn.wixsite.com/website
V1
ISBN: 1983759317
ISBN-13: 978-1983759314

ACKNOWLEDGEMENT

Few books are written in a vacuum and this one is no exception. This would not have been possible without my wife's graceful acquiescence of time. There were many evenings after a long day at work, in which she patiently did anything else other than interrupting my long writing spells.

Also, to my parents, who indulged my passion for history. The visits to the Alamo as a kid, and the special trip to John Wayne's Alamo village, as a teenager, are things I've never forgotten, and believe me, I've forgotten more than a few things.

If my passion for history could ever be considered genetic, then I definitely inherited the gene. To my grandfather, whose passion for history was passed down to at least one of the grandkids. Thank you.

TABLE OF CONTENTS

The Story So Far

SSGT Will Travers couldn't have imagined how wrong a routine supply run could go, as he counted down the days until his National Guard unit would rotate back stateside. That is, until an explosion overturned his Humvee and propelled him through space and time.

When he woke, he was trapped in the body of William Barret Travis, with only a few weeks to go before his fateful death at the Alamo in 1836. With no way to return to the present, and with no desire to become a martyr for Texas liberty, Will could have fled. He had nearly two centuries of history he could exploit. Instead of fleeing or dying at the Alamo, he chose to do the impossible. He rallied every Texian volunteer between the Rio Grande and San Antonio, and met Santa Anna at the Rio Grande where he stopped the dictator with the help of David Crockett, Jim Bowie, James Fannin and seven hundred more patriots.

As Santa Anna brought up his reserves, Will sent most of his men north, to build new defensive positions on the Nueces River. He stayed behind with David Crockett, Juan Seguin and a handful of brave riflemen and gallant Tejano cavalry. They fought a delaying action, leading the might of Santa Anna's army into the jaws of the trap on the Nueces. The flower of Mexico died on the fields of South Texas, as Will led the Texian army to victory.

Victory over the Mexican dictator was only the first obstacle to overcome. Having won the war, Will was determined that he would win the peace. As a student of history, he knew that without a change in direction, Texas would implement a constitution that would trap thousands of slaves and freedmen in one of the most oppressive slave codes in the American South. Indians, like the Cherokee, who were trying to put the pieces of their society back together after President Jackson's genocidal Indian Removal Act, would be driven out of Texas. Thousands of Tejanos, who had lived in Texas for generations, would be forced from their homes, as men like Robert Potter and James Collinsworth strove to make Texas a welcome place for Anglos only.

Will allied himself with David Crockett and Sam Houston to thwart the worst of the pro-slavery faction, and passed a constitution that gave the Cherokee a path to citizenship, and allowed for freedmen to remain in the Republic and for slave owners to free their slaves. For a man of the 21st century, it seemed too little, but it was a start.

The constitutional convention was still in session when an assassin attempted to kill Will. He killed his assassin, and David Crockett used the shock waves sent through the convention to elevate him to the rank of general.

With a promise from David Crockett that the hard-won gains wouldn't be traded away, Will dives into transforming the army, but he has barely begun before the frontier erupts into violence as the Comanche ride out from the Comancheria, attacking Fort Parker on the edge of the Texian settlements.

Chapter 1

May 1836

Will Travers walked beneath scaffolding, where the construction on the Alamo's north wall continued. Since the victory over Santa Anna's army at the Nueces River earlier in the spring, the old mission turned fort had undergone several upgrades. A new, taller wall would replace part of the crumbling north wall, while a two-story barracks would complete its connection with the eastern wall.

Exiting the fort, Will saw two engineers talking to several Tejano laborers. Although too far away to hear, Green Jameson, a contract engineer with the army, gesticulated at a stack of adobe bricks, as he directed the laborers toward a section of the new wall.

Leaving the construction behind, the officer walking beside Will cleared his throat, "You know, General Travis, I'm glad you and your boys stopped Santa Anna down at the Nueces. I can't imagine you'd have been able to hold out here for more than a couple of weeks, if it had come to a siege."

It had taken time getting used to being called William Barret Travis, but Will was nothing if not a survivor. The last four months had proven that. He still wondered if it were a cosmic trick of fate, or the unseen hand of God, placing him and his memories in the body of William Barret Travis five weeks before the Alamo would have fallen. He shook his head at the thought, there was time enough later to get lost down that rabbit hole, and turned his attention to the officer at his side.

Lt. Colonel Albert Sidney Johnston had missed the battle at the Nueces, arriving in Texas the previous month. He had enlisted in the Texian army in San Antonio as soon as he arrived. When Will saw his name on the paymaster's roll, it practically leapt off the page. As a student of Texas history, he recognized that Johnston would have eventually risen to command the Texian army and later go on to command the Army of the Tennessee in the Civil War in a world which ceased to exist when Will's thoughts and mind were transferred into William B. Travis' body. As commander of the Texian army, Will immediately promoted the Kentucky transplant to the rank of Lt. Colonel. Which was how the two men came to be standing on the prairie, north of the Alamo, watching a company of infantry as they drilled.

"At West Point, we studied plenty of tactics, from Napoleon's command of the battlefield with his artillery, to Wellington's counter tactics, and even the tactics used by the red Indians on our frontier, but the use of marksmen tied to several reloaders wasn't something we considered," Johnston said.

Will chuckled, "It was inspirational, I have to admit. Congressman Crockett came up with the idea, and as events have proven, it was very effective."

They fell silent as they watched the infantry company. Some of the men wore gray militia jackets, while others wore blue US army jackets, while many more wore civilian clothing or buckskin hunting shirts. Despite the lack of uniformity, the men were deployed in a skirmish line, operating in teams of four. Will's eyes landed on the nearest team. The four men were advancing on a straw dummy two hundred yards away. The soldier in the lead stopped and fired his rifle. While he stopped to reload, the fourth man on the team moved ahead of the other three and took up the forward position, and fired at the target. The team continued advancing, moving the man at the rear to the front, always with at least one man with a loaded rifle.

Will noticed a thin smile crease Johnston's face while watching the drill. "It's not exactly orthodox."

Johnston shook his head in response, "No, but we're more likely to be fighting the Comanche than the Mexicans next and I wouldn't want to face them with an empty gun in my hand."

About to respond, Will had opened his mouth when, in the distance, he noticed a swirling dust cloud moving southward. He closed his mouth and watched the cloud materialize into a man on horseback, riding at a horse-killing speed toward the fort. The man, with long, graying hair flowing behind him, dressed in a tattered hunting jacket, saw the two officers standing outside of the scaffolding along the north wall. He raced his horse toward them. As the rider jerked the reins, his mount, heavily lathered from the brutal ride, slid to a stop. The rider cried out, "The Comanches! They've killed all the men and kidnapped the women and children!"

Will and the Lt. Colonel ran over to the horseman as he slid from his mount, standing unsteadily. He gasped, and said, "Water, please."

One of the soldiers who had been drilling handed over his canteen. The rider drank greedily as the water he didn't swallow ran down his brown hunting jacket. When he had slaked his thirst, he turned toward Will and said, "Sir, the Comanches, they have attacked Fort Parker, up on the Navasota River. They done killed John Parker and the rest of the men. They kidnapped a couple of our womenfolk and three of our children. Y'all are the army, so you gotta do something!" With that, he collapsed.

With the present drill disrupted by the rider's arrival, Will detailed several soldiers to carry the survivor to the hospital building within the fort. From there, he sent for several officers currently at the Alamo. Later, in his office, Juan Seguin, as senior captain of cavalry and Deaf Smith, as captain of the Texas Rangers within the San Antonio district, joined Will and Lt. Colonel Johnston.

Will knew the Comanche wars were among the most destabilizing events during the brief life of the Republic of Texas, as he recalled from a history he was working hard to change. As the other officers shifted quietly, waiting for Will to start the meeting, he thought about how the Comanche wars lasted into the 1870s before the US government finally forced the remnants of the tribe onto reservations in Oklahoma. That was thirty-five years into a future he was intent on changing.

His thoughts drifted back to the recent constitutional convention in San Antonio and recalled he owed his appointment partially to a commitment to protect the frontier settlements. With that thought in the forefront of his mind, Will said, "We're going to mount an expedition and follow the Comanche back into the Comancheria. We're going to free the women and children they have captured and punish the Comanche." He took a deep breath and continued, "It falls to the four of us to figure out how to accomplish that. What are your thoughts?"

Seguin spoke up, "General Travis, we can ride out with both our cavalry companies, and head north as soon as tomorrow, with eighty troopers."

Deaf Smith nodded to Seguin, "I've got twenty-five Rangers here in San Antonio, who can leave tonight, and another company north of here. I figure we can take a total of fifty Rangers into Comancheria."

Johnston looked between the other men, searching for the right words, "Well, General Travis, we have hundreds of infantry around San Antonio. It would take a few days, but I believe I can take three or four hundred men, if allowed time to prepare."

"I'm not sure we have time for that, Colonel Johnston," Will said cautiously, "We'll likely be going thirty or more miles each day, which makes bringing the infantry difficult"

When he saw Johnston's shoulders slump at the news, Will added, "But, someone needs to stay here in command of the army while I'm gone with Seguin and Smith here."

Johnston smiled feebly and replied, "You can depend on it. I'll keep up with training the infantry, sir."

Will shook his head, "Oh, you can do more than that, Colonel. I want you to furlough every man who won't follow orders or submit to the new training regimen. We've added hundreds of men to the army since we won our independence. I'd rather have fewer well-trained soldiers than an ill-disciplined mob."

After the meeting broke up, Will sat, reviewing a list of invoices he needed to send to the provisional government for payment when Captain Seguin returned. With no one else present, the Tejano used Travis' nickname, "Buck, I wanted to run something by you."

"My family has contacts among the Lipan Apaches, south of here. One of their chiefs is an old warrior by the name of Flacco. He's got a son, by the same name, a few years younger than us and he's a damned fine scout. We could use a good scout, and I believe he'd be reliable."

Will set one of the invoices to the side and said, "That's a good idea, Juan. Get him here tomorrow before we leave."

The next day, Will watched the mixed force of Texian cavalry and Rangers ride out through the Alamo's gate. Deaf Smith's Rangers were festooned with pistols, secured on saddles or belt holsters or frequently stuck in belts. Most carried rifles and a few, muskets. Among the Rangers, no two men dressed the same. Mostly they came from the southern United States, although there were a few who came from Europe or were raised on the haciendas of south Texas.

Seguin's cavalry favored swords and knives, to accompany their pistols and shotguns. Half of his men were native Tejanos, while the rest, like the Rangers, came from the American South and Europe. While most of the men managed to find some sort of uniform, those included old US army, gray militia, and surplus Mexican jackets.

As the last of the horsemen rode out the gate, Will nudged his horse and followed behind. Once on the trail, heading north, he spurred his horse to a gallop, riding to the head of the column where Seguin rode with the Apache scout, Flacco.

The second evening on the trail was warm, as May prepared to give way to June. The mounted column forded the slow-moving Colorado River before setting camp for the evening near a small stockade on the northern bank of the river. From the stockade, Will saw a large man walk out, approaching the camp. Will hurried over, intercepting him. The other man looked him up and down before asking, "You in charge of these men?"

Will dipped his head in acknowledgement and offered his hand, "William Travis, at your service, sir."

There was a glimmer of recognition when the other man heard his name. "I'm Jacob Harrell, and yonder stockade is my family's place. What's the general of the army and all these men doing up here on the Colorado?"

Will's shoulders slumped a bit as he replied, "The Comanche are raiding again. We received word a couple of days ago about a large war band that attacked Fort Parker, up on the Navasota."

Harrell's eyes grew wide and he swore as he looked to the west, to the land of the Comancheria. "I hadn't heard about it." He looked back to Will and asked, "Well, if you're going after them, the least I can do is let my wife know we got company. Will you join me and my family for dinner?"

"I think I can manage that, would you have room at your table for my captains, too?"

Harrell's eyes held a twinkle, "Sure, if they don't mind sharing a plate."

Less than an hour later, Will and Captain Seguin sat at a large table with Jacob Harrell and his family. Deaf Smith passed, muttering about eating beans with his Rangers.

As Harrell's wife, Mary, brought plates loaded with venison and beans to the table, he said, "We've been worried about the Comanche as of late. There are four families here along the Colorado, no more than were at the Parker fort. Apart from the threat from the damned redskins, this land is some of the best we've ever seen. Given time, a real town could develop here."

While Seguin dug in and wolfed his food, Will set his spoon down on the wooden table with the realization that Harrell's homestead was located in the bend of the Colorado River where the town of Austin would eventually grow. "I agree with you Mr. Harrell, and that's why we're headed north to put paid to the Comanche."

When they finished eating, while Mary and several of the Harrell children cleaned the table, Will and Seguin joined Jacob in center of the small stockade, where their host lit a pipe and smoked, "I moved out here to Texas a few years ago, because as a poor dirt farmer in Tennessee, land enough to farm just wasn't available, not at the prices I could afford. Texas has given me the opportunity to have something far beyond what I could have ever scrambled to have in Tennessee, and the opportunity to pass something significant on to my children. Push the Comanche back, General Travis, and give us settlers the breathing room we need, and we'll build something here that'll last."

While listening, Will imagined the stately capitol building standing in the distance, and wide avenues filled with the commerce of the republic flowing through them, instead of the rolling plains and copses of live oak trees which filled his vision. As he recalled from his history, Austin was the project of Mirabeau Lamar, the second president in a republic which wouldn't exist. It seemed Austin would need a new patron and he swore as he looked through the gate of the stockade toward the Colorado river, he would show Crockett the advantages of moving the government out here, away from the populated areas of East Texas.

He refocused on Harrell as the other man finished and said, "Whatever the cost, Mr. Harrell, the army will end the Comanche raids, so that others can find here in this part of the Republic the same opportunity you have."

Six days after leaving the bend of the Colorado River, Will led his mixed command of Rangers and cavalry troopers into a broad meadow containing the burned remnants of Fort Parker, a few miles south of the headwaters of the Navasota River. The fort's smoldering embers no longer sent tendrils of smoke into the sky. Apart from the skeleton of the fort, the only other sign of the massacre was a handful of burial mounds and their wooden markers.

More than a dozen men who were either related to the Parkers or came from nearby farms met Will and his force when they arrived. The leader of the band was an older man, in his mid-fifties. As he approached Will, his face was hard edged and belied his soft-spoken voice, "Thank God you all have finally arrived. We prayed daily for Elisha to get through."

After stretching from the long ride, Will went over to the group of survivors, "He arrived in San Antonio eight days ago. We got here as soon as we could."

"My apologies, sir. I'm Daniel Parker, and these men are my family and neighbors. I implore you, please fetch back our womenfolk and children."

Will took off his hat, knocking the trail dust from it, and ran his fingers through his damp, red hair, "I'm General Travis, sir. I wish we had been able to get here earlier. But now we're here, we'll be heading into the Comancheria to find your women and children."

Parker's shoulders sagged, and a couple of his relatives guided him over to a stump, where he sat down. Will thought the older man was out of breath, but when he lifted up his head, his eyes were swimming in tears as he said, "General, had you arrived when we did, you could have helped us bury our relatives. Oh, dear God in Heaven, what those savages did to John, Silas and the others, it's enough to make the hardest heart weep."

Without any prompting, Parker continued, "We found my brother, Benjamin's, body where they killed him, in front of the fort. They had pierced him with dozens of spears. I pray he was dead before hitting the ground. They scalped, defiled, and disfigured his body, General. My family, we're men of peace, we came here from Illinois for the opportunity to spread the gospel. But as God is my witness, sir, as wrong as I know it is, I want vengeance, General Travis. Find our women and children, and avenge our father, brothers and sons."

Parker lowered his head into his hands, where Will heard him sobbing. Taking leave from the settlers, he returned to where Juan Seguin and Deaf Smith waited, out of earshot. Smith said, "I've got a few of my boys riding patrol around the fort. Like as not, the Comanche are long gone back into the Comancheria, but we'll make sure."

Chapter 2

The morning following their arrival at the remnants of Fort Parker, Will ordered his command to follow the trail to the west left by the large war party. Joining Will's little army were a half dozen of the Parkers' family and neighbors. Flacco, Seguin's Apache scout, and a couple of Smith's Rangers, skilled at tracking, led the way. Will held no illusions about his own tracking skills, they were nonexistent. Even so, he had no problem seeing the westward trail left by the Comanche war band.

There were no settlements west of the Parkers' fort, but several homesteads were burned husks. The second day out from the fort, as they watered their horses in the Brazos river, one of the scouts rode back along the trail and found Will discussing where to ford the river with Seguin and Smith. "Sir, we found a place a couple of miles north, where we can ford the river. Water's only a few feet deep there." He stopped, opening and closing his mouth a couple of times before he managed,

"We found the body of a woman on the other side of the Brazos, sir. She'd been there for a while."

Will dreaded what they would see when they crossed the river. As they spurred their horses toward the ford, Will muttered to Seguin, "Bad news doesn't get any better by waiting for it to come."

On the west bank of the Brazos, a couple of Rangers and Flacco, the Apache scout, stood over the body of the woman. A blanket covered the corpse when Will and the other officers rode up. When he motioned for the blanket to be removed, one of the Rangers standing beside the blanket said, "General, you don't want to see this. What they done to her ain't fit for Christian eyes."

Flacco glanced at the Ranger disapprovingly and knelt by the body. He said something rapidly in Spanish. When he finished, Seguin shook his head and said, "Buck, it's up to you, but Flacco says it isn't pretty, what the Comanche did to her."

Will paused as his thoughts were drawn back to what seemed a lifetime ago, before his mind had been cast through time, to several years before the transference, when his unit participated in the battle for Fallujah in 2004. The terror of hearing a bullet careen off the concrete inches from where he was sitting was bad enough. Even so, he thought the daily firefights with snipers inured him to death. After finding himself cast back in time, he had taken the battles at the Rio Grande and the Nueces in stride. As a soldier, death was something he had learned to steel his heart against. Now he needed to know into what he was leading the men who followed him, he needed to know what they faced.

When Flacco pulled back the blanket, Will retreated a step. He was no expert, but even to his untrained eyes, the body had been exposed to the elements for a while. While animals had found and mangled the body, what skin remained left little doubt the Comanche warriors had tortured the woman before she died. Before ordering her buried, Will sent for one of the Parker men to examine the body. When he arrived, he threw up his most recent meal upon seeing the body, but after recovering, confirmed she didn't appear to resemble either of the women captured from the fort.

After the woman was hastily buried, and the command was again following the trail westward, the image of her brutalized body kept returning to Will. The number of bodies he saw killed when his unit took part in the 2004 battle of Fallujah was low, and while some of them were badly mangled, they paled in comparison to hers. Despite hearing stories of the Comanche warrior culture, the frequency of which bordered on commonplace, and now seeing first-hand the terror they struck among the settlers along the frontier, Will was still shocked to see the casual brutality inflicted on the woman's body. Somewhere along the way, he decided the author who wrote *"Bury My Heart at Wounded Knee."* obviously wasn't thinking of the Comanche when she penned her book.

The mixed command was a few days further west of the Brazos, and the war party's trail had become harder to track. Flacco told Will it was because various groups had peeled away, going back to their own bands. The Texas plains were hot in June. The command had left the Alamo more than two weeks earlier and the strain of being under a constant state of alertness was beginning to show on the men under Will's command. The day was at its hottest as the sun was tracking across the western sky. The men, in columns of two, wound their way across the prairie. The only tracks in sight were those made by the buffalo. In the back of his mind, Will knew the heat sapped his attention and made all of the men more lethargic.

To the west, in the distance he heard a gunshot shatter the monotonous sound of squeaking saddles. The lethargy fell from Will, as adrenaline coursed through his system. The flurry of shots came from the direction where their scouts were riding forward of the main column. He spurred his horse into a gallop, waving the column of men toward the sound of the gunfire.

The steady drumbeat of more than a hundred sets of horse hooves thundered across the plain as Will led the mixed command over a low rise. In the distance, he saw a dust cloud retreating westward, farther into the Comancheria. A few hundred yards away a horse was down. Will scanned the area, looking for his forward scouts, but apart from the fallen horse and the dust cloud in the distance, the only movement was the tall grass rustling in the sweltering breeze. He let his horse gallop until he closed the distance to the fallen animal. When only a few dozen yards separated them, he saw the bodies of his scouts from Smith's Ranger company, lying in the grass. From beneath the downed horse, which had several arrows protruding from its body, he saw movement as Flacco, the Apache struggled to get out from underneath the dead animal.

Juan Seguin leapt from his horse, rushing over to where the Apache was trapped. He grabbed the reins and tried dragging the horse in the opposite direction from where the Indian lay. Several men joined the officer as they managed to drag the horse from atop the Apache scout. When the horse no longer trapped him, the Apache attempted to stand up, but his left leg gave way, and he collapsed. He landed with only a grunt, and Will couldn't help but to admire his stoic response to his injury and the loss of his horse.

As a couple of men looked to the injured Apache, Will walked over to where one of the Rangers had fallen. A single arrow pierced his side. Despite only a few minutes passing between the time of the gunshot and the column arriving, the man had been scalped, and his clothing ripped from his body. Deep gouges were cut into his legs, and someone had been in the process of cutting off his genitalia when Will's command had crested the ridge, as the job had been abandoned midway. He turned away from the body, desperately willing the image from his mind, and yelled, "Boys, get some shovels. We're going to bury our fallen. We'll not leave them for the Comanche."

Three wooden crosses were a few hundred yards away as the little army camped on the rolling prairie that night. The sky was dark, the distant stars standing sentinel in the night sky against the return of the new moon. Before collapsing into his bedroll, Will had ordered a strong guard to watch over the camp and the horses, which were staked out along a picket line. As he drifted to sleep, his mind was filled with the images of mutilated bodies. He awoke several times when nightmares broke through his restless slumber.

The sound of gunshots startled Will awake when they shattered the stillness of the night. He leapt to his feet and grasped his sword. Standing over his bedroll, he saw other men rising and reaching for their weapons, which they kept by their sides each night. From where the horses were staked, Will heard more shouting and gunfire. "The horses! Juan! Deaf! They're raiding the horses!"

Will ran toward the picket line where shadows moved and rushed around the panicked animals. Only a few yards away, a shadow melded onto one of the horses and he realized it was a young warrior bounding onto the back of the startled horse. When the warrior spotted Will, he kicked his heels into the horse's flanks and charged at him, brandishing a sharp spear. As the warrior lunged forward, Will dodged to the left, coming up on the other side of the horse. Will drove forward with his sword, piercing the warrior in the left side of the rib cage. A look of stunned surprise crossed the Comanche's face as he slipped from the horse, crashing to the ground. Will barely contained his astonishment when the warrior climbed to his feet, grasping his side.

Will scarcely had time to think, "What the hell! I should have punctured something vital."

When the Comanche brought his bloodied fingers away from his wound, he drew a knife from his leather belt and tried circling around Will. Will knew he would never be Inigo Montoya, but between his college fencing days, Travis' own memories and frequent practice, he confidently interposed himself between the injured warrior and the stampeding horses. Rather than attempting to circle around again, the young Comanche warrior sprang forward, arm outstretched, blade first at Will's chest. Will parried the short blade, and reposted. The warrior's shock was complete as he ran himself into the outstretched blade. The knife slid from his fingers and blood bubbled from his lips as the young warrior buckled to the ground, where he quickly bled out.

Will stepped over the body, rushing toward the horses, where he, Seguin and Smith directed their men to corral all the horses they could find. The night's raid appeared to be an unmitigated disaster for the Texians, for as the sun arose less than an hour later, they discovered they lost more than thirty of their mounts. For the Comanche's troubles, Will's men found the bodies of four warriors. As he and his officers took stock of the situation at dawn, they found three more dead and five wounded among their men. The news grew progressively worse, when Seguin reported two of last night's watch were also missing.

Will understood, only too well, the frustration which had plagued the Texian and US armies in the history he had learned, in their fight to pacify the Comanche, for it was now his own. He had ridden into the Comancheria with one hundred thirty riders. Six were dead, five were wounded and only a hundred horses remained. And two of his men were missing. As he looked out across the vast prairie of west central Texas, he felt a sinking realization. He wasn't going to win this fight. He was outmatched and outnumbered. There was a bitter taste in his mouth as he considered he had led the Texas army to victory against the larger Mexican army using tactics which were not entirely dissimilar to those of the Comanche. Now, as the invader, Will knew defeat, lacking the resources and men to successfully avenge the massacre at Fort Parker. But before he would permit himself to withdraw, he owed it to his men to find the two missing troopers.

A day later, and twenty miles south from where they lost their horses, Smith's Rangers found the two men. When they reported back the location, Will led the rest of the command there. Will found both troopers had been stripped and staked atop fire ant mounds. Both had been tortured, their bodies mutilated. One had a bullet hole in his forehead. Will turned to Smith, "Did you find him like this?"

Smith spit a stream of tobacco juice onto the ant mound and shook his head, "No. Poor bastard was still alive when we came upon him. What those red devils did to him was … ghastly."

Will shuddered at the thought. "Did your boys end his misery, Deaf?"

Smith shook his head, "No. Had to do it myself, damn it. General, I ain't doing this anymore. When we return to San Antonio, I'm done, all I want to do is get back to my wife and daughters."

Taken aback by Smith's outburst, Will realized Deaf's frustration was entirely justified. As he played back in his mind the past few weeks, he realized his first mistake was racing north to Fort Parker. Despite thinking he had the resources, circumstances proved otherwise, as a third of the men were riding double, with the loss of their horses. The Comanche never deigned to fight his men on terms remotely equal. The attack against his scouts had potentially crippled his Apache scout and the attack on their horses had effectively ended his campaign.

Seeing no other option available, he ordered his command to ride to the southwest, toward San Antonio. He stopped his horse as his men filed past and turned, looking at the land of the Comancheria. "I swear, I'll be back. And when I do, we'll end, once and for all, these raids on our settlements."

True to his word, Deaf Smith resigned the same day Will's column limped back to the safety of the Alamo's ramparts. To replace him, Will brought to the fort the captain commanding the Rangers assigned to patrol the area between the Nueces and the Rio Grande. Matthew Caldwell was thirty-eight years old and had earned a reputation for being decisive and a hard fighter. Before Will could lead the army back into the Comancheria, he needed to stop the raids. He needed someone like Caldwell to lead the Rangers.

Part of Will was glad the provisional government had relocated eastward to the population center of Harrisburg, on the western bank of the San Jacinto River, around fifty miles north of Galveston. The failure of the campaign to punish the Comanche was overlooked by the provisional government as they were busy scheduling a plebiscite to adopt the recently completed constitution. When he sent a requisition for more Rangers, he was surprised how quickly Burnet authorized the expense, until he realized the acting president wanted security along the frontier to increase turnout for the vote. Even on the edges of civilization, the provisional government wanted as open and democratic elections as possible.

Will and Matthew Caldwell sat in his office, with the window open, letting in hot July air. "I'm not going to look a gift horse in the mouth, Matt. If Burnet has loosed the purse strings, then let's not delay in building up the Rangers."

Caldwell joined Will at looking at map of Texas spread over the large desk and said, "With six companies, we can establish a line of forts along the frontier. General, I'd like to set our northern most fort on the West fork of the Trinity River."

Will arched his eyebrows, as the location was just over the loosely defined border of the Comancheria. "Do you think thirty Rangers can hold the fort that far away from our population centers?"

"I ain't one to underestimate the Comanche. They are fierce warriors. But that fort's going to be full of thirty Rangers, not a few settler families like at Fort Parker. I'll personally make sure them Comanche don't see it as low-hanging fruit when we're done building it."

Caldwell also marked a spot on the Brazos river, fifty miles south of the first marker, and again on the Brazos River at the confluence of the Bosque. The fourth marker was on the Lampasas River, about fifty miles northwest of where Will had met Jacob Harrel on the bend of the Colorado River. The fifth mark was drawn on the falls of the Pedernales River. The sixth mark he placed at the Alamo.

He looked up at Will and said, "With these six forts, we'll hopefully have warning before the Comanche raid into our eastern settlements. Also, these men can, when we're ready to clear the Comanche from Texas, form the core of our mounted force, if you want."

Will nodded in agreement and took the charcoal marker and added a fort at Laredo and another at the mouth of the Rio Grande. "It will be the responsibility of our infantry and regular cavalry to man these two forts, but let's not forget when we're looking at the Comancheria that our back door is the Rio Grande."

7th July 1836

To Colonel William B. Travis

The Alamo, San Antonio, Bexar, Republic of Texas

Your recent inquiry into our patented revolving pistol has come at a fortuitous time, and I and my investors have set a price of $15 per pistol. We will also sell for $1 each extra cylinder for the pistols. I will consider a license to your government for the manufacture of replacement parts for $2,000 in gold, silver, or US Treasury certificates. I urge you send an experienced gunsmith to our facility in Connecticut where we will provide him the necessary dies for the replacement parts, at cost. As a sign of goodwill between the Patent Arms Manufacturing and your government, I am sending with this letter a matched pair of the Patterson Model Revolving pistol as a gift to you. May you wear the pistols with continued success.

Your humble servant,

Samuel Colt

The letter and package's transit between Paterson, New Jersey and New Orleans, Louisiana, was fast, arriving in less than three weeks. But it languished in New Orleans several more weeks before one of the Republic of Texas' small schooners docked in New Orleans for supplies. A week later, the letter and packet arrived in Galveston, and another two weeks passed before a wagon laden with supplies for the army arrived in San Antonio with it.

Will opened and scanned the letter on the 20th of

September, and then gazed lovingly at the blue finished barrels and ivory handles resting in the cherry wood case. He found Lt. Colonel Johnston and they went out to the firing range, located north of the Alamo. Like a giddy child on Christmas morn, eager to play with his new toy, Will charged both pistols' cylinders with gunpowder and seated the lead balls on top of the powder. Finding a tin of percussion caps in the case he gently squeezed the caps onto the cylinders' nipples. He handed one of the pistols to Johnston and then, with the other pistol, stepped up to the firing line.

The target was thirty feet away and Will sighted down the gun, ignoring the lack of sights fixed on the barrel and squeezed the trigger. He smiled at the recoil and unloaded the other four rounds into the target. Johnston finished firing seconds after Will. He handed the gun back to Will, saying, "You can load it on Monday and fire all week, Buck! That was, dare I say it, fun."

After setting pistols back into the case, ready to be cleaned, he slapped Johnston on the back as they walked back to the fort. "Just wait until we get these guns into our Rangers hands, Sid. We'll see about sending a message to the Comanche they won't soon forget."

Chapter 3

The referendum ratifying the constitution passed by a wide margin, and acting President Burnet, in accordance with the new law, set the presidential election for the 6th of September 1836. Will wasn't surprised when Sam Houston and Stephen Austin threw their hats in the ring before the referendum. Henry Smith, a Kentucky transplant, who had been in Texas for nearly a decade, announced his candidacy immediately after the results of the referendum were known. David Crockett announced his own candidacy a few days later.

The presidential election was a few weeks away, when Will took a leave of absence from command of the army in San Antonio, joining Crockett as he campaigned. This was how he found himself in Washington-on-the-Brazos with the Tennessean in mid-August. Despite his keen interest in Crockett's presidential aspirations, on which he feared his command of the regular army rested, something else also brought Will to Washington. During the early days of the revolution, as a result of his divorce, Travis received custody of his son, Charlie, who was eight years old. Travis' memories were of scant help to Will regarding the boy, as Travis had arrived in Texas back in 1831 when the boy was only three years old. Travis had spent only a day with the boy since the child's arrival at the end of 1835, before Will's mental invasion of Travis. Although it pained him, Will concluded Travis was an indifferent father, at the best of times.

Travis had left Charlie with a family friend, David Ayres, almost nine months previous. Ayres was a Methodist missionary and ran a school in town. Will knew the right course of action was to visit the boy and ensure his wellbeing, but a large part of him wanted to leave things as they were and pretend Travis' life before Will was of no consequence. But when he turned the question around, he knew if he were in the same situation as Charlie, it would be a hateful thing to be altogether abandoned by his father.

When they arrived the previous evening, Will and Crockett made camp on the outskirts of the town. "Riding into town on a Saturday morning, while folks are in town from their farms gives a bigger platform, and you'll see plenty of folks looking to be entertained by a politician on the stump." Sometimes Will forgot Crockett was a political animal until the Tennessean glibly reminded him. "Especially if they know they're going to hear the Lion of the West and the Hero of the Revolution."

Will grinned at his friend. Few men could verbally

capitalize words as well as the Tennessean. "I look forward to hearing you spin a yarn or two. Once I track down Charlie, we'll come find you."

Crockett grew serious as he reached across his horse, offering his hand, "Good luck with the boy, Buck. I can't claim to have had the best of relationships with my own boys, so I understand a bit of what you're feeling. Just look for the largest crowd, that's where you'll find me." Will shook hands with Crockett and nudged his horse down the lane, leading to the Ayres homestead.

The road which the homestead faced was more path than road, Will thought as he came upon the split-log cabin David Ayres and his family called home. Next to the cabin, was another split-log structure, most likely the school. Across the road, the missionary from Kentucky also operated a small general store. Will thought it likely between running a school and keeping a store, Ayres made ends meet.

The oppressive heat of summer left the school empty. Will noticed the door swinging gently in the warm, morning breeze. On the porch of the Ayres log cabin he saw a slight boy sitting on a wooden bench, reading a book. The boy's shock of red hair immediately reminded Will of his own. He was slight of build, just as Travis had been as a child. As the boy looked up and saw Will sitting on his horse, the look of uncertainty in the boy's face removed any doubt in Will's mind he was looking at Charlie, Travis' son.

Before this moment, Will had been unable to decide

how he would handle this meeting. Travis' memories were unhelpful, given the man's emotional distance from his son. The look of uncertainty in the narrow face and sorrowful eyes broke his heart. When he dismounted and tied the reins to a tree branch, the boy set the book down and stood. As Will walked up the path leading to the Ayres' cabin, the boy took a hesitant step forward, stopping on the edge of the porch. Will's heart hurt seeing the fear and uncertainly writ large across the child's face. He stopped a few feet shy of the porch, and Will faced the same uncertainty affecting Travis' son. This boy wasn't his own, but by some twist of fate, Will was the only father Charlie would ever know. Whatever choice he made next would define their relationship. He crossed the last few feet separating him from Charlie and pulled the slight boy into an embrace.

Charlie flung his arms around the man he knew as his father. Will felt his cheek become wet as he felt the boy sobbing into his shoulder. The uncertainty returned, as the boy's hurt poured out through his sobs. He had no idea how to comfort the child, but he patted the boy's back and said, "There, there, Charlie. I'm here now, son."

The words came unbidden to his lips, but Will was amazed how quickly the sobbing was replaced by a smile and a hiccup as Charlie looked into his face and smiled, "I've missed you so much, Pa."

He set the boy back on the porch and tousled his red hair. The dam broke, and without really understanding it, Will felt as though he knew his part in this new relationship. "My, Charlie, you've grown a lot since I had to go off to war."

The boy pulled Will back to the bench, where he sat down again. From a hesitant start, when Will asked him about the trip from Alabama, Charlie opened up and told him about the trip westward as well as about life with the Ayres family over the past nine months. Will smiled as the boy prattled on. Like so many young boys before and since, once he started talking, he kept on.

Eventually Charlie wound down and Will asked him if he'd like to go hear the famous Davy Crockett. The boy bounded off the bench, jumping with excitement. "Really, Pa? *The* Davy Crockett?"

Will couldn't help himself, and laughed at Charlie's unbridled enthusiasm. "Yes. He may soon be President of Texas and he's talking to folks at the town green."

After finding David Ayres at the store across the street, and thanking him for his hospitality, Will gave into Charlie's infectious enthusiasm and allowed himself to be pulled out of the store, toward the town's center.

He and Charlie walked toward the green and found Crockett in full politicking mode, speaking, "I also told them of the manner in which I had been knocked down and dragged out, and that I didn't consider it a fair fight any how they could fix it. I put the ingredients in the cup pretty strong I tell you, and I concluded my speech by telling them that I was done with politics for the present, and they might all go to hell, and I would go to Texas. And now I stand before the finest people that

Almighty God has brought to this fair land, and ask that you join me and tell Andy Jackson that he can go to hell, and we'll keep Texas!" The crowd, numbering several hundred men, women, and children, clapped and hollered their approval, as Crockett stepped down from the tree stump.

He was swamped with supporters trying to shake his hand and introduce themselves. It reminded Will of a rock concert. Few politicians elicited the kind of reaction from a crowd as Crockett manufactured. Shaking his head while laughing, Will directed Charlie's attention to Crockett, pointing him out to the boy, "There's Davy Crockett, son. It appears he's a bit busy politicking folks. You'll get a chance to meet him later. He'll be swinging by Mr. Ayres' place this evening."

Hours later, Crockett showed up, gave a short speech on the steps of Ayres' store to his greatly reduced audience, after which they returned to their homes and farms. With his hair plastered on his forehead, and sweat pouring down his face, Crockett ambled across the road, approaching the Ayres' porch, where Will and Charlie had watched Crockett entertain his electorate. Charlie slid off the bench, watching in awe as Crockett moseyed up to the porch. Will nodded to Crockett, "Looks like you had a good time politicking folks around these here parts, Davy. Allow me to introduce Charles Edward Travis to you. Turns out he's quite the scholar and has studiously followed all of your exploits in your book 'Sketches and Eccentricities of Colonel David Crockett,' which I'm sure you remember."

For a fleeting moment, Crockett looked like he had bitten into a lemon. He skillfully slid his smile back on his face and tousled the boy's hair. "I hope you enjoyed reading the book, but those are just stories another writer wrote. Most of those stories are just tall tales meant to give a boy a couple of hours of reading. I think it may have worked here."

Dinner in the Ayres household was a chaotic affair. The meal was served as Mrs. Ayres and her daughters brought a steady flow of food to the dining table. Despite the table's large size, it was crowded with David and his wife, Ann, their three children, Will, Crockett and Charlie as well as a couple of other children who lived with the family. David Ayres sat at the head of the table and after saying a lengthy grace over the plentiful food, engaged Crockett in conversation. In the middle of Ayres' probing questions, several families stopped by to see the famous Davy Crockett. While Crockett deftly answered Ayres' questions, he still managed to make the folks who stopped by feel welcome. Will tuned out the conversation when he recognized most of the Tennessean's answers were part of his stump speech, which Will had nearly memorized by this time.

He had been thinking how much better Ann Ayres' cooking was than what he ate in the military, when his attention was brought back to the conversation upon hearing Ayres ask, "Congressman Crockett, what is your view on how the Republic should spend its money?"

Crockett leaned back in his chair, eyed his empty plate, then pushed it away before replying, "Mr. Ayres, you're a God-fearing man. Even if Buck here hadn't told me about your Methodist persuasion, it's clear by what I've seen this evening. I have no doubt your charity and liberality does you credit. I believe it to be a good and noble thing for you to give as you see fit to those charities that compel you to act. While we have the right, and perhaps a duty to give away as much of our own money to charity, I do not believe that right extends to Congress. As a member of Congress for six years, off and on, I don't believe we have the right to appropriate a single dollar of the public's money to charity."

Ayres looked surprised at the Tennessean, "Are you saying that Congress shouldn't help the distressed people of our nation?"

Crockett shook his head, "That ain't exactly what I'm saying. No, but let me explain it by telling you about something that happened a few years back in Washington City. I was standing on the steps of the Capitol one evening with several other members of Congress when our attention was drawn to a great light over in Alexandria. It was evidently a large fire. So, we jumped into a hack and drove over as fast as that old horse would go. When we got there, I went to work, and as God is my witness, I never worked as hard in my life as I did there for several hours. But, in spite of all that could be done, many houses were burned, and many families made homeless. Some even had lost all but the clothes on their backs. Also, it was still winter, and it was very cold, and when I saw so many women and children suffering I felt something ought to be done for them. Everyone else was of a similar mind, so the next morning a bill was introduced, and we appropriated twenty thousand dollars for their relief. We put aside other pressing business of the nation and rushed it through as soon as we could. I reckon I should correct myself, here. I said that everyone felt the same way, and that twern't completely correct. There were a few, who perhaps sympathized as deeply with those suffering women and children, but who did not think we had the right to indulge our sympathy or excite our charity at the expense of anybody but ourselves.

"They opposed the bill, and upon its passage demanded the yeas and nays be recorded. There were not enough to force a rollcall vote, but many of us wanted our names to appear in favor of what we considered a praiseworthy measure, so we voted with them to sustain their measure. So, the yeas and nays were recorded, and my name appeared on the journals in favor of the bill.

"Later, when I was politicking back in Tennessee I approached one of my more noteworthy constituents, a real bellwether in that area, and I asked him for his vote. He told me that he would not vote for me, telling me that I acted outside of the constitution. I was perplexed as I could recall no vote about the constitution. It was then he reminded me of that vote for twenty thousand dollars. I told him that I owned that vote, he had me there. I asked him why would anyone complain that a great and rich country as ours shouldn't give the insignificant sum to relieve its suffering women and children. Especially when we have a full treasury. I told him that had he been there, he'd have done the same thing."

Crockett paused his tale, when Ann Ayres brought over a large blackberry pie to the table. After accepting a large slice, he continued, "Well my constituent told me that it's not the amount of the money that he complained over. It was the principle. In the first place, the government ought to have in the Treasury not more than is enough for its legitimate purposes. But that wasn't here nor there, as the real reason he was upset was because the power of collecting and disbursing money is the most dangerous power that can be entrusted to men, particularly under our system of collecting revenue by tariff, which reaches every man in the country, no matter how poor he may be, and the poorer he is, the more he pays in proportion to his means.

"What is worse is that our tariffs press upon him without the knowledge of where the weight centers, for there is not a man in these United States who can ever guess how much he pays to the government. He told me that while I had contributed to relieve one, it was being drawn from thousands who are even worse off than the women and children of Alexandria. If Congress had the right to give to their needs, then we could have given twenty million dollars, rather than twenty thousand. If Congress has the right to give to one, then the right exists to give to all and he reminded me that the Constitution never defines charity nor stipulates the amount. That, my friend, Mr. Ayres, opens the paddock to give to any and everything which Congress decides is charity and in any amount they think is proper.

"Can you imagine, Mr. Ayres, what a wide door this would open for fraud, corruption and favoritism, on one hand, and for robbing people on the other? He told me then and there that Congress has no right to hand out charity. Individual members may give as much of their own money as they please, but they have no right to touch a dollar of the public money for charity. If one tenth of all of the houses in Tennessee had burned down, would Congress lift a finger to help? No. No member of Congress would have thought about appropriating money from the Treasury for relief.

"There are two hundred forty members of Congress. If each showed sympathy for the plight of the destitute women and children of the fire by contributing only a week's worth of pay, it would have provided more than thirteen thousand dollars. Also, there are plenty of wealthy men in Washington that could give up twenty thousand without depriving themselves of the luxuries of life.

"He reminded me that the congressmen chose to keep their own money, which I can assure you, many spend frivolously while the folks in Washington City applaud them for removing from them the burden of their own charity, by giving what was not Congress' right to give. The people have delegated to Congress, by the Constitution, the power to do certain things. To do these, it is authorized to collect and pay moneys, and for nothing else. Everything beyond this is usurpation, and a violation of the Constitution. Now I have given you," Crockett continued, "an imperfect account of what he said. So, you see, Mr. Ayers, it is a precedent fraught with danger to the country, for when Congress once begins to stretch its power beyond the limits of the Constitution, there is no limit to it, and no security for the people."

As Will listened, wrapped up in Crockett's words, he realized how far the federal government which he had grown up with, had fallen away from the Constitution, promising people today the rewards of the fruits and labors of a future generation. It took Crockett addressing the issue eloquently with David Ayres to verbalize his own opinion.

The next morning, they saddled their horses, ready to continue the political campaign. After listening to Crockett's views on charity, Will felt his own perspective on it had changed. He couldn't undo Travis' reckless choices which had ruined his own marriage.

"I can't change the past," was Will's first thought, but that made him chuckle, given the past was the very thing he was working to change.

Setting the thought aside, Will decided his own charity would start at home with William B. Travis' son. The boy stood on the porch, looking at the horses. Will walked back to the boy and said, "Charlie, if you want, you can stay here with the Ayres family and attend school. But it would please me mightily if you came with me to San Antonio. We could get a home in town and you can go to school and make new friends there."

The boy's eyes lit up and he jumped off the porch into Will's arms, "Pa, take me home with you!"

Will and Charlie walked into the house. There was packing which needed doing. The day was young and as Crockett was prone to telling him, he was burning daylight. There was an election to win.

Chapter 4

Will sat at the table, a copy of the *Telegraph and Texas Register* lay folded on it. He glanced around the room, with its fresh coat of paint and smiled. Over the past month, since returning to San Antonio, he found a home, recently vacated by a Bexareno, a native of San Antonio, who chose to return to Mexico rather than remain in the Republic. Juan Seguin's father, Erasmo, acted as a broker, selling the home to Will. He found it to be bigger than he and Charlie needed, but the boy was thrilled to have his own room.

He thought it a holdover from his life before, but he was an unabashed morning person, and he delighted in sitting at the dining table, which was simply a large extension of the kitchen, and drinking a cup of coffee while reading dispatches and reports brought home the previous night. Of special interest, the *Telegraph and Texas Register* included the completed returns of the previous week's election. He unfolded the crinkling pages and read the article.

12th September 1836

We are able to assure our readers that one-time

congressman, Colonel David Crockett will be the first elected president of our Republic of Texas. While results are still due in from Red River county, in the northern reaches of the republic, the margin of victory accrued by Col. Crockett provides no possible means for any of the other candidates to seize the election.

The provisional government in Harrisburg confirms nearly six thousand votes in total have been counted. Of this amount, almost four thousand were attributed to Col. Crockett. Gen'l Houston was not able to account for more than a thousand votes. Neither Governor Smith nor Mr. Austin collected more than five hundred apiece.

Señor Zavala, Col. Crockett's chosen selection for vice president remains in the lead, with less than 200 votes separating him from his nearest challenger. We are confident that the votes from the Red River will not substantially change the results, and we believe that Señor Zavala will join Col. Crockett's administration as vice president.

According to acting President Burnet, the transition will occur on the 22nd October, from whence President-Elect Crockett's six-year term will commence. The government will convene also on the same in Harrisburg.

Will set the paper down and said a silent prayer of thanks. Houston's campaign included promises to settle the matter with the Comanche by treaty. He didn't need Travis' memories to know the futility of that course of action. From his own recollection of history, he recalled Houston's attempts had been failures. He thought the lack of central leadership among the tribe was the likely culprit which scuttled Houston's efforts.

He chuckled grimly, as he thought, *"One way or*

another, I'll know soon enough whether my way will be any better than Houston's."

After taking Charlie by the home of Juan Seguin's sister and her husband, where the younger Seguin children played on the weekend, Will headed to the Alamo, where he met with James Neill and Green Jameson. Neill now contracted with the army as an engineer, working with Green Jameson on expanding and improving the Alamo's defenses. He met the two engineers outside the doors to the chapel, where Neill held several rolled schematics on which he was working.

Will anticipated one of the first things Crockett would do after the inauguration would be to review Will's plans for the Comanche campaign, but he knew he also needed to provide Crockett a detailed plan for the Alamo's development as a bastion against invasion from Mexico or incursion from the Comanche to the west.

Using the low wall separating the chapel courtyard from the plaza as a makeshift table, Neill opened a large diagram of the fort, as Will and Major Jameson looked on. Neill pointed to the north wall on the diagram, "We've removed most of the wall, as we can see over yonder, and have started construction on its replacement a dozen feet further out. The arduous task of repositioning the aquacias, north of the fort, has already been completed. So, the wall will still be inside the aquacia network.

Will inclined his head, "It's good work you're doing, James, but you've been working on the north wall all summer. When you do expect to finish?"

Ignoring the map for a moment, Neill pointed

northward, where they could see scaffolding and adobe. "When it's finished this stretch will be a hundred sixty-two-feet long. It'll be twelve feet tall and three feet thick. And, General Travis, I'll have it complete before Christmas."

"You should be prepared to evacuate your laborers, James, when we start the campaign against the Comanche. I may hold you to that timetable, as we may need this old fort's walls before that campaign is over. Now, next to the completed north wall, what is this?" Will pointed to a building extension drawn on the map.

Neill nodded to Jameson, "It's a project I've given to Green to complete."

Major Jameson said, "General, that extension is a barracks. I've been told by Colonel Johnston the fort should need to garrison around eight hundred men, and our existing structures are wholly inadequate for the job. This planned barracks will be two stories, topping out at twenty feet. The outer wall is a simple extension of the new north wall, while the barracks will face the stock pen. When completed it could house as many as three hundred men."

Will nodded, there were other markings on the diagram.

Jameson continued, "Another barracks will run along the south wall, parallel to the chapel's outer wall, and should hold about the same number of men. And the chapel, we're going to repair the roof and will use it either for its original purpose or storage."

Will asked, "What about the façade of the chapel? It could use some repair as well. Any plans there?"

Both Neill and Jameson shook their heads. Neill said, "Hadn't much thought of it, General. Do you have any thoughts?"

With a flash of inspiration, will took the charcoal marker from Major Jameson and flipped the diagram on the back and drew a crenelated hump situated in the middle of the chapel's façade. The other two men bobbed their heads in agreement.

Will smiled and thought, *"This old chapel may never go down as the shrine of Texas liberty, but damned, if I'm not going to make the front of the old church look just like I remember."*

He flipped the diagram back over, "The north wall, the two barracks, and the roof to the chapel, how much time will you gentlemen need?"

Neill rolled the diagram up and said, "Even if the government gives us the money we want, we're looking at two or three years. Longer, if they're tight with the purse strings."

Will grunted. A lot could happen in three years. As they toured the construction, Will prayed the forces arrayed against the republic would give him the time.

After Neill and Jameson left, to continue their work on the north wall, Will closed himself in his office as he reviewed orders which required his approval and did the thankless task of reviewing each invoice requiring payment from the provisional government. One invoice he set aside as he worked through the stack. Once finished he returned to it. It was from a vendor in New Orleans who won the competitive bid for the new butternut uniforms which he and Lt. Colonel Johnston had approved. Each Jacket, pair of pants, and shoes were four dollars, and a black slouch hat was two dollars. Excluding the cost of shirts and socks, each soldier's uniform was fourteen dollars. Even if he only equipped 800 men, it still totaled more than eleven thousand dollars

Long ago, Will conceded it was impossible to translate exactly between the twenty-first century American dollar and the hodgepodge of currencies circulating in Texas, but it hadn't kept him from trying. He considered the comparable clothing in the early twenty-first century would cost more than two hundred dollars, or nearly two hundred thousand for all eight hundred men.

"It's hardly apples to apples," Will thought, *"but it's still a godawful lot of money."*

The chest with gold and silver had been moved to Will's office from the chapel's sacristy, and a few thousand dollars had been used to settle debts with New Orleans merchants so they would continue providing supplies to the three ships of the Texas navy.

A knock at the door diverted his attention from the invoice, and he set it aside. Lt. Colonel Johnston entered. "You wanted to see me, sir?"

Will waved Johnston into the room. "I wanted to discuss our new tactics and get your take on them, Sid."

Johnston settled himself into the chair opposite Will, "The men are taking to them. Despite your order this past spring to clean out the soldiers just looking for their land bounty but have no interest in taking to our new order drill, I've still got close to a thousand infantry in the Army, not counting Seguin's cavalry or Caldwell's Rangers. I've only been able to get about half of the infantry training with the new tactics."

"Once President-Elect Crockett takes office and we have a working congress, we'll request funding for a fixed number of regulars, Sid. When that happens, we'll have a solid battalion of infantry. Looking to the future, I'm concerned our structure is ill-suited to the war we're facing against the Comanche."

Dropping the formality of rank, Johnston cocked his head, "In what way, Buck?"

Will responded with a question, "What's the smallest operational unit on a battlefield, Sid?"

Johnston leaned back in the chair, as it creaked, "Typically the company is the smallest unit to function on a battlefield, although platoons can certainly operate away from the company if called upon."

"True enough. We'll have but a single battalion of infantry, come next year, call it eight companies if David can pry the funds free from congress. We need to demand more from our non-commissioned officers, and show them they can take initiative on a battlefield. I don't want us to be limited to a company of sixty or eighty men being the smallest tactical unit."

Will paused, as his thoughts slipped back to the months before his mind was transported to Travis' body. The fireteam was the glue holding a squad together. The four men in the fireteam each had a separate function, but more than that, they worked closely together. A single fireteam could operate independently to take or hold an objective or work with the other teams within the squad or section. He wanted the men in the Texas army to work that closely together. The weapons were different, the technology 180 years old, but the men, he thought, could be trained.

"We need a new model. I have an idea for a tactical team of men, under the command of a corporal to be the focal point of each platoon. Let's call this team a rifle team. These four men will drill together, work together, and fight together. I want them so well adapted to their team, there's never a question they have each other's backs. Three of these rifle teams will be under the command of a sergeant. These squads, just like their rifle teams, will work together and learn to be integral units. Three squads will form a platoon under the command of a lieutenant, and two platoons to a company." Will drew a breath before continuing.

"Sid, when we take the war back to the Comanche, I want every rifle team to have the confidence that they can hold an objective for their platoon or company. This model will force us to scrap any existing commitment to the tactics of Napoleon upon which both the US and Mexico rely. No more training the men to stand in line, blazing away at an enemy. We are going to focus on small unit tactics."

Johnston stood to his feet, and started pacing behind his chair as he tried wrapping his mind around Will's vision. "That's going to require a lot more drilling, Buck, and more practice on the firing line. We're going to need more gunpowder and lead." He continued pacing, becoming lost in thought about how to implement the new tactics.

Mid-October brought with it a break in the sweltering heat, as summer, which had seemed determined to hold out as long as possible, finally gave up its assault on San Antonio. The day was perfect for a war game. Will joined Johnston on top of the Alamo chapel's southern wall. Johnston had selected two companies of infantry, which had been training in the new "Texas Model" tactics over the previous month.

The hundred fifty men were assembled in two companies of seventy-five men each, south of the fort. They were about to start a two-day war game west of town, one company pitted against the other.

As the soldiers started marching to the west, Will glanced down at a piece of paper he had received from Harrisburg. It was the approval for the new organization of the army. Although only a month old, the new congress had agreed to Will's proposal to fund a single battalion of infantry of eight companies, six hundred men in total. Will tried not to think about the fact that these two companies represented a quarter of the republic's infantry. In addition, congress approved the earlier expansion of the Texas Rangers under Major Caldwell, while keeping two companies of regular cavalry, under the command of Captain Seguin. A battery of artillery, totaling forty men, was also stationed at the Alamo under the command of Captain Dickinson, while another was to be stationed between a couple of coastal forts east of Galveston, under the command of Captain Carey.

The paper in Will's hand was also an irritant. In it, President Crockett explained Will needed to work with Thomas Rusk, whom congress had assigned to organize the republic's militia. Rusk hadn't talked to Will since the constitutional convention, when the two had found themselves on the opposite side of the slavery debate. How was he supposed to work with someone who wouldn't talk to him to organize the militia companies, which varied greatly in their sizes. Worse as far as Will was concerned, was their musters were poorly attended. On paper, Texas militia forces numbered more than four thousand men, and that only counted those present during the Revolution. Thousands more had arrived over the past few months, lured by the promise of cheap land. Even so, he had serious reservations Rusk would be able to muster more than a quarter if things came to a head with Mexico.

It wasn't something he cared to discuss with Johnston yet, so he tried setting the thought aside as he considered things which were actually going the right direction. In three weeks, he had the largest war game yet planned. In addition to six of Johnston's infantry companies, both of Seguin's cavalry would join in, as well as sixty rangers from Caldwell's command and Dickinson's battery. Around six hundred men would participate.

The large command tent Will had previously purloined from Santa Anna was set up a day's march from San Antonio. Will was joined by Lt. Colonel Johnston and Captain Seguin, as commander of the cavalry. Captain Dickinson was present as was Major Caldwell. A half dozen infantry captains rounded out those present, making the tent rather crowded.

Will glowered at Johnston, who he thought looked happier than a tornado in a Texas trailer park. He grumbled, "Sid, you look like a cat that found himself a bird to eat."

Johnston's sly smile spoke volumes. "Oh, please, General. I'm sure if your team had won yesterday, you'd be smiling too."

Will corrected him, "You mean, gloating." But it wasn't something he could deny, so he let the sniping go, even though it grated against him that Johnston's team of three hundred won the war game against his own team. The judge's ruling that Johnston's use of artillery was more effective tipped the balance into the Lt. Colonel's favor. Will tried to be philosophical about the loss. Despite Will's eight years of infantry experience, first in the regular US Army and then later in the Texas Army National Guard, he understood Johnston's formal training at West Point exposed him to a broader range of experiences. It hadn't hurt that Johnston took to the new "Texas Model" tactics like a new convert. Will soothed his wounded pride by reminding himself Johnston was actually a very gifted and skilled officer. In a world living only in Will's memories, he had risen to the rank of full general during the Civil War.

In addition to the tactics, another of Will's innovations was the "after action debrief" he and his officers were conducting. "Captain Seguin, your troopers would have been badly mauled when you attempted to move against company B. Most of the infantry were deployed effectively to counter your attack. Even though the judge ruled in your troopers' favor, I don't think he fully understands the effectiveness of our new model tactics."

Seguin nodded, "I thought the same thing, General Travis. Usually, there's a window of opportunity to move cavalry against an infantry unit after they fire their volley. But with the new tactics, there is no volley, just a constant rate of fire. Each rifle team always seems to have someone ready to fire."

The next morning, Will's six-hundred men quickly broke camp and marched back to the Alamo, less than twenty miles away. Next to him rode Major Caldwell. As the column marched along, the two men talked. "Major, when we move against the Comanche in a few months, in addition to your Rangers, I intend to take four of our infantry companies, Seguin's cavalry, as well as a couple of Dickinson's field pieces. My hope is we catch the Comanche by surprise with these new tactics."

Caldwell replied, "I have to admit, General, if these new tactics actually work, it's going to really change the role of cavalry on a battlefield."

Will agreed, "Here in the west, Santa Anna's lancers are a dying breed. Hell, even back east, I understand the army is looking at dragoons, to augment their infantry. That, I think, is the future of cavalry. Very mobile, but more likely to actually fight on foot once in combat."

The column ate up the distance to San Antonio, covering the score of miles by midafternoon. As Will led the column into the large Alamo Plaza, he saw a half dozen wagons along the western wall. His hopes began to rise as he rode over to the lead wagon. It was heavily laden, with a canvas tarp pulled tightly over the bed. Major Payton Wyatt, acting in his role of quartermaster, looked over the manifest as Will approached.

Wyatt pointed to the wagons, "General Travis, sir. It appears we've received supplies from the United States."

Will untied the ropes securing the first wagon's tarp and flung the canvas back, exposing several long crates, nailed closed. A teamster handed him a crowbar and he pried loose the nails and lifted the lid from the nearest box. He reached in and took from it a carbine. The rifled weapon was just under four feet long. The stock's deep brown wood was polished to a bright finish. The barrel was twenty-eight inches long and had been browned at the armory, giving it a dull, matted finish. Will flipped the block on the breech up, inspecting where the paper cartridge was inserted. As he held it in his hands, it looked and felt deadly. His grin was feral and untamed. The Model 1833 Halls Rifled Carbine had arrived.

The last wagon contained several dozen boxes with the words, 'Patent Arms Manufacturing' stenciled on their sides. Opening these boxes up, they found their order of Paterson Colt Revolving pistols. Will and his command had received two early Christmas presents.

Chapter 5

The ride between San Antonio and Harrisburg was uneventful for Will, Juan Seguin, and his father, Erasmo.

Will thought, "*I could get used to traveling in style,*" at the end of the trip.

They traveled in the elder Seguin's carriage, which was as comfortable a mode of travel for the period as could be had, except for the cold, early-December weather. An hour out from Harrisburg, they traveled through a newly platted town, the developers were marketing it as the new town of Houston, in honor of Texas' first general. Will shook his head at the irony the town was still named for Sam Houston, even though Crockett was considered by nearly all Texians to be a key hero in the revolution. The reasoning behind the developers' decision was lost on Will, as he thought it should have been named after the new president.

The naming of the new town after Houston left Will wondering about the mutability of history. On one hand, in the history he knew, the developers chose to honor Sam Houston for his victory by naming the town after him. Now, their choice perplexed him. If the same rationale was used here, by rights, the town should have celebrated Crockett's name. Will couldn't help but feel a mysterious paradox at work. Texas had won its independence without the fall of the Alamo. Hundreds of men, who otherwise would have fallen at the Alamo or been murdered at Goliad, yet lived.

"Yes," Will thought, there were exceptions like Jim Bowie, and now, he added the town of Houston to that list.

In Will's quest to stay alive, he knew he had changed history. He had spent a more than a few sleepless nights puzzling over how the future would look in a world in which hundreds of men, who would have otherwise died in a Texas Revolution that would never be. Did the world he come from simply cease to be, or did it move along a parallel path after his own transference? He even briefly questioned whether this was still an elaborate dream, even after all these months. These were questions to which he had no answer. To cope, he trusted that God, for reasons he would never fathom, had allowed this to happen. When he allowed his thoughts to wonder about the poor Mexican *soldados* who had died, who otherwise might have survived, he had no answers for that.

He shook his head, mentally shelving the thought as the coach pulled up next to a clapboard building serving as Harrisburg's lone hotel. Now that President Crockett had been in office for almost two months, he wanted to go over the details of the coming Comanche campaign. Since the election, Will's communication with Crockett had been by correspondence, and there were simply too many details to discuss, to leave things even to the speed of a fast horse.

The next morning as they sat in President Crockett's split-log cabin, the president welcomed the three men, "Thank you all for joining me in my humble presidential mansion. As I like to call it, the Texas White House." He swept his hand grandly around the roughhewn logs of the cabin, which served as both his home and office in Harrisburg. The government's tenure in Harrisburg was temporary and they were too cash poor to do more than rent a ramshackle collection of buildings to house the government.

"After many a letter to my Liza, she has agreed to join me here. I suspect the humble nature of my home may have something to do with her decision. She was plum pleased, given the size of the house, there would be no more housework than before."

"Now that I've given you the nickel tour, let's get down to the republic's business. I want to express my thanks to you, Señor Seguin for accepting my invitation. As I mentioned in my letter, you're native to the soil here and your perspective on how the Spanish and Mexican governments have dealt with the Comanche is priceless." From the elder Seguin, Crockett turned to Will and warmly welcomed him, "Buck, it is good to see you, boy. I hadn't realized how much I missed you until now. The last couple of months have found me busier than a one-eyed cat watching nine rat holes. And Captain Seguin, thank you for bringing the perspective of our mounted forces."

After the four men were seated around a large, wooden table, he said, "I had asked Sam to be with us today, but since the election he has chosen to represent Texas' interests with the Cherokee by brokering their tribal claims with our government. Recent correspondence from him has been favorable, but the claims proceed at their own pace."

Switching subjects, Crockett asked, "Señor Seguin, am I to understand correctly you have been in contact with the governor of New Mexico?"

Erasmo Seguin spread his hands and shook his head, "Alas, President Crockett, would that it was so. No. But in my dealings, I have talked with several traders from the Comancheros."

Crockett interrupted him, "How are these Comancheros related to the Comanche?"

"They are mostly traders from *Nuevo Mexico*, mostly from Santa Fe and Albuquerque. They get their name from trading with the various bands of the Comanche. There are many things the Comanche want which can't be obtained from the buffalo, and if they can't raid it from Texas, then they will trade with the Comancheros for it."

Erasmo paused for a moment, before continuing, "There's a story I have heard repeated among these half-breed traders. In 1779, a few years before my own birth, the Spanish governor, a man named Juan Bautista de Anza, in Santa Fe, grew tired of the constant raids on the settlements under his jurisdiction. So, he formed up an army of six hundred men, led them into the Comancheria, and defeated the Comanche in battle."

The other men leaned forward, hanging on his every word, "Anza's army included *Nuevo Mexicanos* as well as more than two hundred Apache auxiliaries. Largely traveling at night, he used his Apaches to screen the main force. They were deep into the Comancheria when they came across a large village. Anza's men attacked the town, capturing many of the women and children. In an ironic twist of fate, the Comanche warriors were at that same time busy attacking Taos. Following the capture of the Comanche town, Anza ambushed the returning warriors, killing their war chief and many men. What followed was a series of raids by Anza's army from Santa Fe. They fought and killed Comanche warriors wherever they offered battle."

Crockett asked, "But how did Anza bring the Comanche to the peace table?"

Erasmo Seguin nodded his head, and stood up. He walked over to the door, which was open and looked out to the west, in the direction of the Comancheria. "Peace with the Comanche, that's the elusive question, Mr. President. It is a question we Tejanos and you *Norteamericos* equally have in common. I read about General Houston's proposal to treat with the Comanche during the election and I think his way is wrong. Unlike the Cherokee, where there is a powerful sense of tribal unity, the Comanche bands owe no allegiance to each other. If it were not for Texas and Mexico, it is just as likely those different bands would war against each other.

"But back to Governor Anza. The first thing he did was have his army take captives, just like the Comanche. This forced the Comanche to trade their own captives for those held by the Spanish. The second thing he did was strategically release other captives with the news that Anza would treat with all the Comanche bands for peace, or none of them. He understood what General Houston never did. The Comanche nation lacks a central voice of authority. Each band is responsible for their own actions and a treaty with one band is not binding on any of the others. To bring them to treaty he had to force it on all of the Comanche bands bordering *Nuevo Mexico*."

Will shuddered at the complexity of the problem. "It looks like we're going to need our own Indians." As he spoke, he experienced an ah-ha moment. Less than a year after arriving in Travis' body, and his modern vocabulary had taken a beating. What would the other men at the table think should he refer to an Indian as a Native American? He shook the moment off, continuing, "Juan, would you see if Flacco's people would be willing to work with us as scouts and guides? Also, Mr. President, would you reach out to Mr. Houston and see if he can talk the Cherokee into fielding a company of Rangers, on the Republic's dime?"

The president chuckled drily. "That's a pretty turn of a phrase for fleecing the treasury." His eyes followed

Erasmo's, as they

looked out the door of the small cabin, looking west, in the direction of the Comancheria. "What do we do with the Comanche when we finally drive them to the peace table, gentlemen? I despised what Jackson did to the Cherokee, but there were existing treaties between the Cherokee people and the federal government, ignored by Andy Jackson. Without a treaty between us and the Comanche, it's akin to having the Mongol horde living in our outhouse."

Will's thoughts, while not as colorful, mirrored the president's. Once again, Will found himself facing a common paradox of history. From what he could tell, the Cherokee were often times more civilized than their white neighbors, having frequently adapted to the dominant culture and religion, while tribes, like the Lipan Apache struggled to maintain their tribal grounds and customs in the lands disputed by Texas, Mexico, and the Comanche. The Comanche defied Will's modern view, and it was evident books like *"Bury My Heart at Wounded Knee"* held no correlation to the Comanche. They were a vastly different people than Will had been taught by Hollywood and school.

Crockett interrupted his thought, "I fear their days of wandering the plains may be numbered. Buck, it would surprise me nary at all, if by the time your boy, Charlie, is married with children of his own the world of the Plains Indians will be over. I'll not deny it, while I have my concerns over how we wage war against the Comanche, I can scarcely sleep at night if we don't look to our own. Because we need to secure the frontier, it will be my policy, as president, to enforce the territorial integrity of Texas, even when it brings us into conflict with Mexico or with the Comanche."

Not for the first time, Will noted how Crockett could drop the rough veneer and allow the well-spoken, self-educated man to shine through. The president continued, "We'll respect and honor every man's private property rights and make a home here in Texas for any tribe that agrees to live by our laws, as it appears the Cherokee will. If we can have peace with the Comanche, we'll make no claim on the plains north of the Red River. But if the Comanche attempt to live or travel south of the Red, they will do so only in peace. If they want trade with us, I'll be glad to put policies into place encouraging trade. But I recall from my days in Washington City words from ol' Thomas Jefferson. 'Millions for defense and not a cent for tribute.' Sam was wrong when he advocated this when he ran against me, and time hasn't made it any more right. We're done trying to buy one band or another of the Comanche off of us to keep them from raiding. All that has done is makes the other bands want to hit us all the harder."

"One last thing," Crockett said, "Buck, you'll need to develop a plan for dealing with the squaws and adolescent boys and old men you may capture. I'm sure some of those West Point boys you've recruited can set up a military prison where they can be housed under the best conditions you can manage. But make sure our own soldiers' safety comes first."

As the meeting came to an end, the president took Erasmo aside, "Señor Seguin, I am in your debt for joining your son and General Travis in meeting with me. I don't like indebting myself further, but I have a request related to the coming war."

As the elder Seguin nodded for Crockett to continue, he said, "When our army is successful in the war against the Comanche, we need to be ready to deal with any captives. Would you consent to using your connections within the Catholic church to establish a refuge of safety at one of the nearby missions where any children taken captive can be taken, where they will be cared for and protected against any retaliatory depredations from our loyal citizens?"

"Think nothing of it, Mr. President." As Erasmo joined Will and Juan outside, He turned and added, "I count it as no favor to ask for an act of charity for those innocents who will pay the price for their elders' war."

Chapter 6

The small room in the newly constructed hotel felt much larger once the Seguins left Harrisburg with the sunrise, returning to San Antonio. Will lingered in town, at President Crockett's behest. He pulled his pocket-watch from his vest pocket and, seeing the time, decided to walk across the few muddy streets to the president's humble house.

He picked his way down the streets, dodging muddy craters in the road, his hands tucked into his pockets, warding off the morning chill.

"Asphalt. That's what I should invent," Will thought as he misjudged his step and felt his bootheel sink into the mud.

"Would make tons of money selling paving material to towns," he muttered, shaking mud from his bootheel.

Crockett, with a buffalo robe wrapped around his shoulders, sat on the porch to his "Texas White House," talking with several congressmen. As Will approached he heard Crockett saying, "I understand the problem with specie, Tom. The fly in the ointment is that without both a tariff and property tax, even as low as what has been proposed, we can't protect our borders or defend our trade at sea."

Crockett grinned ruefully at the other man, before continuing, "It's not like any of us was surprised that Santa Anna was denounced when he got to Vera Cruz or that the Corro administration in Mexico City rejected the treaty Santa Anna signed with us. The truth of the matter is without a standing army and navy we can't protect our trade or our territory. If we can't do those, then we might as well go to Washington with our tail between our legs and hat in our hand."

The congressman said, "What's so bad about that, Mr. President? Annexation would give us room to grow and lower our tax burden."

Crockett glowered, "And for how long, Tom? I know Andy Jackson's on the way out in March and there will be that Van Buren fellow next, and I hear tell he's not sweet on annexation. I'd rather we chart our own path. And part of that path means we must figure out how to pay our own way. Taxes, and I hate 'em as much as you, are a necessary evil. Now, Tom, I'll be glad to talk solutions with you, but I'm afraid that General Travis here and I have a packet-cutter to catch. We're off to Galveston this morning to review the island's fortifications."

Crockett bade farewell to the men as he stepped off the porch into the muddy road, grabbed Will by the elbow and headed toward Buffalo Bayou, where a small schooner was anchored.

"I hope you don't mind the change in plans, but last week, I submitted my budget, along with some new taxes and as you can imagine, I got some of our congress critters angrier than wet hens at me. Getting out of town for the day suits me fine."

They boarded the schooner from a skiff, which transported them from the shore. The boat weighed anchor, and swung around, heading for the open waters of Galveston Bay. The president stood next to the railing, watching the shore slide by as the small double-masted ship picked up speed when the northerly breeze filled the canvas sails. Will finally asked, "Are we really going to check on the fortifications on Galveston or is this just an attempt to dodge a few unhappy politicians?"

"Both, actually. Did you know that Andy Jackson sent his congratulations to David Burnet over our independence? And he sent a personal letter to Lorenzo congratulating him on his election as vice president. But he knows how to hold a grudge. He never has forgiven me for fighting him on what he did to the Cherokee. I heard from Stephen Austin that he's tabled any action on recognizing our independence."

Will grimaced. "Any chance Jackson'll relent?"

Crockett guffawed, slapping his palm on the railing. "Jackson's too pigheaded to do that. But never mind him. Steve has met with Van Buren and has received his promise that recognizing our independence will be one of his first actions come March."

"That's good. How is your former electoral rival doing as Minister to the United States?" Will asked.

"Like a fish to water, I'd say. I know he'd rather be playing the role of impresario, but the constitution's pretty much put paid to that. I expect once Van Buren is in office that Steve's job will get a bit easier. But he's had a fair degree of luck scrounging up a loan here and there and a few gifts as well. That money, as you well know, is coming in handy."

Will glanced down into the murky depths of the bay before asking, "What about Europe? Any word from our ministers there?"

"Word? Yes. Good news? Not yet," Crockett replied. "I wonder if I made a mistake appointing Colonel Grant as chargé d'affaires to the British. I figured being a former subject that he'd do well. But his last letter just asks for more money and gives me empty promises. Dammit, Buck, it's only been a few months, but I have my doubts that I chose well with him."

Will prompted him, "What about France and the Germanies?"

Crockett cheered up at the question, "I'm glad you suggested appointing Mirabeau Lamar as minister to France. That man has fire enough for two men. I can't rightly say that he's making headway, but I received word just last week that he's secured a couple of loans. He has even been able to press the French to allow emigration, which is something I didn't think he'd be able to wrangle. The more of us there are the harder it will be to force us out. The Germanies, I've appointed Edward Harkort to act as our chargé d'affaires there. He's actually still in Galveston at the moment. We'll see him later today. He's been building the new fort there. I don't want to get false hope, but I am trusting that he'll be able to talk more Germans into coming. They're hard workers and if he's any example, they like building things."

When the tiny Schooner docked in Galveston, Crockett led them down the gangplank and across the dock to a livery stable. With rented horses, the two men threaded their way through the crowded streets. As headquarters for the fledgling Texas Navy and the nascent Marine Corps, as well as the best port in the Republic, Galveston had grown rapidly over the past year, as a couple of thousand people called it home and even more transitioned through the town on the way to where they were going.

There were fewer houses as they rode eastward. They crossed over several sand dunes until they arrived on the eastern tip of the island, where an octagonal earthen fort had been constructed. Along each wall a parapet was being constructed. Large canvas tarps were draped over several large coastal guns, in storage until their platforms were ready.

When Will and Crockett entered the fort, Will noticed Edward Harkort approaching. Nominally an engineer under Will's command, he had been working with the Navy to construct this fort since the middle of the year. With a thick German accent, he said, "I'm honored to have you here, President Crockett and General Travis." His words were precise and formal, while his tone conveyed a strong hint of reproach at their unannounced arrival.

Ignoring the German's tone, Crockett waved him off with, "Don't mind us, Captain Harkort. Had to escape all those congress critters in Harrisburg, and thought we'd take a gander at this here fort of yours."

Mollified, Harkort scurried away, shouting at several slaves working on framing one of the parapets. Will cocked an eyebrow at Crockett, "Labor problems, David?"

Crockett's eyes tracked across the fort and saw the slaves. He shrugged, "I left this in the hands of Harkort, Buck. Let's ask him. He's proven to be a trustworthy man."

When asked about the use of slaves, Harkort said, "I was approached by several men of property on the island and asked if I would lease their laborers. According to your own directive, General, I was permitted to use land scripts to pay for labor. But I have also paid each of the negroes two bits each day for their labor. I don't care for what slave labor does to the value of each man's worth, but by using them I have progressed faster than I would have without them. Their owners get some cheap land on the frontier, and these men get some silver in their pockets."

Will opened his mouth to respond, but closed it as he realized Harkort was making the best of a miserable system. On one hand, it gratified him to see Harkort's own distaste for the system, but he was also disturbed how the German compromised with it, and harnessed it to the military's purpose. "Very well, Captain." He almost asked about where he was getting fifty cents per day for each of the slaves, then decided he didn't want to know the answer.

After inspecting the fortification, Will and Crockett rode out of the fort back to Galveston. "Will, people might mistake you for a Yankee rather than a Southerner with your views."

Will grinned sheepishly, "I'd rather they mistake me for a Texan."

The next day Will was back in Harrisburg, sitting in Crockett's small cabin. Ledgers and other recordkeeping books were scattered across the table as he tried to make sense of the income and expenses. After looking over a stack of invoices, totaling more than $50,000, he set them aside and asked, "What has Michel Menard been able to accomplish as treasurer?"

Crockett frowned, "Not as much as he promised. Oh, he's hiring reputable men to act as customs agents at our ports and has actually proposed an idea for selling land to newcomers. But it's not taking off. it's just the hole we are digging ourselves into is so damned deep, that it's going to take a miracle to pull us out of it. The republic is more than a million dollars in debt, and I can assure you that we took in only slightly more than one hundred thousand dollars this year. Who's going to extend credit to a broke country?"

Will whistled appreciatively, and said, "That's no small feat, David. For what it's worth, I think you need to give Menard a free rein with the treasury regarding to customs duties. I'd be willing to bet that more than two million dollars in trade will come through our ports and borders with the United States next year. The tariff alone should be able to generate more than a quarter million dollars. I know it's a drop in the bucket. But it's a start."

As Will continued flipping through the various ledgers, he found one which listed as assets 251,579,800 acres. 26,280,000 acres were marked as distributed, either during the Spanish or Mexican eras. Will showed the information to Crockett, "Here's the long-term solution to our money problems, David. We have more than two hundred and twenty million acres of public land in the Republic. The first thing we need to do is empower Menard's treasury department to collect property taxes. From there, we need to quickly settle as many of the title disputes between people as we can. The sooner a piece of land has a clear title, the sooner it can be taxed."

Crockett shook his head in disagreement, "Buck, I'm not in favor of taxing people coming and going. Won't we make enough just selling the public lands? It seems to me that it would take a couple of life times to sell all the land."

Will glibly replied, "If a man owns six-hundred-forty acres, at a minimum, his land is worth three hundred twenty dollars. That assumes it is truly valued at the fifty cents an acre we're currently selling our public lands for. Now, if the tax on the property is one per cent, this farmer or rancher pays three dollars and twenty cents. That's a small price to pay, David. Especially if we permit the tax collectors to accept grain, corn or cotton in place of hard currency."

Crockett smiled at the thought of paying in kind. "I like that idea. Although how Menard's revenue collectors would manage it would be a sight to see."

"That gives me an idea, David. You should appoint some people to study what it would take to form a commodities bureau."

Crockett eyed Will skeptically. "A what?"

Will continued, "A commodities bureau. Here's what I'm thinking. When people pay their property taxes with commodities, the Commodities bureau could exchange the goods with certificates, not unlike the treasury certificates from the United States. But our certificates would be backed by the value of what was traded. The bureau could sell the commodities that are collected in the States or even in Europe."

Crockett's face was one of surprise. "That sounds like a capital idea. What kind of commodities would we allow people to use to pay their taxes? Because as I understand it, the commodities get passed through your bureau and turned into what is basically currency."

Will gave it some thought and grabbed a stub of a pencil and jotted down a list. When done, he read it back to Crockett, "Of course, the first two are gold and silver. Add to them cotton, wheat, sugar, corn, and coffee, and you have the basis of a basket of commodities. The way to keep it working is the bureau will have to adjust the objective value of the commodities within the basket to keep the related value of the certificates stable."

Crockett rubbed his temples, "That seems complicated."

"In a perfect world, we could rely on a currency backed by gold and silver. The problem is that Texas has neither," Will said, "by trading certificates to our farmers and ranchers for the commodities they produce, it establishes both a value for the commodity being traded as well as for the certificate. What's the most valuable cash crop produced in the Republic today?"

"Cotton."

Will could tell the wheels were spinning in Crockett's head, so he helped to fill in the details, "Let's say we collect ten thousand bales of cotton as payment for taxes. We could then sell it to the British or the Yankees for gold or silver. We turn around and put the gold and silver in our vaults and issues certificates in the amount received."

Crockett frowned. "I can see how it could generate revenue for the government and even how it can put money into circulation, but it's going to take someone special to run this. I don't suppose you'd consider it?"

"I've got more on my plate than I can say grace over, David," Will said, "But I'll tell you who I think would do well with it. Erasmo Seguin. Turn the project over to him, with the authority of the government behind him and I'll bet he'd have it running before the end of next year."

Crockett scrawled some notes down and said, "Enough of this. If I stare at any more numbers I'm going to lose my mind. Did I tell you that my Liza is supposed to be here by Christmas?"

"You mentioned something yesterday, as I recall," Will replied, "But I don't think you said when you were expecting her to arrive."

Crockett stood, and shuffled the ledgers and piles of paper into what Will hoped was a semblance of order. After what seemed like an hour, but was probably less than a minute Crockett confessed, "Buck, I've not been the kind of man that I should have been to Liza or to Polly before she passed."

Will's eyebrows arched as the president mentioned his two marriages, and Crockett hurriedly added, "Oh, I've never been unfaithful to my Liza or Polly, bless her soul. Well, unless it was to the frontier or my itch to travel. But I've been gone from home far more than I was ever there. I told myself I was doing it for her and the children, always to provide a better life, but when I saw you bring your own son back to San Antonio with you, I knew I had missed the mark. When she gets here, I don't want to make a mess of things."

Will smiled and placed his hand on his older friend's shoulder. "I think you'll do fine, David. One thing I have learned over the past year is that Texas is a place for second chances."

Chapter 7

March of 1837 roared in like a lion. A bitterly frigid wind blew across the plains from the arctic north. As Will rode toward the San Fernando Catholic Church he fervently hoped this would be the last cold front of the season. He pulled his coat up tighter around his neck and tried to ignore the blasts of icy wind cutting through his woolen overcoat. Small hands, in woolen mittens, were wrapped around his waist, as Charlie sat behind Will, his feet dangling above the stirrups.

After the Revolution, several prominent members of the San Antonio community came together, pooling resources to establish an academy. Since the closing of a public school a couple of years earlier, the children of Bexar had been without a school. In the previous fall, the academy launched, as a partnership between monied Bexareno interests and the local Franciscan monastery. They leased space from the parish of San Fernando. Most of the students were children of San Antonio's more affluent residents. And, Will, despite his republican sensibilities, found himself, as General of the Army, considered by most, one of the town's more affluent and eligible bachelors. Plus, as Will thought about it, Charlie was thriving, learning, and making new friends.

The seven months since returning home with Charlie had been good for both Will and the boy. For Will, putting some separation between the stress inherent in commanding Texas' army and his home life was restoring a semblance of balance. More than a year had passed since the transference; he long ago decided to make the most of the circumstances in which he found himself. In addition to his military duties, he worked to undo the abandonment issues resulting from the five-year separation the boy had suffered away from his father. It seemed to be working, Charlie appeared to be happy. Will was amazed how quickly Travis' son, now eight years old, adjusted to life in San Antonio. Part of that he attributed to the time spent with the Seguin children. Part of it, Will realized, came from the investment Will made in time spent with Charlie. Will was no expert chess player, but over the winter, he took time to teach him how to play chess, and more than a few cold evenings were spent, the two of them sitting cross-legged before the hearth fire, playing the game.

As the bitter wind whistled across the main plaza, they arrived at the church where they saw several children, bundled in their winter clothing, hurrying into the relative warmth of the building. Will offered Charlie his hand and helped him slide off the horse. As the boy's feet touched the ground, Will echoed words his own father had told him a lifetime ago, "Behave yourself, son. When school is released, go home with Teresa and Jose, and I'll pick you up from the Seguins on the way home this evening."

Charlie stopped and turned to wave, as a gust of wind nearly swept his hat from his head. Grabbing at it before it was carried away, the boy turned and ran toward the church's heavy oaken doors.

Will pulled his reins and wheeled around and pointed his horse toward the Alamo, allowing his thoughts to drift. He returned to his conversation with President Crockett back in December. One of the outflows from it was a bill to implement the Texas Land Office. The TLO had received its charter the previous month.

The plan, when fully implemented, would be to run the sale of public land through the land office. Gold and silver were in very short supply throughout the republic, so with a little prodding by Will, Crockett had convinced Congress to promote land sales through a land bank which "loaned" the funds to settlers to purchase the land. No actual currency would trade hands. The settlers would take possession of the land, and the Land Bank would receive a promissory note from the settler for the value of the land. The notes would carry an interest rate of three percent, which was slightly below international rates, and carried monthly, quarterly, or yearly repayment schedules, as selected by the borrower. Will recalled a letter he read from the

Treasurer of the Republic of Texas, in which the Canadian born Michel Menard enthusiastically endorsed the scheme. The money received from the ongoing payments would flow into the general fund each year.

As he crossed the wooden bridge over the San Antonio River he adjusted the thought. That depends on the effects of the banking crisis. In his history books, he remembered reading about the crisis of 1837 in the United States. While he saw no way to influence the coming crisis, hopefully the steps he talked Crockett into implementing would cushion its effect on Texas in the coming years.

"Maybe Stephen Austin can exploit the crisis and increase immigration into Texas." Will thought, *"Especially from free states."*

For what seemed like the thousandth time, he puzzled over ways to increase immigration from both the free states and Europe. The surest way to end slavery was to make Texas more accessible to Yankee and European immigration.

Realistically though, the best hope in the short run, was to continue expanding the agricultural economy. Before Texas could successfully build industry, there would need to be railroads, and before the railroads would be built, the border issue with Mexico would need to be sorted out. But first, he needed peace with the Comanche.

As usual, when Will passed through the Alamo's gatehouse, the gate was open. Except during times of crisis, the gate stayed open during daylight hours. Six companies of infantry were assembled in the Alamo plaza. The 450 men looked sharp in their butternut uniforms and black slouch hats, each man holding his carbine breechloader at attention. The last of Santa Anna's captured gold and silver had gone to buy the uniforms for the army. Even so, never had the army of the Republic of Texas looked more professional than they did then, standing in formation in the plaza.

Opposite the infantry, on the other side of the plaza, Captain Seguin's two companies of cavalry were assembled. Like the infantry, the eighty troopers were arrayed in the new uniforms. Each trooper carried a holstered Paterson Colt Revolver at his belt and a carbine breechloader in a saddle scabbard. Standing above the plaza, along the west wall, Captain Dickinson's forty artillerymen also stood at attention.

In the center of the plaza Lt. Colonel Johnston stood, waiting for each company commander to report the status of his company. Will dismounted and joined Johnston. "Just a week to go before we head into the Comancheria again, Sid," Will said quietly. "Did the company commanders inform their men that today's drills will determine which companies go and which staying behind?"

Johnston shrugged, "Lots of boys are upset that both of Seguin's companies are going. All of the boys are eager to take the fight to the Comanche."

Shaking his head, Will said, "It's because they don't know better. By the time the campaign is over, most of them will gladly trade places with those who stay."

Johnston issued commands to each company commander for the day's exercise. As Juan Seguin joined them, they followed one company as it marched over to a firing range they had put together a half mile north east of the Alamo. There were several dozen targets downrange of the line, set at intervals between 100 and 400 yards away.

Will had stood on this very line on many occasions, firing one of the rifled carbines at the targets. Today, he watched the men of Company C as they practiced. A corporal, standing on the end of the firing line, opened the breech while pulling a paper cartridge from the black leather box at his hip. He bit the end from the cartridge and poured the powder into the breechblock and then slid the bullet and paper on top of the powder before closing the breech. He next reached into a cap box at his waist and took a percussion cap and set it on the nipple. He raised the rifled carbine to his shoulder and aimed at the target downrange and fired. He flipped the breech open and grabbed another cartridge and ripped it open with his teeth, and repeated the process over again, and less than ten seconds later sent another bullet flying to the target.

As the three officers watched the soldiers at the firing line, Will saw pride on Johnston's face as the paper targets at four hundred yards were torn to shreds. He slapped the other man on the back and said, "Your men are doing well, Sid. That's some of the finest shooting I've seen."

Johnston pointed to his men, and said, "They're good men, Buck. But you should know we're finding that when we get out much further than three hundred yards, the amount of gas escaping the breech reduces the bullet's power."

From the firing range, Johnston led them over to a field southeast of the fort, where another company was simulating an advance over broken ground common across the Great Plains. As they watched the company go through open order drill tactics, Will watched the quartet of soldiers closest to them and observed as the rifle team split into two, 2-man teams. The first two men dashed forward twenty or more feet before seeking the meager shelter behind thistle bushes. The two men behind them raced forward, rifles at the ready as they too sought out a place from which they could fire from cover. While the exercise was "dry fire" it was clear the idea behind the fire team was working.

Will and Johnston followed Seguin back to the Alamo where they climbed to the top of the chapel, where they were able to watch the two companies of troopers skirmishing against each other, east of the fort. Seguin was quick to point out, "We're not able to exactly imitate the four-man teams on the firing line, as we need horse handlers, but other than that, my troopers are turning into some good dragoons."

As was Seguin's habit, he talked about the tactics his troopers were using, while Will and Johnston watched and occasionally made notes or asked questions. After the skirmish ended, the officers climbed back down to the ground and escaped to above the hospital, to Will's office. "Sid, I'm impressed with what you've done with the infantry. I'm going to leave it in your hands which four companies will accompany the cavalry and Rangers into the Comancheria next week."

Johnston smiled broadly and said, "I think I can manage. Much of the credit belongs to you, Buck. I can't help but wonder what they would say at West Point about our tactics. With them, it was always about mustering your infantry into line of battle and throwing as much lead at the enemy's line. Can you imagine a line of Comanche infantry?" He laughed at the image.

Will found the image equally ridiculous and smiled. "It begs the question, I wonder how these tactics would fare against the US or even a European army."

Johnston shrugged, "I couldn't rightly say for sure. But in a lot of ways these tactics are an evolutionary development building on the tactics you and President Crockett used on the Rio Grande last year. We saw how well Santa Anna's army managed against them."

"Fair enough Sid. But we had them at a severe disadvantage. They were charging across a couple of hundred yards of river. I don't think it would have been as nearly as one-sided if the river hadn't been in the way." Will paused, thinking about what he was trying to say and then looked between Johnston and Seguin, continued, "I don't want us to become complacent or think that because we're Texians and have repeatedly defeated Santa Anna and his famous army that we'll always be able to do it. I also don't want us falling into the conceit just because the Comanche aren't civilized they can't beat us.

"If you have any question about that, I have a mountain of reports over the past half year from Major Caldwell and his Ranger companies about how the Comanche have reacted to his forts."

Both the other officers swallowed hard. They had read the reports from the Ranger companies. There were several large raids attempted on the Ranger forts, and it was only the arrival of the revolvers which had allowed the Rangers to keep the Comanche on one side of the walls of the forts and the Rangers on the other. Even so, Johnston said, with an air of informality, "When it comes to comparing our soldiers against the US or even against Europe, you have nothing to worry about here, Buck. I served in the United States Army for seven years before coming to Texas and you have developed the most demanding and rigorous training regimen I could ever have imagined. It's not the hours on the firing range or the frequent war games pitting company against company that we've waged over the past six months. No, it's these long marches, carrying full packs that we've been doing almost weekly. Hell, if you'd told me two months ago we would be able to take these companies here and rouse them before the sun was up and march them up the north to that little town on the Colorado River. Waterloo, I think. Eighty miles away! I'd have laughed and said it couldn't be done."

Will's feet tingled painfully as he recalled the

memory of the march. There was no regret in the decision, however, they had taken no horses with them, and every officer joined in every bone-jarring step along the way, both directions in less than six days.

Johnston continued, "It's not something I enjoyed, but the ability to move our infantry across country quickly will come in handy soon, I suspect."

Will said, "Sid, if memory serves me correctly, wasn't it George Washington who said, 'To be prepared for War is one of the most effectual means of preserving peace?' I know peace can only be had with the Comanche when they agree to our terms, but when peace has been achieved, I believe a well-trained and well-equipped army will keep the peace. At least I hope so."

As was typical of Texas weather in the winter, the morning of the 6th of March dawned with temperatures hovering a few degrees above freezing. But by mid-morning, it was twenty degrees warmer as the column of infantry snaked along the road heading north, kicking up dust as six hundred feet trod steadily forward, followed by two horse-drawn field guns. Seguin's cavalry and a couple of dozen Lipan Apache warriors ranged ahead of the column and to either side.

Thinking back to the early morning, before leaving the Alamo, Will replayed the image in his head. As was becoming the norm, there was little fanfare as wives, sweethearts, and children bade husbands, lovers, and fathers goodbye in the predawn darkness that was punctured by lamps hung around interior walls of the Alamo. The lamps cast a gloomy glow as Charlie grabbed Will by the hand and pulled him down to the child's level and gave him a fierce hug. The boy's lips trembled as he tried to keep the tears from flowing down his cheeks. "Pa, please come back. I don't want to be alone again."

Will returned the hug with his own bear hug and then held the boy at arm's length, willing his words to be true, "I'll be back soon, son."

As the morning sun climbed higher in the sky, the prospect of leaving his son in the company of the Seguin children didn't seem fair, but, as he kept his horse moving forward in the center of the trail, he couldn't keep the thought out of his mind that there was never a good time for a parent to ride off to war, leaving a child to face an uncertain future.

When the little army stopped for lunch, about twelve miles north of San Antonio, Will climbed down from his horse and grabbed a meal with several officers. As they talked, one mentioned the date was the 6th of March 1837. Will was struck by the fact it was a year to the day after the Alamo had fallen in the history he remembered, but would never be here. He looked at the well-equipped and uniformed men around him and compared them to the ragtag force which had defended the Rio Grande and Nueces Rivers from Santa Anna's professional army. "We *have* come a long way," Will said to no one. With lunch over, he mounted his horse and led his command northward.

If things went according to plan, Major Caldwell would meet Will's column at the Ranger compound, Fort Bee, on the Brazos River, where the Bosque flowed into it, with 120 of his Rangers. A battalion of militia cavalry had been assembled at Columbus a week earlier and should be waiting for his command at the bend in the Colorado River, where the army's quartermaster company had stationed a half dozen heavy-laden supply wagons.

The plan was simple. The militia battalion's purpose was to secure the army's supply line. Even though supplies had been pre-positioned at Fort Bee, Will was under no illusion that more supplies would be needed to keep his army in the field. The militia would hold a few locations between the Colorado River and the Comancheria, and would also provide mounted escorts for supply wagons moving behind his column.

Any doubt Will may have harbored about the army's ability to quickly cover ground, fell away as it marched north. The army's training was paying dividends. Three days after leaving the Alamo, the army was camped along the Colorado river, eighty miles to the north. Six days after that, on the 15th of March, Will's column arrived at Fort Bee, where they met Major Caldwell's command of Rangers. Each Texas Ranger carried one of the new revolver pistols and from looking at their weaponry, the pistols had already seen plenty of action. Additionally, Sam Houston came through, and roused the Cherokee to field a Ranger company too, and they came with another thirty men.

While waiting for some of the supplies to arrive, Will held a council of war. Attending were the executive officer for the infantry battalion, Major Payton Wyatt, Major Caldwell, and Captain Seguin. During the earlier planning stages, Will decided to leave Johnston in command of the Alamo, and bring his second in command, Wyatt. They decided to spend the next few days integrating Caldwell's Rangers into several tactical scenarios, to allow the Rangers to adjust to Will's force.

When he was satisfied the mixed command was ready, on the morning of the 21st of March, Will led his army of more than five hundred men back into the Comancheria.

Chapter 8

By the eighth night, Will was getting used to the long, nightly marches. Since leaving Fort Bee, Will's force followed the meandering path of the Brazos River to the northwest. Caldwell's Ranger companies, working in tandem with the Apache scouts and the Cherokee Rangers, scouted ahead of Will's Infantry, while Seguin's cavalry covered the column's flanks as they snaked along the river each night. According to Flacco, who had returned to lead the Apaches despite his permanent limp, most Comanche bands camped along the many rivers crisscrossing the Comancheria. As the sun rose on the morning of the ninth day, with the command more than 120 miles into the Comancheria, Will called a meeting with Majors Caldwell and Wyatt, as well as Captain Seguin and Flacco.

Will was effusive in his praise. "I can't say enough good things about our Apache allies and Cherokee Rangers. Both have impressed the hell out of me by the way they have aided your Rangers, Matt, in screening our main column."

Caldwell smiled wanly, stifling a yawn. "General, I know the Cherokee ain't plains Indians, like the Comanche or Flacco's people, but I want you to know that as scouts go, a fair number of them are better than many of my Rangers. Once we've done whipped the Comanche, I'd think mighty kindly on you if you was to ask Congress to expand the Frontier Battalion to include a full company of Cherokees."

Will spread his hands, "From your lips to God's ears, Matt. Getting Congress to authorize another company of Rangers may be a sticking point. You've got no idea how hard I had to fight to get Congress to authorize the supplies we needed for our present campaign. What about spreading thirty or forty through your existing companies, though?"

Caldwell scratched at his week-old beard, scowling as he considered Will's idea. As he pondered it, his features softened, and he replied, "It might could be a good idea, General. I got me some excellent men under my command, but I do believe they might learn a thing or three from adding a few Cherokee into each of the companies." He paused and gave Flacco a long, hard stare, which the Apache returned in equal measure. Eventually he continued, "Might be, some of Flacco's braves might want to join too."

Flacco's stare remained fixed on the Ranger, but he replied in Spanish. With a twinkle in his eye, Seguin quickly translated, "Flacco says his braves might be able to teach Caldwell's women how to be warriors."

Caldwell's eyes grew wide with surprise before he burst out laughing, doubling up with mirth. Will wasn't sure he saw the hard-bitten Ranger wipe a tear away when he said, "Like as not, Flacco, your boys could. The offer still stands."

He turned his attention back to Will and said, "I know a few of my boys will throw Texas-sized conniption fits, because the Indians ain't white enough, but hell, I already got me a few Mexicans serving in my companies what can outride and outshoot most of my other boys. When it comes to the Ranger whose got my back, General, I'd rather have the best. When I scratch a Ranger's skin, what I expect to see is the mettle of his courage." Caldwell yawned again and took his leave. Part of his Rangers acted as mounted pickets throughout the day, and he still needed to make sure they were in place before he could rest.

As Caldwell moved off, Juan Seguin smirked and said, "General, you are the sly one, you are."

Will looked at Seguin quizzically, "What do you mean, Juan?"

"If you get your way, the Rangers, they'll be the frog in cool water, not noticing the fire under the pot, as it warms the water, until its eventually boiling."

Will wasn't sure where Seguin was going with it, but the captain continued, "In a couple of years you'll have the Rangers completely mixed, with Anglos, Tejanos, and Indians serving next to each other. I wouldn't be surprised if you turn all of us into abolitionists."

Will wasn't sure he saw the connection and asked

about it. Seguin happily explained, "On the surface, there's no evident connection, but below it, I see where you're going. During the Revolution, at the Rio Grande and Nueces battles, all of the infantry were white men, while my company of cavalry were all Tejano. You've already done it with my cavalry, when you reorganized the army last fall, and half of both companies are Tejano and the other half is Anglo. I have no doubt you'd have done the same with the infantry, except there aren't many Tejano volunteers who want to serve. But that'll change, and I've no doubt, you'll slide them into the existing companies."

Will finally realized where Seguin was taking the conversation and smiled coyly at the captain. "Juan, you of all people should understand how Texians like yourself benefit from such an arrangement."

Seguin snorted, "Texian now? When did I go from being a Tejano to a Texian?"

Will patted him on the back as he spread his blanket roll on the ground, "To me, they're not exclusive of each other."

Will wasn't sure if Seguin bought his argument, but as the Tejano captain went to check on his men, Will heard him whistling a merry tune.

Will thought, *"This is good. When we expand our infantry I'll make sure we recruit from all of our immigrant communities, whether they're originally from Mexico, Ireland, or Germany. Hell, maybe even go out of my way to recruit from among the Cherokee, too."*

Will stood before a group of students, spinning the classroom's globe. "Can anyone find Iraq on the globe here?"

He was halfway through his semester of student teaching history. Few of the students in his class could have found the country on the globe. Despite his love for history, he felt a real frustration with the lack of interest on the students' part.

With no takers, he lowered the world map from its spring roller and pointed to the middle east. "Next to Iraq is Iran. Can anyone tell me the ancient name for Iran?" Still, no takers.

He heard what sounded like a firecracker, and he turned his head searching for the sound. More firecrackers exploded.

Will was shaken awake, with the image of the classroom fading into the recesses of his memories. His wide brimmed hat fell from covering his face, revealing an agitated Major Wyatt standing over him. Although the Major's body was blocking the direct sunlight, Will could tell the sun was at its apex in the sky. He heard a distant crack of a gunshot shatter the stifling silence of the prairie. Wyatt said, "There's trouble behind us. It's some of our supply wagons, a few miles back. One of our Apache scouts saw the Comanche riding toward them."

Major Caldwell ran over to where they stood. He was strapping his gun belt around his waist as he ran.

"General, I've got a company ready to ride. I'll lead 'em out!"

Will waved him along as the Ranger ran to his horse. Turning around he saw Major Wyatt who had collared the battalion's bugler. He called out, "Major, sound assembly. Get the men into a defensive perimeter!"

The Infantry formed a loose perimeter, each company defending a side of the square, in the open order skirmish tactics in which they were trained. The two artillery pieces were in the center of the square, unlimbered and ready to fire. But time passed slowly for Will as he reached into his vest pocket frequently, looking at his pocket watch to check the time. The occasional faint sound of gunfire echoed in the distance.

Nearly two hours passed before a solitary Ranger galloped back into camp. When he saw Will and the other officers, he sawed on the reins and headed toward them. "Gen'ral, we whupped 'em and whupped 'em good. There must have been forty or more Comanche that attacked our supply wagons. We had to have killed a dozen or more afore they took to showin' us the daylight between them and their saddles."

Nearby soldiers, hearing the news, cheered. Will was tempted to let the men celebrate, but as Major Wyatt and the other officers restored order and refocused their attention at the prairie around them, Will decided discipline was more important. If there were any Comanche observing his command, there was no sign of them and Caldwell arrived back at camp with his men an hour after his messenger. He maneuvered his horse through the skirmish line of infantry and came up to Will, and gave a casual salute. "General Travis, the supplies will be here by this evening. The Comanche caught the waggoneers and militia by surprise. Ten were killed and another four were wounded by the time we arrived. If we hadn't caught the Comanche by surprise, they would have looted and burned the wagons. Although the Comanche retreated with their wounded and some of their dead, I think we killed seven or eight warriors and probably wounded an equal number."

Will nodded, accepting the discrepancy in casualties between the excited messenger and Caldwell's calm report. "That was well done, Matt. I want our Apache scouts to see if they can follow whatever trail the Comanche leave. Tonight, we'll follow it and God willing, they'll lead us to a Comanche camp."

The Apache scouts followed the trail left by the retreating Comanche warriors, and by the time the sun dipped below the western horizon, Will's command followed behind their Apache allies.

Despite being driven away from the wagon train by the unexpected arrival of the Rangers, the Comanche warriors were confident as they retreated. Yes, they were learning to hate the Rangers and their dreaded pistol which fired many times. Time honored tactics which used to work when fighting the white devils were no longer effective. But as these young warriors traveled across the prairie they gave little thought to pursuit. This was the Comancheria. This was their land and they were the undisputed masters. Older warriors, more experienced in fighting these new Texian interlopers would have urged more caution, and watched for pursuit. But this raid, undertaken by youths and young men, were overconfident when they returned to their camp along the banks of the Brazos River.

The Apache who followed the bloodied warband never approached close enough to be seen, but Flacco's scouts easily followed the fresh hoof prints across the prairie, until in the early hours before dawn they found a large Comanche village spread along the south bank.

The Texas Rangers were the next to arrive while the sun was still a couple of hours away from rising. The infantry, flanked by Seguin's cavalry, arrived in the window of the night, before the first warm glow began to lighten the eastern sky. Will tasked Major Wyatt with deploying his infantry in an arc to the south and west of the village, still more than a thousand yards from the river. He sent Major Caldwell's Rangers across the Brazos, covering the most likely route of retreat. As Caldwell prepared to follow his rangers north, Will grabbed him by the arm, "Capture as many as you can, Matt. I don't want a massacre."

The rugged Texian nodded, "I'll not risk my men, General, but I'll make sure they don't get their dander up."

Will waved as the Ranger followed his men, who were circling around the village. Seguin's cavalry took up position, a company on either side of the infantry battalion.

As the eastern sky began to glow with the promise of the morning sun, Will found Major Wyatt with his men, and said, "It's time, Major. When we get into the camp, I want us looking for captives, and capture any woman not under arms as well as any children. As for the warriors, give them the same mercy the showed us at Fort Parker."

The butternut clad soldiers within hearing of Will growled in agreement as Wyatt issued the order to advance. Across a front more than six hundred yards wide, the Texian infantry moved forward, more than seventy rifle teams advancing in a thin skirmish line, each team working closely together. Will watched one such team, as two men sprinted from behind some scrub brush to a clump of hackberry trees, while the others covered their advance. Then these two raced forward, passing through the small hackberry grove, while the two in the tree line covered their comrades' advance.

The dawn's peace was broken by an angry cry from the village as a Comanche warrior stepped from his teepee and saw the advancing infantry. A moment later, a scattering of rifle fire slashed out from the advancing Texians, riddling the loan warrior, who fell back against the teepee, knocking one of the support poles down, causing the shelter to lean precariously to the side. The camp broke into pandemonium as warriors spilled from the teepees with spears and bows and arrows in hand.

A few even carried muskets. Following fast on the warriors' heels, their wives and children wore alarmed expressions as they saw the advancing Texians for the first time. Many of the band's most vulnerable members fled to the bank of the Brazos, splashing across it at the shallowest spots. Warriors who stopped to pull back their bows and fire at the steadily advancing infantry, quickly drew the aimed fire of riflemen. With a precision which comes from long practice, the infantry advanced into the camp, and tendrils of flames sprung up as they set the teepees ablaze.

To either side of the infantry, Seguin's cavalry spread out, and attempted to turn any running Comanche back toward the camp, frequently using their revolvers, whenever a warrior would stand and fight.

As Will and Wyatt followed behind the Infantry, they found dozens of old men as well as women and young children under guard. On the northern bank of the river, Caldwell's Rangers rode into view, corralling even more prisoners before them. Following earlier orders, many of their riflemen were dragging the dead warriors into a line. Will was distressed to see among the dead many of their wives where they had been struck down, still clutching knives, spears, or bows in their lifeless hands. As Caldwell's rangers rejoined the main force, he came up to Will and saw the many women among the dead. "It's hard to imagine, General, but they are a warrior culture. Like you, I had hopes that their women would surrender when it was clear they were defeated, but as you can see, in too many cases, they chose to die with their men."

Will gazed across the long line of warriors who had been slain. Fifty-three warriors were counted among the dead. Additionally, thirty-one women were killed, when they joined their husbands, brothers, and fathers in defending their camp. Four children had been killed in the fight, the unfortunate collateral damage when war is visited upon the innocent. Despite the depredations visited on Texas settlements by their fathers and older brothers, the children were carefully laid to rest in hastily dug graves. The rough men who placed them in their final resting place mourned the senseless loss of life. The Comanche adults were dumped into a common grave.

In all, a half dozen warriors were captured, too badly wounded to flee. Four elderly men and thirty-nine women of varying ages, and twenty-three pre-adolescent children were also captured. As they were chained together, Will watched. The human misery among the Comanche was palpable. The old men, unable to fight any more, glared angrily at Will's Texians. The women either mourned their dead husbands or scowled at their captors, hatred in their eyes. The youngest children cried while those older were afraid. Everything they knew had been brutally ripped from their young lives.

For a moment Will questioned the strategy upon which they were embarking. Seguin rode up at that moment and saw the look of distaste on Will's face.

"Juan, are we doing the right thing? Look at them," Will said, waving his arm toward the prisoners.

Seguin looked them over and quietly said, "They are a sad sight, General Travis. It reminds me of something that happened a few years ago. My father and I led a part of my father's vaqueros after a Comanche raid destroyed some farms nearby. We caught up with the war party and killed some of the warriors and rescued their prisoners, our neighbors." He lowered his voice further, and continued, "Buck, the women they captured had been raped repeatedly, and beaten. The children were terrorized. I know for a fact that several of those young ones still wake up sweating, screaming from their nightmares. Both women, who we rescued, good Catholic women, committed suicide. They couldn't live with what they went through. They were buried in unconsecrated ground; the church makes no excuse for suicide. I owe it to those families, just as you owe it to the Parkers, to end this savage war. Look at that." He pointed to the burning camp, drawing Will's attention to the loot from many Texas farms, littering the ground, as the teepees were consumed by fire.

Seguin continued, "It wasn't a complete success, either. A few of the warriors avoided our cavalry and Rangers. We think some of their women and children also managed to escape."

Will's spirits rose when Crawford and Wyatt came over gave their own reports. One Ranger had been wounded when trying to stop one of the Comanche women from fleeing. He had been stabbed in the leg.

His companions were not able to find her, but they stopped his bleeding and brought him to the battalion surgeon. Wyatt told him three of his men had been injured by arrow fire. They too were with the surgeon and were expected to recover. The Major was positively beaming as he recounted to the other officers how his men swept across the prairie, using the terrain to their advantage as they assaulted the village.

Before the prisoners were marched away into captivity, Will freed the oldest man, who was bent with age, arthritis long ago stealing his mobility. As many of the Comanche who ranged the western reaches of the Republic, the old man spoke passable Spanish. Will asked Seguin to translate, "You are free to go. Find your fellow Comanche and tell them we have destroyed your band, killed your warriors, captured your women and children, just as you have captured our women and children. If you want yours returned to the Comanche people, all of your chiefs from all of your bands will come to San Antonio with all your captives."

With eyes still blazing in anger, the old man spat in the dirt at Will's feet and said something in Spanish. Then he turned on his heels and started walking west, along the Brazos. Will turned to Seguin, "What was that about?"

Despite his swarthy complexion, Seguin colored a bit, "Ah, Buck, I don't think it has an English equivalent."

Chapter 9

The sun hung at its zenith in a cloudless sky as a company of Seguin's troopers escorted the Comanche prisoners. They anticipated crossing paths with militia cavalry within a day or two, and trading their prisoners for supplies. Despite the pleasant weather, the prisoners kicked up a cloud of dust, as they trudged along under guard. They were tied to each other by a rope at the waist and a shorter rope between their ankles made it impossible to take anything other than short steps. Most of the troopers wore wary expressions, keeping a close eye on their prisoners.

Will watched the prisoners as they retreated into the distance, until only a pillar of dust remained. He fervently hoped the troopers would be able to rendezvous with the militia, hand off the prisoners and hurry back. Being down by forty men wasn't ideal, but it would have to suffice until the troopers returned in a few days. That made keeping a weather eye for any other Comanche warriors even more important. With that in mind, his army settled in to sleep until nightfall. They camped less than a mile away from the remains of the village. He had Major Caldwell deploy some of his Rangers to patrol while he sent most of his Apache allies to follow any promising trails.

That night, the Apache warriors returned as Will's army broke camp, Flacco found Will as the army continued its northwesterly route along the Brazos. The Apache was practically dragging Juan Seguin along when he approached Will, "Traveling along this river may yet lead to another Comanche camp," Seguin translated, "But with the current migration of the buffalo, there's a good chance we'll find another camp along the Leon River."

Will asked, "How far away is the Leon?"

Seguin and Flacco discussed the answer in Spanish, "less than fifty miles."

From their northwesterly march, the order was given, and the army veered away from the Brazos, heading to the southwest.

The next night, halfway across the prairie separating the two rivers, Will located Major Caldwell as the little army continued its trek to the southwest, "Matt, I've not taken the time to see how your companies are handling these scouting duties ahead of the army. Mind if I joined you tonight and observe?"

Already riding ahead of the force, Caldwell called over his shoulder, "Sure, General, if you can keep up, you're welcome to ride along with my boys."

He caught up with the major and rode along with

him and a company of his men as they scoured the terrain a few miles ahead of the infantry's line of march. Few clouds hid the sparkling stars and the moon was a thin sliver, low in the western sky. The prairie grass was swept by a cool northerly breeze, and the rhythmic swishing sound lulled Will into a near slumber as his horse plodded along behind Major Caldwell.

An echoing shot shattered the quiet of the night, causing Will to jerk his horse's reins as it grew skittish. A flash of white flew by him, as he glimpsed a shadowy figure rise from the tall prairie grass. With a dawning realization, Will realized he had nearly been struck by an arrow. The company of Rangers were surrounded by dozens of darting figures, some afoot, and even more approaching on horseback. He drew his pistol and fired at the shadowy figure. He saw it descend below the top of the grass but couldn't tell if he'd hit it.

Major Caldwell, pistol in one hand and reins in the other, circled back to his side, "General, our best bet is to pull our men into a circle. I don't fancy our chances scattered about like we are."

He swung down from his horse and shot at a shadowy figure who had ridden up close, bearing a heavy, steel tipped spear. The rider dropped the spear and slid to the side, as the horse raced past. Will jumped down from his mount and joined Caldwell as the major called out for nearby Rangers to join him.

Despite the dim moonlight, Will saw one of their flank riders, hatless, racing toward them, chased by several warriors, brandishing spears and bows. The

Ranger hugged his horse's neck, as he made the smallest target he could atop his mount. Arrows sped above him as he kicked his horse, urging it to go faster. Will could make out the Rangers' black mustache and pale face as he approached the dismounted officers.

An arrow punched through his throat, blood splaying across the neck of his horse, as his arms went slack and he slipped off the back of his mount. Will stood shocked as the riderless horse reared up, a dozen feet to his front. A mounted warrior came up beside the horse and made several attempts to snatch the reins slapping in the wind. Will shook the shock from his face and hastily snapped a shot which flew through the space between warrior and horse. Breathing in sharply, he steadied his hand and fired a second time, catapulting the warrior off the back of his horse.

The multiple shots from Will's pistol caused the other warriors following behind the first to pull up short. Rather than find out how many more rounds Will had, they wheeled about and rode back the way they had come. Will turned to Caldwell and saw the Major had found a half dozen more Rangers, who had dismounted and joined them. The Major deployed four of the men forward, with their carbines. Will straightaway recognized the small group tactics he and Lt. Colonel Johnston had been teaching to the infantry. The Rangers were not as smooth nor as coordinated as the foot soldiers, but Will's lips skinned back into a vicious grin, as two of the men fired at targets well beyond the range of the revolvers, while the other two held their fire.

It was good they had done so, as several mounted warriors raced toward the dismounted men with lances lowered, thinking the Texians were busy reloading their guns. As the distance rapidly narrowed, the other two men raised their rifles and fired, toppling two more warriors from their saddles. Across the prairie, Will could hear the frustration in the voices of the Comanche warriors, still determined to press home their attack.

The ringing of a horseshoe striking a rock behind him, made Will turn his head. Less than a dozen feet from him, slinking through the tall grass, he saw a warrior, crouched low, racing toward the horses. Will snapped the gun up and fired directly at the warrior, and the hammer fell on the percussion cap, but nothing happened. The warrior sprang toward Will when he realized he had been discovered, steel bladed knife glimmering in the faint starlight. With no time to shoot again, Will threw the pistol into the warrior's face.

Stunned, the warrior dropped his knife, but his momentum carried him into Will, and the two crashed to the ground. Despite blood running down his face from a gash to his cheek, the warrior recovered and grasped for Will's windpipe.

As the warrior's fingers, slick with sweat, grabbed his throat, Will saw the warrior's head less than a foot from his own. He smashed his fists into the Warrior's elbow, bringing the sunburned face closer. With all his might, Will swung his head forward, his forehead crashing into the warrior's nose. The satisfying crunching sound of the cartilage breaking was music to Will's ears as the warrior's grip loosened. Ignoring the stars dancing in front of his eyes, Will focused on the face looming over him, and drove his right fist into the ruined nose. A sharp pain traveled from his knuckles up his arm, but the warrior attempted to roll away, as blood ran down his chin.

The warrior jumped to his feet, and saw Will's revolver lying on the ground. As he lunged for it, Will drew his saber. The Comanche held the revolver in both his hands, pointing it at Will, and pulled the trigger. The hammer slammed down as the warrior cringed in anticipation of the explosion which would send a bullet flying at Will.

When the hammer snapped down on the empty cylinder, Will leapt forward, his saber outstretched, and caught the still cringing warrior in the stomach, driving the blade through. The grip was just a few inches from the belly when Will stopped moving forward. The warrior sank to his knees and Will retrieved his revolver from where it fell.

After the bloody work of removing his saber, he rejoined Major Caldwell where more than a dozen Rangers stood in a semicircle, weapons at the ready. A few arrows landed in front of the band of Rangers and several men returned fire. It appeared the Comanche realized there was nothing more to be gained and after a few more arrows landed harmlessly in front of the dismounted force, the shadowy figures turned and faded back into the night.

The sliver of the moon descended below the horizon, and from the direction of the main column, the blast of a bugle alerted Will and the Rangers to the approach of Seguin's cavalry. Spread out to the north, Will watched the troopers, advancing in a long single line, stretching across more than a hundred yards.

The site of the Comanche ambush now secured by more than a hundred men, Will let Caldwell alone, allowing the commander of the Rangers to assess the damage sustained. By the time the infantry arrived, Caldwell confirmed eight of his men were dead or missing. Of the Comanche, they found four dead. Will ground his teeth, wishing he could find out how many of their dead and wounded the Comanche had made off with.

With the arrival of the infantry, Will decided they would rest until the next evening. The Rangers buried their dead, and patched their wounded. Will grimaced as the regimental surgeon sewed the cut on the back of his hand closed. It wasn't the sutures which hurt, but the trauma inflicted by the sawbones when he dug out the bits of cartilage. Will tried to put the pain out of his mind, reminding himself it was better the fragments had come from the warrior who nearly killed him.

The next morning, as the sun crested the eastern sky, Will's army arrived on the banks of the sluggishly flowing Leon River. Flacco and his Apache warriors had been right to think they would find a Comanche camp here, but the camp was abandoned. From the number of firepits and how much prairie was trodden, the camp had been large; possibly two hundred teepees. Now, it was just open prairie along the banks of the river.

The Comanche left a reminder of their recent departure. Hanging between two poles, less than six feet apart, was the body of one of the Rangers, who had gone missing in the previous night's battle. His skin had been torn to ribbons, the ground below his naked body, soaked in blood. Next to him, another figure had been hung similarly. This was the naked body of a young woman, not likely eighteen. Her body was horribly disfigured, burn marks ran along both her arms and her body. Her nose had been burned off, exposing bone. Her hair was closely shorn, but unlike the Ranger, her scalp was intact. Blood caked her thighs, evidence of her lowly place within the society which had cast her aside like refuse, in its effort to put distance between itself and the Texian army, seeking vengeance.

The soldiers, who make their camp in same fields which until a day ago, contained the Comanche village, burned with anger toward the men and women who casually desecrated the bodies of their prisoners. Will worried that when they found their next Comanche village, his men would retaliate against the Comanche. He found Captain Seguin and the Apache, Flacco studying the camp.

As they discussed this, Seguin translated Flacco's words, "They do this to terrorize their opponents. They believe if they can strike fear into the hearts of their enemy then they will be victorious."

Flacco's eyes followed the trail westward, staring hard, as though still following the retreating Comanche. "They have chased my people out of our hunting grounds, and forced us to rely upon the Spanish, then the Mexicans and now you Texians. We Lipan feared no man, we waged war against the Spanish and their Indian allies and they knew we were fierce warriors. When the Comanche came, in my Grandfather's time, they made everyone fear them. This is their way. They kidnapped our children, made slaves of our women and killed our warriors, until we grew weak."

Through Seguin, Will asked, "What now, Flacco?"

"We go now, and find the Comanche. When you next march, we will not fail you. The next camp be full of Comanche." With that declaration, Flacco turned and strode away, and a short while later, his band of warriors rode to the west.

Will allowed his army time to rest, while waiting for the Apache to return. Two days after they rode out, a pair of Apache raced into camp and reported Flacco had located the Comanche who had fled their camp along the Leon River. Before the last glow of day slid below the western sky, Will flung his army west, as the Apache warriors led them across the prairie. For most of the night, the trail left by the Comanche was easy to follow, despite the dark sky of the new moon. Long before dawn, Will lost the trail, but the Apaches continued along, certain in retracing their route.

With the coming dawn, Will's army made camp and waited. Flacco's men all returned to the camp before the next nightfall, reporting the location of the newly erected Comanche village. The encampment was on the north bank of the Sabana River, a meandering tributary of the Leon.

In the darkness of predawn, Will's army quietly approached the sleeping encampment. Before sending the Rangers around the camp, to cut off the retreat, he met with his officers. "Same as before, gentlemen. I want prisoners." He focused on Major Wyatt. "Your boys will lead the attack. I know they've got their blood up, but we don't want to kill any noncombatants. Make sure your officers pass it along."

Sorrow crept into the major's eyes. The brutal executions they had found earlier weighed heavy upon him. "The boys got their blood up, but I'll make sure their discipline holds. There will be no massacre."

Acrid black smoke billowed into the sky. Nearly two hundred teepees were on fire. A company of infantry guarded their prisoners, who huddled in a circle, tired and scared. There were fourteen elderly men, fifty women and fifty-three children. The children ranged in age from infants to preteens. After watching the men of the village die where they stood, defending against the overwhelming force brought to bear against them, many of the survivors were in shock.

Will had ridden through the smoldering camp; the dead were still strewn where they had fallen. Will had watched the infantry fan through the camp, their discipline barely holding, as officers screamed the command to take prisoners. Even so, no warrior survived. No matter the orders, Will found several bodies which had been bayoneted repeatedly. The officers could not be everywhere at once, and when the angered soldiers could, they had visited back upon the Comanche warriors the same ferocity they received. It reminded Will of the terrible images played endlessly of the helicopter pilot dragged through the streets of Mogadishu. It was an image that as a soldier in the twenty-first century had plagued him and other soldiers. And now, here in nineteenth century Texas, his own soldiers hadn't hesitated to repay the Comanche in the same brutal coin in which they had been paid.

He turned about and came back to where the soldiers guarded the prisoners. While most of the children wore vacant looks, shock still etched on their innocent faces, the old men nursed the bruises that arose on their arms and legs where the soldiers had grabbed them, forcibly propelling them to the area where they now sat. They saw an overwhelming number of soldiers surrounding them and they sat on the ground, dejected in defeat. Some women were as shocked as the children, and others as dejected as the old men, but others glared at the soldiers and cursed them in Comanche.

In addition to the seventy-five prisoners taken on the banks of the Brazos, now Will's army had an additional one hundred seventeen. Will considered dispatching more of his mounted troops to escort the prisoners back to San Antonio, but then decided it would leave him with too small a force. He recalled what happened the previous summer when he brought his army north, unprepared for the war, and decided the main objective of capturing enough prisoners to draw the Comanche people to the peace table had been achieved.

The hardest part in leaving the still smoldering camp was the decision to leave the bodies where they fell. Even though he could have issued the order, when confronted on the issue by Seguin, Caldwell, and the Apache, Flacco, all had argued that leaving the bodies was a calculated signal to the Comanche. Seguin summed up the other men's position when he said, "General, this is like war in the old testament. When the army of Israel won, they tore down the buildings and salted the ground. It was a signal to their enemies they were willing to wage total war. The other bands will come, they will see the utter destruction of this band, and they will know that if they will not agree to a peace, we are willing to show them the same mercy they have shown us."

The army's return to San Antonio took another ten days, as Will placed caution to the side and ordered his army to march by the most direct path through the Comancheria. There was little doubt the Comanche watched his army's southerly march, but his army's vigilance discouraged any attempt to free the prisoners. By the time his tired and dirty army marched through the gate at the Alamo with their prisoners in tow, the

Comanche would be coming.

Spirit Talker walked among the remains of the village along the river. The fires had long burned out, but the bodies remained. Ravaged by the wind, rain, and sun from above and coyotes and wolves on the ground, the many warriors who had died defending their village still bore the wounds of battle. Spirit Talker was used to it. He had seen it, many winters before in his youth, when he had taken horses from the people called the Mexicans. But the savagery visited on some of the warriors reminded him of the raids between his people, the Penateka against the Lenape. He spat on the ground as his thoughts ran to the treacherous Apache.

This was not the work of the Apache, though. The iron shod hoofs stamped into the mud along the river left no doubt those who called themselves Texians were the perpetrators. Next to him walked Buffalo Hump. The two men were as different in appearance as in temperament. Spirit Talker had long given up the raid. Arthritis made it impossible now for him to pull the war bow, and made his steps slower than they used to be. It was fitting and right that he now guided his band in peace. Buffalo Hump still walked tall and straight. Forty winters old, he was still bold and decisive. Spirit Talker could not deny his companion was a fine war chief for the band.

But, he was worried. This was the second village attacked by the Texians. In the first attack a few days before the Texians left no doubt it was revenge for the attack on the fort belonging to the people known as the Parkers. He came to stand before a young woman, lifeless, body ravaged by scavengers, the dagger still gripped in her hand. He turned to Buffalo Hump, "You want revenge my young friend. You see what the Texians have done to our people in this village, and I see it in your eyes. You want to take many scalps and prisoners."

Buffalo Hump pointed to the woman, "They kill even the women who have many years of child bearing ahead of them. They have no appreciation for our lives or our children. How many of our People have they taken into captivity?"

Spirit Talker shrugged, "Too many. Listen to me, Buffalo Hump. Like you, I want revenge. I want the Texians to know the sorrow of the loss of their women, but that way may lay our destruction."

Buffalo Hump shook his head. "Don't let the voices of old women keep you from seeing our way forward, my old friend. We shall let all of the families and bands among the Penateka know and invite the Nokoni and Tenewa bands to take many horses and women from the Texians."

Spirit Talker turned on the younger man, "Would you toss all of the women and children of the people prisoners of the white man on the fire? That way is impetuous. There are no old women's voices rattling in my head, when I counsel caution. Yes. Rally the other chieftains among the Penateka and we shall go find out what the Texians want in return for our women and children."

Buffalo Hump stormed away, stopping after a few feet, and turning, "I will not stop you, Spirit Talker, but while you counsel peace, I will prepare for war. I do not trust the white man. They eat away at our hunting ground, and drive away our buffalo."

Spirit Talker waved the younger man away. Understandably he was angry. The casual way the Texians had left the People scattered among the remnants of the teepees was a stark reminder they were willing to learn from his warriors. He had heard of the raid on the Parkers' Fort. They had built on the edge of the Comancheria. Many warriors had felt a stern message needed to be sent to the white men who were flooding into the land to the east. Now, Spirit Talker scanned the broken remains of the village. The Texians had heard the People's message and had responded in a way which threatened the very existence of the People.

"*No, we must try to find peace with the Texians*." Spirit Talker thought, "*Or there will be no future for our people*."

April gave way to May and life returned to normal as the Alamo's garrison drilled and trained. Most of the Rangers had returned to the forts along the frontier. East of the fort, a large paddock had been constructed, where the captured Comanche men and women were kept as prisoners. As an act of compassion, Will ordered blankets and tents provided to give the prisoners protection from the elements. The Comanche children were being kept at the decaying convent at the Mission Conception in town.

Soldiers guarded both locations. While watching a platoon march from the Alamo to relieve the guards at the paddock, Will couldn't help noticing the soldiers' uniforms were worse for wear, having been in the field for more than a month, but there was something else about the men. The way they marched out the gate, there was a cool determination and purpose in their steps that said these men knew they were now veterans.

He followed the men toward the paddock. As the days wore on, he wondered how long before the Comanche either came raiding or came to negotiate. As he arrived, the soldiers were changing the guard and the relieved soldiers marched back to the fort. As he looked through the slats at the women and old men, he couldn't help thinking of the old daguerreotype photographs he'd seen of the prisoner of war camps during the civil war. Despite regular food and the tents providing cover, the air of human misery hung palpably over the camp.

"Sweet Jesus, this is worse than the internment camps where the Japanese were imprisoned in World War II." Will thought to himself.

Not for the first time, he said a prayer the Comanche war would end soon. While his heart beat with compassion springing from his own twenty-first-century values and renewed faith, he couldn't avoid the actions required by the standards of 1837. It was one more example of how he had changed since the transference into William B. Travis' body and he didn't like it.

Two weeks after the army's return to San Antonio, a dozen Comanche showed up outside of the walls of the Alamo, holding shields painted white, symbolizing peace. Will was called to the wall, as dozens of soldiers ran, with carbines in hand, and took up their positions atop the wall. A few hundred yards away, Will noticed a platoon of Texas cavalry shadowing the Comanche delegation. He was relieved the Comanche hadn't come this close without being spotted. An old man, his long hair pulled back, sat on his horse at the head of the group of Indians. The image of the prisoners wallowing in the paddock a few hundred yards away was all the motivation he needed to see if the Comanche could be reasoned with.

Juan Seguin was already at the gate, sword clipped to his belt. Will eyed the saber and quipped, "Ever show up to a knife fight and have a gunfight break out, Juan?"

Seguin smiled sheepishly and unclipped the scabbard, and after handing it to a nearby soldier, followed Will out the gate.

Spirit Talker sat atop his horse looking at the long walls, ringing the large fort. In his youth, he remembered coming here and trading with the Spanish for food, horses, and weapons. The transformation of the walled complex was disconcerting. As the gate swung open, he saw two men walk out. The taller of the two was pale skinned and he was bare headed with hair the color of fire. The shorter of the two wore a black, wide brimmed hat and was swarthy. Spirit Talker was sure he was a Mexican. It was strange the White man and Mexicans were both part of what they called Texas. More disconcerting, were the uniforms both men wore. They were the color of mud. The Spaniards had worn bright blue and red uniforms, as had the Mexicans after them. Spirit Talker had assumed it was the nature of both races to announce to their enemies their presence by being more colorful than the birds of the air.

"The Texians were proving to be different birds," Spirit Talker thought drily.

Before they could speak, Spirit Talker addressed them in Spanish, "You have destroyed two of our bands and have captured many of our women and children. I, Spirit Talker, have come on behalf of the Penateka to negotiate a peace treaty and end the fighting between the People and the white man of Texas. I also seek the release of my people you hold here."

The shorter of the two mud draped men spoke in the language of the white man. The taller of the two men listened and then the silence grew long as Spirit Talker waited for him to respond. Finally, after what seemed too long, he spoke one word. There was no need for a translator, "no" was the same in Spanish as in English.

Spirit Talker blinked. He expected something. A

119

counter-offer or some proposal. He held his hand open to the men below him, "I have come in peace, as is the custom between all men. In our battles with you Texians and the Mexicans before you, all have found it good to seek peace. We have always been willing to sell back any captives you wish to buy. You have many of ours and we wish to trade for them."

Through the Mexican, the White man said, "It is true that if we wished we could trade captives with you, and I have no doubt you would be fair in returning to us an equal number, if you and your band have them. And you and I may even agree on a peace between Texas and your band. But I don't care to have a peace treaty with only your band. I will have peace with all the Comanche or none of them. That is your choice to make."

This was unexpected. Even before the time of his grandfathers, it was custom for the Spanish and Mexicans to seek peace and provide gifts to the People. It was how it had always been. "I am but one among several Penateka chiefs. I can make peace with you and my own band. The other chiefs keep their own counsel and do as they choose."

The man with fiery hair replied, "I am aware of that. I will give you time to consult with the other chiefs of the Penateka Comanche. Let them all come to negotiate peace or let them select a few among them to act for them. Be warned. Any band who attacks a Texas settlement or our farmers, will receive the same treatment that we have given out over the past month."

Spirit Talker looked searchingly into the eyes of the fiery haired chief, looking for a sign of compromise. Finding none, he nodded his head, sadly, and pulled the reins to the left, guiding his horse away from the walls of the old fort. He had hoped for more. The greatest strength of the People was its defused governance. Each band followed its own leaders. When there was disagreement, as was common between the proud warriors of the People, rather than battle within the band, it customary for the band to split. The land of the Comancheria was wide and rich in game and buffalo. Until now. The White man pushed into their land and took that which didn't belong. Looking back at the faces of the warriors who rode with him, their faces told him all he needed to know. An ill wind blew from the south. It chilled his neck. It was the winds of war.

Chapter 10

2nd of May 1837

To the officers and enrolled militia of the Republic of Texas for the militia districts of San Antonio, Goliad, Victoria, Gonzales, and Bastrop.

In accordance with the Militia Act of 1836, revised 3rd of April 1837 by 1st Congress of the Republic of Texas, you are hereby ordered to report to the prescribed armories of each respective district and assemble in San Antonio no later than 24th May 1837. Call to service is 90 days or the duration of the current campaign, if shorter.

Signed,

General William B. Travis, Commander Army of Texas.

Nearly a month had passed since Will watched the Comanche chief, Spirit Talker, ride away empty handed. The late May sun stood high in the Texas sky, as the temperature hovered near ninety degrees. For what seemed the millionth time, Will wished for air-conditioning. It was silly, he realized, to miss air-conditioning most of all. There were so many other more useful things he should miss more. Internal combustion engines, for instance. Paved roads would be nice, too.

Still though, when he considered the current situation, he was well ahead of where Texas could be. The army was equipped with the most state-of-the-art weapons in existence in 1837, and the tactics were at least a generation ahead of other nations. The finances of the Republic were still shaky, even though large strides had been made over the last six months. The most recent edition of the Telegraph and Texas Register reported the Texas Land Bank had issued loans for more than a million acres since opening, valued at more than half a million dollars.

Even the Commodities Bureau was slowly growing, as property taxes came due, and the taxes often were paid in kind. Juan Seguin had told him just a few days ago, one of the larger plantation owners had paid his taxes with twenty-five bales of cotton, which the bureau had already sold to a New York based company. Those bales were on their way north to be turned into textiles. The Commodities Bureau received $1,200 in silver and in turn, put into the general fund an equal value of cotton-backs, as folks were calling the new currency. The cotton-backs were then used to pay the bills of the republic, often finding their way into the pockets of Will's soldiers each payday, and from there, into general circulation.

Will would make do without his air-conditioning.

"All things considered," he thought, *"things are shaping up much better for Texas than in the world I left behind."*

He stood on top of the chapel's wall, admiring the roof covering the chapel's nave. Heavy support beams ran over the chancel, but the roof was not yet extended that far. Below, the dirt ramp which once held several east facing guns was gone. In its place, a large wooden platform ran the width of the chancel, a dozen feet above the floor. Three heavy guns faced eastward. Gun ports, which had been hastily dug through the thick adobe walls in the days before Will's arrival at the Alamo well over a year before, had been squared and thick shutters added, to protect the platform from the elements once the roof had been completed.

Flashes of light in the distance caught his attention, and Will looked up to see coming down the Gonzales road a column of mounted men. Behind them rolled several wagons. A flag fluttered in the warm breeze, at the head of the cavalcade. A particularly warm gust made the mounted force's flag dance in the wind, and Will could see a single star in a blue field in the upper left corner of the flag. Thirteen red and white stripes horizontally crisscrossed it. As the mounted men came nearer, Will saw most of the men wore blue jackets. One man, riding next to the standard bearer, wore brown buckskins. With a sinking feeling, Will had a strong suspicion of who was leading the column and hastily climbed down a ladder and ran to the Alamo's gate.

As he reached the gate, he watched as President Crockett rode through it, with a company of Texas Marines trailing. From behind him, Will heard Lt. Colonel Johnston walk up, muttering about where he'd find a place to bivouac the marines.

Will turned and quipped, "Sid, it looks like our president has decided to come a-calling and he brought his own honor guard."

Johnston grunted. "I hope he left a decent force to defend Galveston. Won't do us any good to beat the Comanche if we let the Mexicans through the back door."

Crockett rode across the plaza until the last of the marine detachment passed through the gate, and then swung around and trotted over to Will.

Ever the soldier, Will snapped a sharp salute. "President Crockett, sir! We had no notification of your visit. Otherwise we'd have turned out the garrison in your honor."

Crockett shrugged, "Guess it's a good thing I just came then. I can't stand all of the hoopla that some of those fine folks back in Harrisburg think a government needs." Then, as if reading Will's mind, "Anyway, I brought my own honor guard with me. Please see to the needs of these fine Marines, General Travis."

Will turned to Johnston, who shrugged and said, "I'll see to it, sir. Where do you want to bivouac them?"

Will pointed to the north. "Put them in the first floor of the North barracks. They can share the space with Company C." Then he turned and ran to catch up with Crockett, as the president led the way up the stairs to Will's office.

Following on the heels of the president, Will entered his office to find Crockett settling himself into Will's chair. Shaking his head, Will leaned against the table and exasperatedly said, "David, please tell me you didn't ride two hundred miles just so you wouldn't miss a fight."

Crockett grinned ruefully. "A man must do what needs doing, Buck. Now that Liza, Bob, and Becky have arrived, the house is overrun with would-be suitors. Anyhow, you know me too well. I would have hated to miss out on this here shindig you're about to have. Also, as Commander-in-Chief, it's only right that I come out here and inspect the army, right, Buck?"

The smile faded, and he continued, "Well, that's what I told those bright plumed Congressional popinjays back in Harrisburg. The truth of the matter sets elsewhere. You and I both know your raid into the Comancheria was approved by Congress. They were mighty pleased with how it started. Hell, they read your dispatches into the congressional records each week. But they wanted to keep the army raiding through the Comancheria, killing the Indians until they're gone. Lots of congresscritters were unhappy you ended the campaign when you did, to say nothing of the stink they raised about paying for your prison camp, either. Lots of good folks in Congress think the only good in'jun is a dead in'jun."

Will glowered. "Let them think that, as long as they pay the bills." But softened as he asked, "Is it that bad in Harrisburg, David?"

Crockett howled with laughter. "Hell, Buck. If it were only that bad. I got plantation owners like Robert Potter grousing about the property tax he's saddled with paying. Then there's the Galveston merchants screaming about the tariffs. Congress is screaming about the expenditures for the army and the navy. The only good news is Lamar wrote from France saying he is hopeful for recognition soon. Come '42, if Houston wants the presidency so damn much, I'll go to stumping for him."

Will chuckled at Crockett the raconteur. "Don't. Sam'll make a beeline strait for Washington. Right after he disbands the navy and cashiers the army. But never any mind about the Raven. I told those fools in Congress that staying in the field inside the Comancheria was costing us men, weapons, and supplies. It's damned hard to defend a moving supply train without drawing down our forces. The mounted militia we had was damned near useless. By the time we had nearly two hundred prisoners, it would have left us too exposed to have sent back a force with the second group of prisoners.

"The fact is, I delivered our message. The Comanche know we have lots of their women and children prisoner here in San Antonio. After meeting their peace chief, Spirit Talker, I believe the Comanche will try to take them back by force before they consider peace. God knows I wish they'd listen to reason and negotiate."

Crockett nodded, grimly. "I know, Buck. Sam even sent a couple of his friends among the Cherokee to see if the Comanche would listen. They didn't. I allow I have fought in a few Indian fights back east, but none of those tribes come close to the fierceness and ruthlessness of the Comanche. They take an all or nothing approach to life, Buck. Not unlike a few of our own congresscritters." He deflated at that. "Dammit all. If we don't win a resounding victory here soon and bring the Comanche to the treaty table, I'm not sure that a majority of our illustrious Congress won't be calling for a war of extermination against them. More than any other reason, that's what brought me here. I can't let that happen."

Will pulled the door closed and locked it. As he took hold of Charlie's hand and walked toward the road, he looked back at the low adobe building, a block away from San Antonio's main plaza. The windows were shuttered and padlocked. Their home sealed against their return. A glance to either side, revealed other families packing their belongings. San Antonio was fast becoming a ghost town. Word had reached San Antonio yesterday in the guise of a Ranger from the fort on the Pedernales Falls, of Comanche bands joining together on the frontier. There was little doubt the target was their fair town.

Only the distance of a city block separated their house from the plaza, so Will and Charlie walked there. The tower of San Fernando Church provided a clear view not just of the plaza, but the prairie surrounding the town. A sentry stood in the belfry with a telescoping spyglass, looking first to the north then swinging the lens to the west.

Dozens of wagons crowded the plaza. Frazzled looking women, both Tejano and Anglo, were attempting to keep control of their children. In front of the governor's palace a small company of San Antonio militia stood by their horses, waiting to escort the civilian caravan east to Gonzales. It was second nature for Will to assess the men standing under the Texas flag. He was shocked to see how young they were, before surmising the officer in command of the militia company was sending his youngest and least experienced out of town, ostensibly to protect the women and children of San Antonio.

There were heavy militia patrols east of San Antonio, and the presence of the young soldiers was superfluous. At least that is what Will's analytical side contended. The part of him that worried, as a parent, was glad to see they would accompany the civilians to Gonzales.

Corralling Charlie, Will walked over to the very young-looking officer. "Lieutenant."

The young man turned and seeing Will in his butternut officer's uniform with the gold stars on each of his shoulder straps, threw a hasty salute. All the young men, boys really, wore the grey militia jackets still favored by the Texas militia. They wore an assortment of hats and the pants ran the gamut of civilian clothing. "General Travis, sir! Lieutenant Carlos Bustamante at your service, sir."

Will kept the smile from his lips as his attention was drawn to the young officer's attempt at a mustache, but the down on his upper lip was all he could manage. "Lieutenant, how many men are assigned to your command?"

The eager youth replied, "I have thirty men here, General Travis, sir."

Will let the smile crease his face as he listened to the young officer's enthusiasm. "As you were, Lieutenant."

He took Charlie to a wagonful of the Seguin clan's children, where he lifted the boy on to the back of the wagon and tossed Charlie's bag of clothes beside him. As the Seguin children climbed into the wagon bed, Charlie's eyes started streaming and he pleaded, "Pa, do I have to go?"

Will picked him up and hugged him and said, "Hush, Charlie. We'll both be safe. You know I have my job to do here, and you'll go with the Seguins and all these other fine folks." Will gestured toward Juan Seguin's eldest daughter, Antonia, and said, "After all, all of these pretty ladies need brave lads, just like you, to keep them safe."

Charlie wiped the tears away with his arm and sniffled as he tried to put a brave face on for both his father and the girl a year older than himself, who sat down beside him, her feet dangling from the back of the wagon. Will smiled at his son, who at nine years of age, was growing into the image of his father. No matter how Will ransacked Travis' memories, he couldn't fathom how Travis could have so thoroughly abandoned his duties to his children and to their mother. He tousled the boys' hair and stepped back as the wagon lurched forward, heading out of San Antonio to safety.

As he watched the wagon roll away, carrying the child who was more son to him than the boy had ever been to his own father, a noise startled him from his reverie. He turned and saw Crockett stroll up beside him. The older man joined him and together they watched the wagon disappear around a corner, following the road eastward.

"Not many things are harder to behold than watching them go when they're so young, Buck. I spent so much time traveling, hunting, exploring, and yes, politicking, I never saw any of my children's first steps."

Will glanced at his president and saw Crockett wearing a melancholy expression, watching each wagon roll out of the plaza, heading east, to safety. "I didn't know, David. I'm sorry."

Crockett smiled, sadly. "I didn't learn of my Polly's death until weeks after it happened. Had I been the dutiful husband and father, I'd have been there. I don't know if I could have stopped it, but at least she wouldn't have died without hearing me tell her how much I loved her."

This wasn't a side of Crockett he'd seen before. Uncertain what to say, he simply watched the last of the wagons roll around bend in the road.

The silence lingered after the last wagon was gone. Clearing his throat, Will forced a jovial tone into his voice. "And here I thought you were escaping the family hearth to get away from all the trappings of family. I'd have never imagined the famous Davy Crockett going soft on me."

Crockett let out a loud harrumph. "Damned if I know if Davy Crockett is going soft, but David, well, David knows better to speak of himself in the third person." Both men laughed, and turned to leave the plaza. Crockett was in a talkative mood, as they retrieved their horses. "I've spent less than half my life at home with Liza, the woman I love who gave me three beautiful children. My boy, Bob is almost twenty-two years old, and I barely know the man he's becoming. Becky is nineteen years old and I've sent more suitors packing since she's arrived than I'd ever dreamed of, as not a single one of them is worth spit. Hell, Buck, my youngest, Matilda ran off with her beau when Liza packed up the house to come here to Texas. That's a kick in the pants. My own baby girl didn't want to come out here with her family. I can't tell you how much that hurt, Buck."

The last year and a half had allowed Will to get to know Crockett well. This was the first time he'd ever heard Crockett talk about his love for his family. The other times, it was jokes and fun. One benefit of soldiering Will had learned to appreciate over the past decade was it allowed him to keep his emotions at arm's length. Out of his depth, Will reached over and put his hand on Crockett's shoulder. "A wise man told me once, to be sure that I was right and then go ahead. I'd say he gave me good advice."

Crockett turned to Will, "Good advice, I would have been a better father had I taken it more often."

As they rode back to the Alamo, Crockett stopped on the wooden bridge over the San Antonio River. Water flowed quickly over the rocks and pebbles lining the river bed as it gurgled along. He looked down, watching the river flow by. Finally, he said, "I'm glad I came to Texas, Buck. It's given me and now my family a chance for a fresh start. I know I can give them a better life here, if I don't wind up killing every blasted ne'er-do-well who comes a-knocking on my door wanting to come courting for my Becky."

He nudged his horse along, and the river fell behind them as they approached the walls of the Alamo. "You know, General Travis, there's one young 'Buck' that I know I wouldn't object to should he come calling on my Becky."

Chapter 11

Twenty-five-year-old Ben McCulloch pulled his horse out of the line of march, which allowed him to watch the men of the Gonzales Military District kick up dust as they marched west, toward San Antonio. Forty mounted riflemen and a little more than a hundred men afoot had responded to General Travis' command. He knew it should have been more, a lot more. As the elected officer responsible for maintaining the militia roll, it had fallen to him, as Major of Militia, to muster the district for military service. He was piqued by the poor response from the men of the district. More than four hundred men were listed on the militia roll, and far fewer than half had even bothered to answer the call to arms.

When he wasn't so angry, he tried to put himself into the shoes of those who hadn't turned out. More than half the men who failed to show were married men with wives and children and they were relocating their families away from the frontier, to the east. Word had arrived at Gonzales a few days before the mobilization order that the Comanche had attacked a few farms west of a tiny hamlet on the Colorado River called Waterloo.

As the last of his small force filed by, McCulloch edged back onto the road, following behind his command as they rode toward the Alamo.

Later in the week, Major McCulloch watched as his men joined with the Militia districts of San Antonio, Goliad, Victoria, and Bastrop. They were deployed on the field south of the Alamo, a little more than five hundred men. They were a ragtag assortment, some few dressed in militia jackets of gray, but far more wearing the clothing of their civilian occupation. Their weapons were a hodgepodge of rifles, muskets, and shotguns. Many wore the fearsome Bowie knife at their belts.

McCulloch glanced down at his pocket watch and saw it was time. He yelled, "By the left face! March!"

The men who styled themselves as the 2nd Texas provisional Infantry shifted from parade rest to columns of four men each, and began marching past the ten-foot-tall southern wall of the Alamo. Will stood on top of the wall, above the gatehouse. It was all he could do to keep the disappointment from his face as he saluted Major McCulloch's command. Between the five military districts, which had been mobilized, their paper strength was over twelve hundred men. But only five hundred had answered the call, and nearly half of them had been from the San Antonio district. Goliad, Victoria, and Bastrop each had sent around thirty men or so.

With a neutral expression on his face, Will couldn't stop thinking the poor turn-out bade ill for Texas the next time Mexico decided to invade. Given the poor state of the militia, he was glad there were six hundred regulars already assembled at the Alamo. Standing next to Will were Lt. Colonel Johnston and President Crockett. As the militia finished their parade in honor of the president, Will turned to the other men and said, "Only four out of ten men mobilized. I don't want to minimize the challenge posed by the Comanche, but what will this kind of turn out mean to us when we face an existential threat from Mexico?"

"Nothing good," replied Johnston. "Their drill is nearly non-existent, and we just can't trust them to turn out in significant enough numbers as to be useful."

Crockett shook his head, "I'm not sure if I should ask you what you have in mind or how much this is going to cost me, Buck."

Will smiled contritely, "I'm just thinking out loud about taking a small number of our better militia units and turn them into something that organizationally would fall between the regulars and the militia. Kind of a national guard, of sorts."

Crockett blanched, "That could get expensive real quick like."

"David, look at those boys out there. If they're defending San Antonio, they might be alright, I know a few of them were with Ben Milam when he took the city away from Cos two years ago, but I don't trust their training to commit them to a standup fight against the Comanche, even less if they're called to face the Mexicans in a pitched battle." Will turned to Johnston. "Sid, how many men are enrolled throughout our entire militia?"

"Maybe a bit over five thousand men, General."

Will nodded at Crockett while waving at Johnston. "See, David. Maybe this year or next, we just set aside an equal amount of men as guardsmen as are regular. They're volunteers, part of the militia, when it comes right down to it, but we could equip them and train them, and even more importantly, give them professional officers. No more turning an election for officers into a popularity contest."

Crockett still remained skeptical, "The fly in the ointment is cost. We already spend a half million each year on the army. Asking anything more of Congress may be asking them to swallow an alligator. How much would this cost us?"

Will glanced over at Johnston, who pulled a scrap of paper from his vest pocket, and opened it. "This is purely hypothetical, Mr. President, but for a thousand guardsmen each year, you'd be looking at eighty thousand dollars give or take a bit."

Crockett chuckled as he looked askance at the two officers. "Eighty thousand dollars here and another eighty thousand dollars there and soon enough you're talking about real money."

The lieutenant lifted his black, wide-brimmed hat from his face with one hand and wiped away the sweat from his face with a red checkered handkerchief. His charcoal black hair had streaks of grey shooting through it. Summer, it appeared, had arrived early in south Texas. Lieutenant Gregorio Esparza had ridden with Juan Seguin since before the Revolution and after victory over Santa Anna had stayed in the cavalry. At first it was out of loyalty to his friend, the land grants in lieu of pay wasn't anything his wife, Ana had much use for. He had lost track of the number of times she had asked him how to prepare the land grants for dinner. But when the government started paying in cotton-backs at the beginning of the year, she stopped complaining.

New reports had trickled in over the previous couple of days regarding Comanche raids on homesteads on the Colorado River, to the north. Esparza's platoon of twenty cavalry were deployed in two squads of ten men each. His men had been mounted since before dawn and were keeping a watchful eye on the fords, along the Guadeloupe River, where the trails led north from San Antonio.

Esparza and the squad with which he rode, watched a ford which had cedar elms growing along its banks, as well as various shrubs. There was more cover along the opposite bank than he liked, and he turned to the squad's sergeant, Gustav Fredericks, saying, "Sergeant, you see that elm on the other side of the river? All that scrub brush so close to the ford bothers me. What do you think about putting a couple of our men opposite it. Putting some guns on the right spot on this side could negate anything coming from the other side."

Fredericks gave a precise salute, and with a thick German accent, said, "Yes, sir, Lieutenant. Private Garcia, come with me."

The sergeant followed the wagon ruts down the river bank, scouting positions where he could place his men into cover. Several arrows arced out of the very area Esparza was studying. Unlike many cavalry troopers, the sergeant was a large man and two arrows took him in the chest, flipping him off the back of his saddle, in a somersault, where he landed on the river bank with a bone-jarring thud. Private Garcia wheeled his horse around and ducked his head low against animal's neck. Arrows sped over his head as he dug his heels into his mount, beating a hasty retreat toward Esparza and the rest of the squad.

From the northern side of the Guadeloupe River, more than a dozen Comanche warriors plunged their horses into the shallow water, as they screamed insults and waved muskets, bows, spears, and clubs at the troopers. Esparza grabbed his carbine, and confirmed that the percussion cap was in place. There were more than enough targets to pick from. What was the expression used by General Travis? Target rich environment. But when he saw a warrior rise from behind the brush, he inferred he was seeing Sgt.

Fredericks' murderer. He raised his rifle at the same time the warrior drew back his bow, aiming at the retreating private. Both weapons fired at the same time. Both aimed true. As Private Garza jolted in his saddle with the arrow's impact, the bullet struck the warrior in the throat, spraying blood as the carotid artery was severed. The warrior tumbled into the shallow water, dead before his body splashed in the river.

An arrow protruding from his back, Private Garza managed to guide his horse back to the squad. Esparza grabbed the private's reins and turned. "Let's get moving, boys! Let's find the other squad and send these bastards back across the river." With that, he dug his spurred heels into his horse's flanks and urged it to a gallop. The other seven troopers raced after the officer. Each effort to veer back to the river was met with a shower of arrows, driving them to the southwest, toward San Antonio. Glancing behind him every few minutes, he saw more than a score of Comanche spread out behind him and his men. As a pointed reminder, they were racing for their lives, every few minutes, one of the warriors let loose an arrow, which fell behind him and his men.

As the race lengthened, he lost count of the number of arrows shot from the Comanche still pursuing his squad of men. Esparza guessed his men had been riding hard for at least thirty minutes when to his right, he heard the sweet sound of hurried bugle note. A quarter mile away he spied a half dozen troopers from his other squad. Behind them, he saw even more Comanche warriors pressing them. He pointed toward the other squad and angled his own horse toward his other men. A short while later, he and his men combined with the other half dozen troopers, as the remnants of the platoon came together.

As the two small groups merged, the fourteen troopers urged their horses to greater speeds. The band of warriors chasing Espinoza's squad was joined by an even larger group of Comanche, who were hard on the other squad's heels. Even as their mounts ate away the miles, the horses grew fatigued. A hurried look behind showed the Comanche warriors mounted on their sturdy mustangs. As his own platoon's speed seemed to slow, with their mounts' exhaustion, the warriors' arrows no long fell short. Now they landed amid his diminished force.

Lieutenant Esparza felt his mount shudder and stumble. He looked behind him and saw an arrow protruding from his horse's rump. His mount took several more strides before the front legs collapsed. As his horse crashed hard into the ground, Esparza, the son and grandson of vaqueros, used every skill he possessed to leap clear from his horse. As his body slammed into the ground, he tucked his chin into his shoulder and let his momentum carry him forward as he careened along the ground.

With only a moment before the Comanche would overrun him, he drew his revolver, and aimed it at the nearest warrior and squeezed the trigger. The pain in his arm shot through him and his aim was off. Instead of hitting the warrior, the bullet struck the horse squarely in the forehead. As the animal collapsed, the Comanche was flung head first over the horse's head. Landing just a few yards away from Esparza, the Lieutenant heard the loud pop of a bone cracking. The warrior rolled to one side, and as he attempted to spring up, his left leg collapsed. Behind the warrior, Esparza saw a wave of Comanche approaching. He resolved to sell his life dearly, knowing he only had a few seconds to dispatch as many as he could. He resolved to start with the one before him. Esparza drew down upon him and before he could pull the trigger, a hole exploded in the warrior's chest and he fell dead.

Most of the other men of the Esparza's command had turned around and came back for their commander. A dozen of his troopers had dismounted and ran up behind him. In their hands, they carried their carbines. As they joined him, they fired at the rapidly approaching Comanche, emptying saddles. Rather than ride in among the Texians, they wheeled to the right and left and returned fire, sending arrows into the midst of the troopers. Esparza fired again and again at the Comanche as they completed their encirclement of his tiny island of troopers. When the hammer slammed down on an empty chamber, he turned and saw several of his men were down, arrows sticking from their bodies.

One of the fallen still had his pistol in its holster. He lunged for it, feeling an icy tingling along his spine as an arrow sped through the air, inches above his back. He yanked the pistol from the dead man's holster and seeing the weapon was loaded, turned back to face the rain of death falling among his men. Now with half the command down, the Comanche were emboldened in their attack. He saw one warrior toss his bow onto his back and lower a lance as he dug his heels into his mount, flinging both rider and horse toward Esparza and his men. The Lieutenant pointed the pistol at the charging warrior and sent round after round at the charging foe, finally sending the warrior tumbling from the saddle. The horse veered to the right, as the Comanche warrior rolled to a stop at Esparza's feet.

What seemed like an eternity had been less a couple of minutes. He stood with two remaining troopers, firing at the charging Comanche warriors. What had started as a wave of Comanche warriors, lapping around the tiny island of Texian soldiers, crested and swamped the island. Only the sea of warriors remained.

A tsunami's wave eventually crests, and the wave of warriors who overwhelmed the island of Texian cavalry, carried forward, leaving the obliterated remains in its wake. Spirit Talker and several of warriors who were veterans of twenty or more winters of warfare, first against the Mexicans and now the Texians, approached the carnage. More than a dozen of the Texian cavalry were dead, but they died hard. He saw just as many of the People's warriors broken upon the ground. These warriors would never ride again, and their wives and children would mourn for their husbands and fathers. Spirit Talker remembered his own youth and recalled his own disdain for such thoughts. But now, with so many winters behind him now, such a loss hung heavy. Not only for the dead did he mourn, but for every dead warrior there was another too badly wounded to carry forward the fight. They too would burden the People, unable to raid, to collect more horses from the Texians and Mexicans.

As Spirit Talker rode through the site of the battle, he saw the troopers carried pistols, just as deadly as those used by the hated Rangers. This was unfortunate. If all the Texians on horse now used these pistols, how could the People stand against them? In addition to the pistols, he noted the muskets carried by the troopers were different than those for which the People had traded. One of his men held it and looked it over carefully. As Spirit Talker watched, he flipped a trigger under the gun and an iron block slid open at the breech of the gun. With his finger, the old warrior felt down the opening and grunted in realization. "It's where they put the bullet and powder."

The old peace chief shook his head. He had never seen the like. "What does it mean, Night Owl?"

The warrior closed the breech and pointed the gun at some imagined target across the prairie before replying. "They can fire these guns faster than before. I don't know how much faster, but enough that it worries me."

Without needing to give an order, Spirit Talker watched as his men collected both the pistols and the carbines from the dead. "We need to learn more about these weapons. The Texians have changed the rules by which they are fighting. Even if we win today, we will eventually be overwhelmed if we don't learn about these changes."

As the veteran warriors rode on, following after the blooded warriors now a couple of miles ahead, Spirit Talker worried. He had advocated peace to the various bands. Had told them it was better to trade away their many prisoners and reclaim those of the People now held in San Antonio. But the younger war-chiefs wanted blood for blood. Too many of the People had been killed in the recent incursion by the Texian army for the People to seek peace. The new musket worried Spirit Talker and he wondered what they would find when they reached San Antonio.

The sun had climbed high into the eastern sky as noon approached, but Will had been up since before dawn. He had made the decision to relocate Major McCulloch's militia from the field west of the Alamo to the northern side of San Antonio. Since the revolution's end more than a year earlier, the town had grown and the development north of the plaza was exposed to both the northern and western approaches. Will knew McCulloch was at work turning newly constructed houses on the north side of town into fortified bastions, given the number of people who had rode to the Alamo, complaining the militia were turning their homes into forts. The number of complainants would have been much higher if most of San Antonio hadn't heeded the command to evacuate.

One such time, found Will working with Lt. Colonel Johnston, as they studied a map of the Alamo complex and the surrounding land. The corral which played host to the misery which was the imprisoned Comanche women and old men, had been prominently drawn on the map. As the two officers discussed tactis, two well-to-do looking men approached. When the older of the two spoke, he had a clipped upper-class English accent. "What in heaven's name are you thinking, letting that rabble in San Antonio, tear into our homes? Barely completed, and they've smashed my windows and dug up my Libby's azaleas. This is a travesty. What are you going to do about it?"

Will's eyes blazed, as he turned to face the foreign-born man. Before he could respond the other man spoke. He was younger by at least a decade from his companion. In a soft Georgian drawl, he added, "General, we have been turned out of our homes by your militia. Not only that, but your officer has purloined my property and has put my slaves to work without compensation."

Will snapped at the two men. "Why didn't either of you answer the militia's call? You're both of age." Before either man could respond, he continued, "Failing that, why didn't you evacuate when the alcalde ordered the evacuation of civilians?"

The Englishman replied, "And leave my new home unprotected, I won't countenance any such thing! And now your *militia* have ruined it."

"Then I suggest you return and defend it with them, *sir*." Will's voice dripped with scorn.

The foreign-born man huffed and stormed off, cursing Will to any who would listen.

The Georgian stayed in place. "What about my property, General?"

Will found resisting the urge to strike the civilian hard, but finally managed to reply, "If your property survives the coming battle, I'm sure Major McCulloch will return them to you. If you're concerned about your property, my suggestion is the same to you as it was to your friend there," he pointed to the retreating back of the Englishman, "join with the militia to defend your homes. Now if you'll forgive me, I have a battle to plan."

After the two civilians left, Will shook his head and looked back to the map. No sooner had he and Lt. Colonel Johnston identified each company's position than a cry from above the gatehouse broke their attention. As Will looked up he saw a lone rider galloping through the gates. The horseman, wearing the same butternut uniform of both infantry and cavalry, saw Will and Johnston as they made their way toward the gate, and he pulled his mount up before them and saluted, "Corporal Ambrose Davis, reporting. A Troop. Esparza's platoon, sir! We was attacked by lots of Comanche, sir! I think I'm the only one to get away,

General. The Comanche, they're on their way!"

Chapter 12

As the trooper's words echoed in his ear, Will's thoughts flew to Major McCulloch's militia on the northern part of town. The trooper was spent from his ride, but the town needed to be warned. He cast about, trying to find Captain Seguin. The Tejano officer ran toward them once he spotted the winded trooper. Before Will could issue any orders, Seguin cried, "Corporal Davis, where the hell is Lieutenant Esparza and the rest of your platoon?"

For the second time in as many minutes, Davis relayed the information. As Seguin stood there, slack jawed, trying to accept a quarter of the regular cavalry had been wiped out by the Comanche, Will interjected, "Juan, get one of your men over to Major McCulloch. I want him to know they're on their way!"

The fiery Tejano nodded curtly, snapping back to the present. He shouted orders and moments later another trooper was racing across the ground between the Alamo and the town.

Will turned to Lt. Colonel Johnston. "Have the bugler sound an officer's call and then assembly."

A couple of minutes later, Will and Johnston were surrounded by every officer in the fort above the rank of lieutenant. A dozen men listened to Will as he barked out orders. The previous month's extensive drilling paid dividends as the officers listened to Will lay out the strategy for the coming battle. Now, though, it was no drill.

"Captain Hays." Will addressed a young Ranger officer, part of the two companies Major Caldwell had dispatched from the Frontier forts, "You and Captain Wallace will deploy your Ranger companies north of the prison compound. Your men will act to delay the Comanche while our infantry deploy. With a casual salute, the young man, leapt onto his horse, and galloped through the gate and westward to his command.

Will turned to Seguin, "Pull your men back from before the Comanche, Captain. We're not going to lose any more soldiers piecemeal if we can avoid it."

Seguin nodded sadly. "I've known Gregorio Esparza since we were boys. His father worked for my father. When this is over I'll need to call on his wife and tell her. I'd rather fight Comanche all day than face her."

Will wanted to take the time to tell Seguin it was alright to mourn his friend's death, but a great deal rested on the captain's ability to recover the men from their exposed positions north of town. Morosely, the Tejano captain grabbed the reins of his horse and pulled himself into the saddle, and galloped through the gates, heading north in an effort to save the rest of the Republic's regular cavalry.

"Colonel Johnston, I want you to detail a company of infantry to deploy along the north wall of the Alamo. They'll stay here along with the artillery under Captain Dickinson."

A glance at the north wall of the Alamo revealed the old crumbling wall replaced by a taller wall built a dozen feet further to the north, running more than one hundred sixty feet in length. Connecting it to the eastern wall was the northern barracks, which was under construction. The barracks would eventually be two stories tall, twenty feet in height. At the moment, the first floor was complete, but its exterior wall was not quite as tall as the rest of the northern wall. Seventy-five riflemen along the wall, wasn't many, just one man ever four feet. Even so, Will thought the main thrust of the Comanche attack would be directed at the paddock where the prisoners were kept.

Will pointed to two of the infantry captains. "You'll be under Colonel Johnston's direct command, and you'll be stationed to the northeast of the prisoners' camp." At three other officers, he pointed and continued, "Your three companies will report directly to me. We'll hold the ground directly in front of the camp. Get going. Take up positions about a hundred yards directly to its north."

As the last of the officers hurried away, leaving Will alone for a moment. He turned around, the gate now empty, as the officers and soldiers hurried to their assigned positions. The Alamo plaza was one hundred fifty yards long between the gate and the north wall. In a world existing only in his head, he imagined what it must have been like for the one hundred eighty souls who died trying to hold it, clinging mistakenly to an idea that Sam Houston would come to their rescue. It was but a fleeting image, and his mind returned to the present where he watched the men of the reserve infantry company running across the plaza, racing to the northern wall, where they would act as both the army's reserve as well as their left flank. The confidence they bore as they climbed the ladders reminded Will, any enemy would face a very tough fight against his Texians. With that, he swung up into the saddle and turned toward the gate. He had a battle to fight.

He joined the three companies to the north of the prison camp, where he found Major Wyatt already guiding the deployment of more than two hundred men into defensive positions. As he joined the major, his attention focused on the company directly to their front. The captain deployed his eighteen rifle teams forward a short distance. Each four-man team found what cover the open prairie provided.

"Damn it to hell," he thought, *"I had the time to prepare this land and now, we defend ourselves out in the open!"*

As Will watched the soldiers, he realized he had made a mistake. There had been plenty of time to prepare. While he had prepared and trained his men, he realized now, he should also have prepared the ground on which they would be fighting. He watched his soldiers crouching down behind the scrub brush and shrubs which dotted the prairie, and realized he could have prepared foxholes, trenches and other defensive fortifications.

From the north, a flurry of shots rang out. It was too far away to tell if Seguin's cavalry or the Texas Rangers were tangling with the advancing Comanche warriors. To the right of Will's three companies, he saw Johnston's hundred fifty men crouching low amid the tall prairie grass. Even as the horsemen retreated before the Comanche, it was reassuring see the infantry in as good a position as circumstances allowed.

The mounted men in front of the infantry turned out to be Hay's Rangers. As the youthful captain came within hailing distance, Will called out, "Take up our left flank. Tell Captain Wallace I want his men behind Johnston's men. Tell them I want an eye kept on the prisoners. Where's Captain Seguin? I want him between your company and the Alamo."

Hays waved and wheeled around, eager to pass along the orders. A moment later, a couple of dozen Rangers split away from the others, riding hard to the rear, in the direction of the prison camp. Back to the north, the flurry of shots grew to a crescendo as Seguin's cavalry attempted to disengage from the pursuing warriors. Several troopers from the cavalry galloped by, relief on their faces as they saw the waiting infantry spread out across the prairie. A loud boom echoed from the Alamo's north wall. One of Captain Dickinson's nine-pounder cannons fired at a target beyond the retreating troopers. It was quickly followed by the other cannon on the north wall.

After several tense moments, as the cavalry under Captain Seguin disengaged from the Comanche, Will realized he had been holding his breath. He exhaled as he watched Seguin and several dozen troopers ride by the left side of the infantry. When the last of the retreating cavalry passed by, Will felt the thrill of battle rise up within him. He resisted the urge to cry out to the waiting soldiers. Breathing deeply, he calmed his racing nerves and simply nodded to the officers commanding each of the companies, sending them a prearranged signal. In turn, the one close by ordered, "Aimed fire, men!"

From behind the thin line of infantry, Will wasn't able to see distinct targets, although along the line nearly two hundred yards in length, several men, either better shots or overly eager, fired their carbines.

Finally, through a haze of dust, more than a hundred Comanche warriors materialized. They brandished bows and arrows, spears and here and there even muskets. If he survived the fight, Will resolved to find out if those guns were trade weapons. He'd be damned if he'd let any merchants operating in Texas sell guns to the Comanche. From those first hundred warriors, Will felt a bit daunted as their numbers multiplied in number. Even though it was situated more than a hundred yards behind Will's line of infantry, when the warriors spotted the prison camp, the shouts and taunts from the Comanche grew in volume. In contrast, the officers and NCOs in Will's thin, butternut line offered quiet words of encouragement to their own soldiers.

Although it was only a few minutes, time seemed to stand still as the number of Comanche warriors to their north grew by what Will imagined was ten-fold. From a hundred warriors, less than a quarter mile away, they soon became more than a thousand. After their taunts, shouts and catcalls reached a fevered pitch, hundreds of them surged forward, in defiance of their well-versed tactics of hit-and-run. As they closed the distance, the volume of fire ratcheted up. From Will's position, right behind the thin line of soldiers, he watched as sheets of flame lashed out from infantry.

Among the hurtling rush of Comanche, dozens of warriors were knocked from their saddles, hit by the aimed rifle fire, lashing out from the Texian soldiers. A man mounted on his horse is a big target. Unfortunately, most of the target is horse. Even more warriors fell from their horses, when the beasts were hit, sending both mount and rider crashing to the ground. No matter how many saddles had been emptied, even more mounted warriors were streaming in from the north. Will tried to swallow, his mouth felt as dry as sandpaper. He drew the five-shot revolver at his hip and waited.

The four men assigned to the C team, second squad, first platoon of company D, 1st Texas Infantry saw the charging mass of warriors raging like a tempest toward them. The NCO in command of the rifle team was a corporal, who drew a bead on a horseman a couple hundred yards away and fired. Immediately, he cracked open the carbine's breech, out of which smoke curled, and took a paper cartridge from a large, cartridge box at his belt, tore off the end of the paper with his teeth and crammed the remainder into the breach-block's tube. He slammed the breech closed, and took a percussion cap from a small, leather cap-box and pushed it onto the nipple and waited. The number two man in the rifle team, fired his carbine at a target, more than five hundred feet away, and rushed to reload. When he was finished, the corporal fired again. Their other teammates alternated firing with each other, too. Across the three companies, a total of fifty-four rifle teams coordinated their fire, sending hundreds of rounds into the charging horde of warriors.

Even though the Comanche warriors preferred, and in fact, had perfected the hit-and-run tactics which had sent tremors of terror through northern Mexico and Texas, there was nothing wrong with their courage this day. Most of them were seasoned warriors and had been on many a raid. Until the last few months, their tactics worked well. Until now, most battles were small affairs, skirmishes, seldom more than ten or twenty on either side. Before, the white man would fire his muskets and then he would have to stand to reload. It was easy to ride in and skewer him as he reloaded. The Texian army's invasion earlier in the spring had changed the nature of the war. Two villages destroyed, more than a hundred warriors killed. The Texians had changed the way this war would be fought, and the brave Comanche warriors were doing their best to adapt to the change.

They showed their courage as their horses pounded across the three hundred yards, determined to close with the hated mud-colored soldiers. Hundreds of lead rounds had crashed into the charging warriors, from the thin line directly before them. The number of empty saddles was proof of the accuracy of the rifle fire. Less than a hundred yards to go, and if it were possible for the infantry to fire even faster, they did. Too many bullets found their targets, too many saddles were emptied. Despite their courage, most of the Comanche veered to their right and left, angling to flank the thin line of soldiers. If they couldn't go through the Texians, they would go around. The prison camp was nearly within reach.

Many, though, riled by the punishment they had endured, propelled their mounts forward, closing the last couple of hundred feet. Scores of warriors crashed into the waiting line of Texian infantry. The Texians' open order tactics left little room between the line of infantry and Will, who was standing just a few yards behind them. He saw a warrior, spear in hand, ride by a soldier, lunging out, catching him in the chest, as he tried scrambling out of the way. No sooner had the soldier fallen, the warrior toppled from his horse when another soldier fired his rifle, point-blank into his face, blowing bone and brains out the back of his skull. Dozens of individual fights sprang up, as warriors closed with the soldiers. Soldiers reached for Bowie knives at their belts, as Comanches grabbed their own knives and war clubs as combat degenerated into scores of melee fights.

Where they were able, each rifle team rallied into a tight formation, each soldier guarding the others' backs, in an outward facing square. The Comanche warrior, lord of the plains, was adept at one on one combat, but the Texians rifle teams turned the weight of the fight against them. Rather than facing a soldier in single combat, often a warrior was set upon by two or even three men from a single rifle team. Less often, a group of warriors would roll over the small team formations.

The thin line held. The tactical cohesion of his men impressed Will. For each fallen soldier in butternut, there were more fallen Comanche warriors. The warriors who threw themselves at the line of Texian infantry had endured too much and as they fell back, they hurled arrows toward their foes.

More than two hundred warriors swung to the infantry's left flank. As they raced to the left, their attention was pulled to the corral holding the prisoners. Some of the warriors, who galloped by the infantry, sent arrows plunging into the line of soldiers. In return, those soldiers who were able, reacted by shooting back at the fast-moving targets. Along the eastern wall of the Alamo, a few men from the reserve company fired into the charging mass of warriors. Here a horse was hit, throwing its rider as it crashed to the ground and there a warrior toppled from the saddle as a bullet found its marks. But most of the warriors surged onward, toward the prison camp.

With only yards to go before reaching their goal, the Comanche slammed into Hays and Wallace's rangers as well as the remnant of Seguin's cavalry, who opened fire with their revolvers. Less than eighty Texians faced off against more than twice as many Comanche. Four hundred rounds of .36 caliber ammunition smashed into mass of Comanche warriors in just a few seconds. From after-action reports filed by the Texian officers, no rational person could fail to acknowledge the unsurpassed bravery and determination of the Comanche warriors. They were nearly without equal. But leather shields provide no protection to flying bullets and there comes a point at which no amount of bravery or resolve can overcome lethal firepower. Like a car hitting a brick wall, the Comanche found that point on that late spring day in 1837. The flower of the Comanche nation died on the green prairie, amid the blooms of the bluebonnet fields, outside the walls of the Alamo. They were killed in numbers they had never experienced.

Not far away, to the west, a few hundred warriors bypassed the attack on the prison camp, and rode for San Antonio. Convinced their comrades would overwhelm the Texians at the prison camp, these warriors rode for plunder. They knew they would find gold, food, and horses in the town. Instead, as they crossed the first street in town, the dozen houses, which fronted the street, erupted in gunfire. Major McCulloch's poorly trained militia had knocked out windows and climbed onto roofs, intent on turning every home into a fortress.

Ignoring the houses along the center of the road, the warriors fanned out, lapping around the ends of the street. Dozens of warriors rushed the last house on the western end. It was a small home of adobe construction. A heavy wooden door barred the entrance. From its few windows poked a dozen rifles. From atop its flat roof, another half dozen men fired into the mass of warriors. For each gunshot from the windows, a half dozen arrows responded. In only moments, the gunfire slackened, and warriors crawled through the windows, taking the fight to the beleaguered Texians.

Major McCulloch, from his perch atop the center-most house on the street saw the concerted attack on his flank. The militia holding the dozen houses along the street represented half his strength. But one street over, the remainder of his militia forces were assembled. He scrambled down a ladder at the back of the house and ran between two newly built homes. Across the street, he found a company of militia from Gonzales.

"Get up, men! The enemy is on our flank!"

The citizen soldiers leapt to their feet, and shouldered their weapons. Armed with a flintlock pistol and Bowie knife, McCulloch led the way, at a jog.

As the men from Gonzales, sixty strong, rounded the street corner, they ran into a dozen warriors, who, content to leave their companions rampaging through the last house on the street, were seeking other houses to loot. McCulloch raised his pistol and fired it point blank into the face of a warrior and as the Comanche fell, he stepped around the body and used his knife to parry a war club aimed at his head. A youth, not yet full grown, had attempted to bash in his head. Had the club been expertly wielded, the leader of the Texian militia would have fallen there. As his men were swarming through the Comanche warriors, McCulloch used his weight to barrel over the youth, sending him sprawling to the ground.

As the Comanche warriors spilled out of the house they had overran, they saw the charging Texians. This was not the easy pickings they had expected. Rather than stay and fight, they fell back the way they came, collecting their wounded as they retreated. McCulloch's company quickly recaptured the last house, finding nearly twenty of their militia dead in and around the building.

More militia filtered between the houses behind their line, reinforcing their comrades along the town's northern line. With the Comanche in full retreat, McCulloch called his men back. "Let them go, boys. We stopped them."

McCulloch surveyed the street. Dozens of bodies, mostly Comanche were scattered along its length, but plenty of arrows had found their targets through the windows of the houses in which his men had made their stand.

A stump of a live oak held a prominent place in one of the yards. As the adrenaline wore off, the major sat on the stump, "We did it. We stopped them cold."

To the east of the Alamo, Will watched as the Comanche warriors slipped away, first in twos and threes, and then in larger groups, moving back to the north. The nearest were a few hundred yards away, and as they retreated, they paused long enough to check those on the ground, collecting their wounded. The bloodied men in the line watched the warriors as they headed north. "If any of those bastards come within arrow range, boys, take 'em out. They may be the bravest of the brave, but they need to know Texas owns this battlefield." Will hated himself for giving the order, wondering if a larger measure of compassion was in order.

That evening, crowded in Will's office, he was joined by President Crockett, Lt. Colonel Johnston, Majors McCulloch and Wyatt, Captain Seguin and Captains Hays and Wallace of the Rangers. Crockett sat in Will's chair and looked over the reports collected by the officers who were present. "Tarnation, Buck. But damned if this fight isn't something they'll build monuments about in a hundred years."

He picked up a report and read, "A hundred and seventeen confirmed Comanche Killed. Forty-three more wounded were captured. God knows how many of their dead and wounded they escaped with. Hell's bells, men, they ain't been whipped this bad even by that governor from Santa Fe, who whipped them all those years back."

Captain Hays, the youngest man in the room by a half dozen years, spoke up cautiously, "Mr. President, me and Bigfoot, I mean, Captain Wallace here, have our Rangers following behind 'em and it looks like they could have another two hundred wounded and dead they done escaped with, sir."

As Crockett smiled expansively at Hays' words, Will shuffled through the various reports on the table until he found the one he sought. "Here's the report on our own casualties, sir." Will handed it over to Crockett. "Our regulars did very well. Most of our dead came from Lieutenant Esparza's platoon, this side of the Guadeloupe River. All told, thirty-one regulars were killed and another thirty wounded. Unfortunately, our militia forces suffered heavy losses, when some of the Comanche attacked San Antonio. Fortunately, Major McCulloch's forces held them at the northern edge of town, but at the cost of twenty-eight killed and forty-nine wounded."

The men standing around the table were silent as each remembered those counted among the dead, whom they knew. Will finally broke the silence. "It's likely true, we probably killed or wounded over three hundred Comanche warriors in today's fight. But before we break out the jugs and celebrate, let's not lose sight of the fact we suffered nearly a hundred and forty casualties, too. Not even during Santa Anna's misbegotten invasion last year did we lose so many."

Somberly, Crockett stood and said, "General Travis, I agree with you. Our casualties are only light when compared against those suffered by the Comanche. You and your officers did all that was asked of you by me and Congress. I'll be sending my own full report to Congress on this campaign and I know they'll be thankful for what you boys have done." He paused for a moment, and it looked like he swallowed something unpleasant, as he turned to Major McCulloch, "I got my start in politics commanding militia, just like you did, Ben. For years I always thought we could call up the militia and raise an army whenever we needed. Our fights against Santa Anna last year didn't do anything to change my mind. But now, damned if I think the same thing anymore. Buck here, I mean, General Travis, has been bending my ear ever since we sent that puffed up Jackanapes back to Mexico about the need for a more robust militia. After this, I think it's time to do something about it."

He picked up another piece of paper from the table up, "Ben, I know you asked for a command of a Ranger company, and honestly, I've got all the Ranger captains I need right now." He nodded toward Hays and Wallace. "But what I don't have is someone who can turn our militia into a real army at need. Well, except you. I expect I can force this through Congress, Ben, I'm going to appoint you General of the Texas Guard. Rusk will continue to command the militia, but between his unorganized militia companies and Travis' regulars, I want something betwixt and between the two. I'll smooth Tom Rusk's feathers. You'll report to General Travis, here, just as he reports to me. He's developed some smart new tactics. He took what we did against the Mexican army and improved on it against the Comanche. Take that training manual I know he's been working on and give Texas a guard that can stand with its regulars."

Chapter 13

After the meeting, Will returned to the battlefield, east of the Alamo. The Texians' wounded and dead had been removed from the field. Across the prairie dozens of horses remained where they had fallen. Gruesome work remained to remove the dead animals. Some of the Comanche dead were still strewn on the battlefield, where they had fallen. Others, perhaps a few dozen, had been tossed together in a pile, within view of the prison camp. The women inside the camp were visibly distraught over the bodies of the warriors so near.

He wasn't sure who was overseeing the cleanup of the battlefield. Will had left it to Johnston to delegate. He found a soldier loading an assortment of weapons into a small handcart and strode over to him. "Who's in charge of the burial details, Private?"

When the soldier saw Will, his eyes flew to the stars on his shoulder boards. He dropped the spears he had been carrying and saluted. "Sir, Lieutenant Davis is in command. Last I saw of him, he was over by the corral. I think he was talking with one of the officers from the Marines." The company of Marines, which Crockett had brought with him, were guarding the prison camp. Will found the infantry lieutenant talking with his counterpart from the Marines.

The Marines wore blue uniforms, sourced from the same suppliers which provided the United States Marines their uniforms. Rather than buttons with eagles and anchors, the buttons on the Marine lieutenant's uniform gleamed with a large star, behind which was fixed an anchor. The infantry lieutenant, wearing his worn, butternut uniform, stopped talking when he saw Will approach. Both young men snapped to attention and saluted.

"As you were. Lieutenant Davis, how long until you're finished with the cleanup?"

The young officer said, "I've sent for some wagons from town sir. We've got to butcher some of the horses, before we can get them cleared off. I've collected the Comanche dead over there." He pointed to the pile of bodies. "Once the boys are finished collecting them, I was going to burn them."

Will's first thought dredged up a memory from his own past, before the transference. He was in high school. It was spring break and his parents had taken him to San Antonio. They had toured the Mission Trail and had finished at the Cathedral of San Fernando. In the cathedral's vestibule, a large marble sarcophagus purportedly held the cremated remains of the Alamo defenders. His second thought was to knock the young officer to the ground. He wasn't about follow in the footsteps of Santa Anna by burning the bodies of fallen foes.

Will took a deep breath. He'd already fought one duel because of his temper. He'd be damned if he would allow his temper to get the better of him now. After slowly exhaling and wrestling his temper back under his control, he said, "Lieutenant, take a look at those folks behind the corral fence. Now imagine they aren't wild and savage Comanche women and old men. But instead are the folks you grew up with. Now, how do you think they'd feel about seeing the bodies of their loved ones piled a couple of hundred feet away?"

Davis looked toward the pile of bodies and then back toward the imprisoned Comanche. "But, General, sir, they're just Indians."

The young officer was about to continue as Will cut him off. "What about you, Lieutenant? What does it make you?" Will pointed to the women behind the fence, "Never mind about them. What does it say about us if we casually burn their bodies. In front of their women. Is that a story you'd want your folks to read about in the newspaper?"

A light came on behind Davis' eyes as they grew large. "Ah, I didn't think about it like that. No, sir. I don't recon I'd like my folks reading about that."

Will glanced between the prisoners and the pile of the dead. "I don't really care how you think of the Comanche. There's much I admire in their fierce warrior spirit and their determination to protect what they see to be theirs. But the way we treat their dead says absolutely nothing about them, and everything about us. I'm not asking you, Lieutenant, to treat their bodies with any compassion out of respect for them, but out of your own decency."

Nodding, Davis said, "I see your point, sir. What do you want me to with them?"

"Bury them. A common grave is fine. But do it away from the corral."

The next day, the Protestant soldiers who died in the battle were laid to rest in a new cemetery, east of the fort. President Crockett had signed an order creating Texas' first national cemetery for the men who died serving under the Republic's flag. A single ceremony was held for the thirty men buried there. It was conducted by the 1st Texas Infantry's Methodist chaplain and a Baptist preacher, serving with McCulloch's militia. The ceremony's simplicity was in its brevity. The Baptist preacher read from the epistle of John 15:13, "For this corruptible must put on incorruption, and this mortal must put on immortality." He closed his Bible, and looked around at the soldiers gathered around, "These men we bury today are gone from among us, they now stand before the throne of the Almighty. Each of us should look to their example, as Jesus said, 'Greater love hath no man than this, that a man *lay down* his life for his friends.' Those who knew these men well, I trust will take comfort in this, that each man did his duty to God, Texas and his comrades."

After the end of the service, Will hurried back to the

Alamo, where he collected his horse and, along with Lt. Colonel Johnston, rode into town, in time to attend the Catholic service, held in the cemetery of the Church of San Fernando, near the square. As they rode out of the Alamo, deep in their own solitude, Will's thoughts went to the brief words from the preacher. Even before, during his time in the Army and then the National Guard, chaplains reminded their flocks God was on their side. He was sure the medicine men among the Comanche promised the war bands the Great Spirit was on their side. As long as men rode to war, they claimed the mantle of God.

Since first joining the army after 9/11, his interest in church had waned. While the transference into Travis' body led him to think about what caused him to be flung into the past, it was taking responsibility for raising Charlie which had brought him back to his Methodist roots. When he had taken the boy in, they began attending the small Methodist congregation in San Antonio. He wasn't sure if it was because of his renewed faith or despite it, but Will decided God was less interested in the affairs of nations than in the condition of the human heart. It left him no closer to explaining why God would transfer his mind and thoughts into William B. Travis, but he'd long ago given up rationalizing that thought.

The service at San Fernando, while very different from the one earlier, with the priest intoning in Latin, Will was still struck by the similarities. The sixteen caskets were already in the ground, mounds of dirt to the side of each grave. A majority of those in attendance were Tejano, but the diversity of the crowd of soldiers reflected the diverse composition of the Texian army. Irish and German-born soldiers were mixed in among the Tejanos, as the men from Gregorio Esparza's cavalry platoon were laid to rest. Scratching below the surface, Will found no fundamental difference between the Catholic service or the Protestant service he watched earlier. Sure, the Latin rites spoken were different than the preacher's words, but their intent was the same; to give those who remain the opportunity to say goodbye to those who had died. At the heart of the matter, Will realized, they said the same thing.

Spirit Talker rode beside Buffalo Hump. Both men had journeyed the last few hours in silence. Behind them came the remnants of their war band. Like a wet blanket, defeat lay heavy upon the warriors. As he glanced over at the war leader, Spirit Talker could scarcely imagine at the turn of events which had led to the People suffering their worst defeat in memory. Before they had ridden from the Comancheria, he had tried to warn Buffalo Hump of the inherent risk of an attack on the Texian fortress in Bexar. But Buffalo Hump had stubbornly refused to listen, and had told him, "Our warriors demand blood for the attacks by the Texians. They are old women, hiding behind their walls. Our warriors are brave and fearless. We shall ride into their town, with all our bands. Once we free our people held by those cowards, we shall loot and kill those we find in their town."

He shook his head at the memory. Buffalo Hump turned and said, "You were right. They were ready for us. How could our attempt to rescue those captured go so wrong?"

In a universal sign of resignation, Spirit Talker shrugged. He had warned the younger war chief, but decided now was not the time to remind him of that. "The Texians are growing in power, my young friend. We are not. Every day, wagons cross the rivers or ships enter their ports. All of them bring more white men. They will have our land, no matter what we do."

The heavy sigh which escaped Buffalo Hump's mouth was loud. "If it hadn't been for those pistols and rifles we would have won. Those pistols their horsemen carry have killed too many of our warriors."

Spirit Talker did the only thing which made sense. He nodded. After a moment, he said, "It isn't just the weapons, though. Those who fight on foot are not the cowards we thought. I watched them stand against our attack. Our arrows killed or wounded many of them. But they stayed and fought. Each man worked with his friends, so that someone was always ready to shoot at us."

The war chief said, "But even their guns, they fired them fast, far faster than our men with muskets can fire."

The old peace chief brushed aside the comment,

"Their new rifle is formidable, I agree. But don't forget how each little group worked together, far more closely than anything I've ever seen before by those who fight on foot."

Both men fell silent as they urged their horses forward, moving to the northwest, back into the land of the Comancheria. How much longer they would be able to lay claim to the land was something Spirit Talker could no longer predict. Of the eighty warriors who had ridden with their band toward San Antonio, now only fifty were able to fight. Every other band was in a similar or worse situation. Behind them, more than a mile to their rear, Texas Rangers shadowed their retreat since the previous day. They were few in number, no more than a dozen. But even Buffalo Hump was reluctant to lead his warriors to what seemed likely to be certain death. The Texas Rangers' mastery of the pistol with many shots had thoroughly changed the dynamic of warfare on the plains now.

Fifty winters before, he recalled his first raid. He was more than a boy, but not yet a man. The Apache were terrified of the Comanche. It was good. Horses were easy to raid. The Spanish gave them horses and grains to keep the People from attacking. The Apache cowered in fear.

"*Yes*," Spirit Talker thought, "*It had been good to be one of the People*."

The empty saddles accompanying the band didn't just represent remounts. No, they were a heavy reminder that one of every six warriors who rode to San

Antonio was now dead. Before the latest war, the Comanche were to be feared. Now, the People feared the Texians.

As if reading his mind, Buffalo Hump said, "The Texians hound us even now." He pointed to the small cloud of dust behind them. "They attack our camps and take our women and children."

It was simply the truth, Spirit Talker thought. *"They learned well from us."*

As the sun kissed the western horizon, the two chiefs watched two horsemen approach their camp. Both wore the wide brimmed hats favored by the Rangers. At their hips were the pistols which caused the People so much grief. One of the riders was pale skinned; a white man. The other, darker complexioned. He was a Tejano. Waved forward, the two men approached, holding their hands in the sign of peace. The dark skinned one spoke in the language of the Spanish. Both chieftains understood.

Spirit Talker called back, "What words do you have for the Penateka?"

The Ranger replied, "Pass word to all the bands of the Penateka, riding the Comancheria. Texas seeks a treaty, an end to the violence which has taken too many of your people already."

Buffalo Hump grumbled at his side, "There are only two of them. Give me a chance and I'd have both their scalps hanging on my teepee."

Spirit Talker eyed the younger chief and saw only resignation. His were empty words.

The Tejano Ranger continued, "Meet with us where the river we call the Bosque meets with the Brazos on the second full moon from today. There is a Ranger fort there, named Bee."

The Ranger waited until he saw Spirit Talker's nod of acknowledgement and then the two men wheeled around and galloped to the east.

This scene was played out across the Comancheria a half dozen more times, as other war bands were given the same message.

Chapter 14

The hot July sun beat mercilessly down on Will's head. His hat rested on the saddle horn as he looked through the telescoping spyglass at a Comanche war party approaching Fort Bee at a slow gait. Even their ponies looked tired and exhausted in the wilting heat. So far, nearly a dozen bands had arrived over the past twenty-four hours. Although the warriors' countenance remained fierce and defiant, their chieftains, older and wiser, carried an air of resignation as they made camp at the confluence of the Brazos and Bosque Rivers.

Watching over the gathering were the Texas Rangers. Company B normally had thirty men assigned to it, but in the week leading up to this gathering, Major Caldwell had arrived with an additional sixty from the other forts along the frontier. Additionally, Captain Seguin and his remaining company of cavalry trailed behind Will, as they escorted President Crockett to the meeting.

Fort Bee was a typical frontier fort. Four wooden

palisades surrounded an area which contained a small parade ground and a corral for the Rangers' horses. Two blockhouses were at opposite corners of the fort, providing a three-hundred-sixty-degree field of fire. Along each side of the fort, a few cabins were built into the side of the interior walls. Also interspersed between the cabins were narrow wooden platforms, where riflemen could stand to fire through slits, cut in the wooden palisades.

While Seguin's cavalry bivouacked outside the fort's walls, Will joined Crockett and Major Caldwell on the ground floor of the blockhouse nearest the gate. The room took up the entire bottom floor of the building. A rough wooden table had been set up along one wall, and a cot for the president along another. As Crockett settled into a chair, which creaked as he sat, he said, "Major, how are things along the frontier?"

Caldwell sat at the table, cleaning supplies scattering before him, as he cleaned a spare cylinder. He looked up when addressed. "Mostly quiet, sir. I've received reports from our fort on the North Fork of the Trinity saying they've seen signs the Wichita have crossed the Red River, heading north. If their client tribes see the writing on the wall, then I hope even the Comanche should see reason. Otherwise, why would so many of their chieftains show up here?"

Will was about to add his own thoughts to the conversation when the door swung inward. Sam Houston stepped into the room, accompanied by a slender Cherokee, dressed in brown wooden pants and a gray jacket, and closed the door behind them. "Gentlemen. The Cherokee have arrived."

Both Will and Caldwell were surprised to see the Texian commissioner to the Cherokee show up. Crockett climbed to his feet and offered his hand to his fellow Tennessean. "Sam, I'm glad you got my letter. How many men were you able to bring?"

As Houston sat on the edge of the Table, he said, "We raised a company of Rangers, by God. And I've brought them with me. I'd like to introduce De-ga-ta-ga Waite. He's just arrived from Georgia, leading more than a thousand of his people west. The Cherokee counsel of Texas has appointed him commander of their militia."

Will stared at the dark-skinned man before him and saw a soldier. The gray jacket he wore bore Georgia militia buttons. His hair was combed back and cut below the collar. For reasons he couldn't put his finger on, Will felt as though he had seen the Cherokee before, but no amount of sifting through Travis' memories brought an answer to the niggling question of who he was.

As Houston took the last of the four chairs, the Cherokee extended his hand to Will. "De-ga-ta-ga is 'one who stands.' My Christian name is Isaac Stand Waite."

As Will shook his hand, the name connected in his mind. There was a Confederate general in the Civil War named Stand Waite. He was the only American Indian to rise to the rank of general during the war. Will wasn't sure he was the same man, but at thirty years of age now, it was certainly possible.

"We had been evicted from our homes in Georgia, and were on our way to the Indian Territory to the north, when the Raven here," he indicated to Houston, "implored us to come to Texas. He said Texas would protect our property rights which Georgia has failed to do."

As the meeting broke up, Will was joined by Waite in the small parade ground. "I've heard much about you, General Travis, over the past year. Even during the tragedy of our eviction from Georgia and our travel west, I heard of your victory against Santa Anna. Since our arrival in Texas, your exploits against the Comanche have been warmly received in our towns."

As the two officers, one white and the other red, stood under the night sky, talking, it was clear Waite was articulate and well-educated. Will liked him. As they walked across the parade ground Will learned Waite had also brought a few volunteers who wanted to serve in the Texas army. Will's eyes lit up at the prospect. "Hell, yes, Mr. Waite. You bet I can find a place for them to serve."

The following morning, all the significant bands of Comanche were represented by a total of fourteen chiefs. They were assembled beneath a tall live oak tree, growing beside the languidly flowing Brazos. They sat on blankets in a wide semicircle. Across from them, also under the branches of the same live oak, Crockett,

Houston, and Will sat in wooden chairs. Behind Will stood Juan Seguin, who could translate from Spanish. Houston had brought a Cherokee youth with him, who stood by his side. The teenager had been captured by the Comanche several years earlier, but traded back to his own tribe later. He spoke fluent Comanche.

Houston leaned toward Crockett and whispered loud enough for Will to hear. "Always pays to know what they're saying. A lot of them speak Spanish and I'm sure we could negotiate with them in that language, but this way seems better, don't you think?"

Crockett rose from his chair and stepped forward. "I am David Crockett. I am the elected chief for all the people of Texas. I have come here to meet with you, the chieftains of the Comanche People, in the hope that we can find peace between our peoples." When this was translated he sat in his chair and listened as the Cherokee youth translated each chief's introduction and greeting. The last to speak was the eldest. "I am called Spirit Talker. It has been more than fifty winters since my first raid. I agree with your chief. We want peace, too. But peace should start with goodwill. Show us your goodwill by freeing our wives and children. It isn't right for the Comanche to be imprisoned behind your walls."

When the youth finished translating, Crockett tilted his head in agreement. "Chief Spirit Talker, I have heard you give good counsel to those in the Comancheria who will listen. Over the many years you have served your people, the Apache and Cheyenne have learned to fear your name. I share your desire to see all prisoners returned to their families; both yours and ours."

Spirit Talker nodded his agreement. "We agree to release those of your people who we have taken captive. Our chiefs have decided all our white prisoners will be released as soon as you release our wives and children."

Crockett turned and sat back in his chair. "It isn't enough. War between your people and ours is inevitable as long as we look at the same land and say it is ours. We have defeated the mighty Mexican army and our treaty with them defines our boundary. The people of Texas will not rest until all of the land south of the waters we call the Red River is under our flag."

As the youth finished translating this into Comanche, Crockett's words were met with dark looks and scowls. Another stood up and spoke, "I am Buffalo Hump. I command the war band of the Penateka Comanche. You cannot eat a flag. We follow the buffalo, and it provides all our needs. We have always followed the buffalo and without it, you would have us die."

After hearing the translation, Houston laid a restraining hand on Crockett's arm. "May I, David?"

As Crockett acquiesced, Houston rose and walked to the middle of the circle made by the two sides. "I am called the Raven by my brothers among the Cherokee. Among the Texians I am called Sam Houston. Until recently I was the war chief of my people. I see things differently than you, Buffalo Hump. If the buffalo provide your every need, why do you wear that calico shirt?" Turning to another chief, he pointed, "Why does he wear a leather belt and carry a steel knife?" He pointed to a third and said, "Even the horses you ride originally came from the Spanish."

As he watched the Comanche grumble, he resumed, "If the buffalo is the only thing the Comanche need to survive, why do you burn our homes to the ground and carry our women and children into captivity? I have checked, and let me tell you, they are not buffalo!" As the words were translated, several chiefs glared back at him, while others laughed at his wit.

Spirit Talker neither glared nor laughed, although his lips curled up at the translation. With the sound of joints popping, he stood and said, "The People do not change quickly or easily. I think that you, Raven, adopted by the Cherokee, would understand that. Yet, it has become impossible to ignore that you Texians are like the flood after a spring rain. You wash over the land and change it. Even since the last winter, we are fewer in number than we were. You are more. I speak only for my band. I see you have the power to attack us whenever we attack you. And when you attack, you kill many of the People. Your guns which speak many times makes sure of that. Maybe it is time the People and Texas no longer wage war against each other. But we need the buffalo."

Houston had returned to his seat, and Crockett now stood. "Peace starts with the release of all prisoners. We will agree to release all the Comanche we have captured, if every band agree to release all whites and Mexicans you have captured or adopted."

Crockett's words elicited consternation among the chiefs. Buffalo Hump stood and explained, "Many among the People who were once white or Mexican do not want to leave the People."

From his seat, Houston burst out into laughter. "I can relate to that. I ran away when I was sixteen years old. Those years among the Cherokee were some of the best of my life." But he grew serious. "However, as our president has said, this is a requirement. If those who you adopted wish to return to live among your people, then we will not stop it, when they are counted as adults among our people. Our laws do not recognize a child's right to make such a decision.

Will watched the chiefs as they listened and then discussed the matter among themselves. It struck him, each of these were intelligent men. Some of the concepts about which Houston talked were odd to them, such as the legal rights of children. But even so, they talked among themselves, sometimes amiably and at other times, contentiously. But in the end, all the chiefs reached consensus. Both sides would trade back all prisoners and adopted children. Neither side would take as slaves those from the other side.

After both sides had agreed to the prisoner swap, the issue of land remained. As the sun dipped below the western horizon, Spirit Talked said, "I fear the easy part is now behind us. I can't argue we use more than just the buffalo," he fingered his cotton shirt's embroidery as he spoke, "but we need the buffalo to survive."

The other chiefs nodded their heads in agreement.

"We have decided, we agree the land below the river of the red clay flies your flag. But, the buffalo do not know your flag or our shield. They go where the Great Spirt leads. They are our life, to keep us from them is to hold a knife to our throats."

Crockett said, "It isn't our wish to see the Comanche no longer riding the great plains or no longer hunting the buffalo."

He turned to Will and Houston and asked, "What if we allow them to hunt below the Red River, but to limit their villages to north of the Red River? They can still hunt the buffalo, but their towns stay north."

Will and Houston readily agreed. Such a treaty could buy Texas twenty or more years before the issue resurfaced. A lot could change in that length of time.

Crockett turned back to Spirit Talker. "Your hunting bands can travel below the Red River, following the buffalo. But your villages must stay north of the river. If any of your warriors attack any Texian farm below the Red River, then the warrior's band will be required by this treaty to turn him over to Texas for justice."

While there was unhappy muttering among the chiefs, Spirit Talker said, "It is good to respect each other. The People will agree to this, provided the same rule applies to Whites or Mexicans who attack us north of the river of the red clay. If you agree to surrender to us any who attack our villages, then we can have peace."

Crockett looked to Will and Houston and saw agreement on their faces. "We agree."

Will shuddered at the thought of Comanche justice, but the alternative was worse. When he considered the attack more than year before at Fort Parker, the alternative was far worse.

As the meeting broke up around midnight, Will walked with Crockett back to the fort. The president confessed, "I don't know if I'll be able to force that last provision through the Senate, when they ratify the treaty. We have a mite different idea about justice than they do. But it's a fair deal to both sides."

Will agreed. "David, if the Senate ratifies this, I think we could see peace for a generation with the Comanche. The challenge for the future comes back to the issue of land. Our view of land ownership is alien to the Comanche, far more so than how the Cherokee see private property rights. Unless they change, as we grow, eventually we're going to come into conflict with them again."

Crockett said, "Maybe even sooner than that. The Comanche don't have a clue about the Adams-Onis Treaty. Steve Austin has notified the Van Buren administration we have agreed with the terms of the treaty, as it defines our national boundary with the United States. Somehow or another, men like Spirit Talker and Buffalo Hump will have to understand the world around them is changing. If they raid into the US, they may find that The United States will give them less of a fair shake than we have."

Chapter 15

The road from San Antonio to Harrisburg remained rough and uneven between the two population centers. But Will found the ride relatively smooth, as he sat opposite Erasmo Seguin in a plush carriage. The coiled springs under the carriage absorbed the worst of the jostling as the iron rimmed wheels dropped into the poorly maintained road's potholes. He had been summoned to Harrisburg along with Señor Seguin to meet with President Crockett.

"Are you sure you don't know why the president has summoned us, Señor Seguin?"

The elder Seguin exhaled noisily. "General, for the last three days, you have plied me with the same question. I am as much in the dark as you about why President Crockett has summoned us."

As the weak, December sun retreated across the western sky, the carriage rolled through the rapidly expanding warehouse district which ran alongside Buffalo Bayou. As the carriage rolled to a stop in front of the town's only hotel, Erasmo and Will alighted from it and walked into the ramshackle building.

The next morning, the two men met with President Crockett in the log cabin which served as both his residence and office. Since Will's last visit, another room had been added, accessible through an open-air dogtrot. As Will and Señor Seguin joined Crockett around the familiar large table which sat in the middle of Crockett's office, a young woman came through the door with a wooden pitcher in hand. As she set the pitcher on the table, she produced a few battered tin cups from her apron and placed them next to the pitcher.

Since the arrival of Crockett's family earlier in the year, this was Will's first opportunity to see the young woman the president affectionately called "my Becky." Her face was thin and angular. Like her father, her eyes were blue and her hair the color of roasted coffee beans. There was no doubt in Will's mind as to why Crockett had been turning away suitors. The president's daughter's slight frame and pretty face caught Will's attention. In a town, like Harrisburg, with far more eligible bachelors than available single women, Will thought Becky Crockett could have the pick of any of them.

As she turned to leave, Will's eyes followed her to the door. When she stepped through, she looked back, and saw Will staring at her. As she closed the door, the last image Will had was a smile on her face.

Crockett cleared his throat. "Ah hem. Buck, you

know, she'll be at the Christmas party at the Liberty Hotel tomorrow evening. You might consider staying for a couple of days before returning to San Antone."

Will's cheeks colored when he realized his interest had not gone unnoticed. "A party? I, uh, don't know. Señor Seguin was kind enough to provide his carriage for our trip here. If he needs to get back to his affairs, I may not be able."

The elder Seguin enjoyed watching Will's discomfiture. "I'm sure my business interests will wait a few days. My Josie would not forgive me if I didn't bring back a detailed account of what the ladies of Harrisburg are wearing at such festivities." He paused, savoring the awkward look on Will's face, before turning serious. "My business interests, or rather the Republic's interests are what you wanted to talk about, Mr. President."

The levity forgotten, Crockett said, "Señor Seguin, between your reports and those from our soldiers stationed at Fort Moses Austin, near Laredo, I have concerns over the allegiance of some of the Mexicans who've been coming into Texas."

"I wasn't aware my reports would be of concern, Mr. President."

Crockett pushed a few pages toward the elder Seguin. "Your reports are focused mainly on the Bexar district, and I don't know that there's a direct threat from Mexico as far as the folks coming across the Rio Grande. But as these other reports indicate, we have some evidence Mexico's got agents in Laredo and possibly in other towns in Texas. As a best guess, over the past two years nearly two thousand people have crossed the Rio Grande into Texas. That's an awful lot of opportunity."

Crockett continued, with a report from the Rangers. "I'm a bit concerned there has been an effort to have an election in Laredo, where they want to vote on returning the town to Mexico."

Seguin's eyes arched in surprise. "I hadn't heard of that."

Crockett nodded, "Given our presence nearby at Fort Moses Austin, several families, if I have heard correctly, have moved back across the river. They've taken to calling the town on the southern bank, *Nuevo Laredo*."

Listening to Crockett and Erasmo Seguin talk, Will was puzzled, "David, does it bother you they are moving back into Mexico?"

Crockett smiled wryly. "Only my ego, Buck. Apart from that, no. If they don't see themselves as Tejano, then let them live in Mexico. I'd far rather our Tejano community be loyal to Texas, and it's a good bet, those who relocate themselves south probably aren't going to share that loyalty."

Seguin shook his head. "I pride myself on keeping a close eye on things within my community and my information from Laredo is sparse. I will ask my son-in-law, Jose, to go down Laredo way and see what he can learn about the latest Mexican government trying to stir things up, Mr. President."

Crockett smiled widely at the older Tejano. "Erasmo,

please my friends call me David. And between the three of us, I'd just as soon set aside titles."

Erasmo smiled in return as Crockett set the reports from Laredo to the side. "I can scarce wait to see what your son-in-law finds out. The other reason I wanted to meet was to discuss the status of the Commodities Bureau."

Seguin's smile faded. "And here I thought it was going to be all fun, Mr. ah, David."

Crockett said, "I confess, the reason I asked Will to join is for two reasons. Most of the money we raise flows into paying for our army and navy. The second is, he's pretty good with figures, and this was his idea."

Will and Erasmo had spent much of the three days on the road discussing this very subject. Since the elder Seguin's appointment as chairman of the Commodities Bureau, he had taken to the task like a fish to water. The bureau's cotton-backs had been circulating for most of the year. With the fall crops harvested, property taxes had been largely paid in one of the fifteen commodities which made up the basket of commodities on which the currency was based. Additionally, the Texas Land Office's bank had also received loan repayments in commodities when the farmers or ranchers were unable to pay with gold or silver.

Seguin said, "Between all of the commodities which have passed through the bureau, we have issued more than half a million dollars in commodities certificates in 1837. Although we're still a few weeks away from the new year, we anticipate doubling the number of certificates in circulation next year."

Crockett was scratching his chin, reviewing a ledger full of figures. "But, we only took in around quarter million dollars in taxes and loan repayments from people. Where did the other quarter million come from?"

"Gold and silver payments from the tariff and gifts and loans from the United States. Even now, eighteen months since the end of the Revolution, we've still received aid from quite a few folks in the United States."

Crockett chuckled. "You're not joking. I received a draft drawn from a bank in Philadelphia from a group called "Philadelphians for Texas Independence" in the amount of ten thousand dollars. It was accompanied by a letter from none other than Henry Clay."

Will was astonished. "What would the Senator from Kentucky want with Texas?"

Crockett replied, "Henry has ambitions for the presidency. If fools like Collinsworth and Potter keep yammering for annexation, and feeding Southern Democrats' thirst for another slave state, there are going to be northern and western interests, led by men like Henry and other Whigs who want to limit the power of Southern Democrats. This little gift is just his way of telling me to stay the course. Now back to the Commodities Bureau. Erasmo, what are your people thinking about 1838? Do they really expect to issue a million dollars in cotton-backs?"

"The short answer is yes," Seguin said, "The longer answer requires we look at the sources of revenue we expect to receive next year. So much of the land granted under the impresario system is still a mess. In my discussions with your secretary of Treasury, neither of us expect to see more than forty thousand dollars in revenue from real estate taxes. But the opposite is true regarding the Texas Land Bank's loan repayments. We expect to receive more than a hundred and fifty thousand from loan repayments alone. Nearly all of these are paid by commodities. Our bureau sells some of the commodities within the Republic; some, like payments in grain, get transferred to the military, but most gets sold in the United States or Europe. For example, our tax on physical property, which includes Lumber and Grist mills as well as slaves, brought in nearly a hundred and seventy thousand dollars this year. Nearly all of that was paid for with commodities. Cotton, specifically. There were plenty of buyers for that, all of them with gold and silver in hand."

Seguin's command of the figures made Crockett's eyes glaze over. "So, in short, what's it mean for next year, Erasmo?"

"Excluding loans or gifts from abroad, we should raise around half a million dollars in taxes and fees."

Crockett grunted. "That's still going to mean a lot of loans from banks in the United States and Europe."

Seguin nodded. "If Michel Menard in our Treasure department is correct, we'll probably need more than seven hundred thousand dollars in loans."

Crockett groaned. "That's not a number I'm going to dangle in front of Congress. They'll give off a stink like the polecats they are."

Seguin gave a half-hearted smile. "Look at the bright side. If our growth continues, we expect to reduce new loans to less than ten percent of the budget by 1842."

Crockett crossed his arms on the table and lay his head on them and complained, "Great. We fix the budget, but the next president gets the credit. Where's the justice in that?"

The next evening, what passed for the hotel's dining room was bedecked with festive bunting and candles. Trestle tables lined one of the walls, piled high with food. It seemed as though most of the government of Texas was assembled in the room. The wives of those who were married, were resplendent in a rainbow of reds, greens, and blues. The finest fashions available in the stores of New Orleans were on display.

As Will joined the Christmas celebration, he tugged at the hem of his dress uniform. it was a frock length jacket several shades darker brown than his fatigue jacket's standard butternut hue. When he entered the room, most eyes followed him as he made his way to where President Crockett and his wife and daughter greeted those arriving. Gone was the homespun hunting jacket, and in its place, the president wore a black dress jacket and matching cravat. His waist coat was black satin, contrasting sharply against the white silk shirt he wore.

As Will proffered his hand, Crockett looked a little sheepish. As they shook, Crockett leaned in. "My Liza insisted we all dress for the occasion. When a woman gets an idea in her head, it might as well be set in stone."

To his left, his wife looked over sharply. Her sigh was one of someone used to hearing Crockett's sharp wit. "And well we do, otherwise you men would be completely uncivilized. When we were younger, back in Tennessee, David would rather have been bear hunting than socializing. He's traded his bears for politicians. I've yet to figure out how to serve one up so as you'd want a helping." She smiled warmly at Will as she continued, "General Travis, it is a pleasure to finally meet you someplace other than my husband's cluttered office."

Will took her white gloved hand and brushed his lips against the silk material. The first lady was several inches shorter than her husband, but was still a tall woman. Her thin frame would have been considered frail, except for a sturdiness she wore like an armor. A life spent on the frontier, suffering through years of Crockett's wanderlust, had hardened her to the difficulties of privation and want. Had Will not already met her at the cabin the Crocketts called home, he would have thought her underdressed in the simple blue satin dress she wore. But he decided it suited her demeanor.

Will's eyes lit up as he stepped to Mrs. Crockett's left

and stood before Rebecca Crockett. The nineteen-year-old woman smiled shyly and curtsied in her green gown. Will found his voice and asked, "If I may, would you consent to dance with me this evening?"

Rebecca's cheeks colored as she covered her mouth with her hand. "General Travis, I'd be honored to give you the first dance."

As Will stepped away from the first family of Texas, Crockett detached himself and stepped over to him. "Before things get away from us, I want to introduce you to a man who has set up a hospital here over in Houston."

He led Will over to a man in his early thirties. His brown hair was slightly receding, and his face was framed by an equally brown beard. As Crockett and Will approached he smiled and extended his hand, "Dr. Ashbel Smith. General Travis, I presume?"

Will shook hands with the doctor, and from the dredges of his own memory from a world gone forever, recalled an Ashbel Smith was one of the founders of the University of Texas and wondered if he was one in the same. Crockett said, "Buck, weren't you were telling me recently the army could use a Surgeon General? I reckon I don't know nothing about medicine, but I have heard plenty of good things about Dr. Smith here, and if you're of a mind to, I'd happily move his appointment through Congress."

The young doctor looked embarrassed at Crockett's praise, but managed to respond, "I'm honored to serve my adopted country in whatever way I may, General

Travis."

The two men agreed to meet again later to discuss the opportunity. As the room filled up with government dignitaries, Will found Crockett had again abandoned his post near the door and migrated to a table, where a large, earthen jug sat in the middle. With a smile on his face, Will ambled over to the president as Crockett poured an amber liquid into a dainty tea cup.

"Evening, Mr. President. I see you've found a suitable beverage."

Crockett handed the tea cup to Will, "Here, Buck, take one of these blasted cups and let's get drunk together. Damned if I know why our womenfolk love putting these shindigs on, but my Liza conspired against me with Lorenzo's Emily and they invited half the government."

In one corner of the large room several musicians were practicing on their instruments. Will spotted Crockett's wife, Elizabeth talking with Emily de Zavala and several other women. Next to Elizabeth Crockett stood Rebecca. Every look Will stole made him want to get close to her. Standing across the room, Will was able to see how much Crockett's daughter favored her mother so much so he was a little taken aback by the similarities.

Crockett nudged him, saying, "If I didn't know better I'd swear I was looking at my Liza twenty years ago."

Will nodded. "She's a looker. That's for sure."

Crockett jabbed him in the ribs, "That's my daughter you're ogling, Buck." Will looked quickly at Crockett, but seeing the twinkle in his eyes, smiled back.

"Indeed it is, Mr. President. And a very fine looker she is." He stepped away as Crockett's elbow came back up. "As a matter of fact, finding my position here under attack, I shall strategically retreat to yon corner of the room, where I think I have just caught the eye of a pretty young lady." Crockett laughed and waved Will away.

Will sidled up next to Rebecca Crockett, and said, "If I could redeem the promise of that first dance, Miss Rebecca, will you dance with me?"

The young woman blushed when she looked up at Will and smiled, "Oh, General Travis, I would be honored."

He guided her onto the dance floor where, as a festive Christmassy tune started up, Will showed Rebecca he was a better soldier than a dancer. As the song ended, Rebecca fanned herself, and stepped gingerly away from Will's feet. "Would you fetch me a cup of punch, General?"

Over at the punch bowl, as Will filled a small cup, Crockett came up and slapped him on the back, "Buck, I swear, I do believe that you've two left feet."

Will smiled, sheepishly, "Well, what can I say? I wanted badly to dance with her. And badly I did."

The cantina was nearly empty as Jose Flores sat at a table, cleaning the remnants of a small bowl of beans with a corn tortilla. He kept glancing toward the door, waiting. He had been in Laredo since his father-in-law returned to San Antonio before Christmas. The town was torn between the majority of the people who wished to return to Mexico, and a smaller minority who saw confusion and turmoil to the south and stability to the north. He had been in Laredo ostensibly to manage several business matters on behalf of his father-in-law, Erasmo Seguin, but over the past few months, it was clear, more was going on below the surface than met the eye.

The door swung open and a brown-haired man in his early twenties strode through it. Flores looked him over, the revolver at his belt confirmed he was the man on whom Flores was waiting. Captain Jack Hays had arrived. The Ranger scanned the room before his eyes landed on Flores. He walked over and sat opposite of the Tejano.

In a low tone, Flores said, "It's worse than I suspected, Captain Hays. There's an agent of Mexico, in town. I've managed to find out his plans."

Hays nodded. "Do we need to bring in soldiers from the fort?"

"No, not yet. That would scare him away, and leave him to try again somewhere else. Better to give him enough rope to hang himself here."

Hays agreed. "What do you know about this agent?"

"He's a large landowner from Nacogdoches," Flores said, "In the elections last year, the influx of immigrants to the area caused him to lose his election as county judge. His name is Vincente Cordova. It is my understand that he will be returning tomorrow evening with guns and gold for the faction here who wants Laredo handed over to Mexico. There are a handful of Santa Anna's veterans who have settled here, and Cordova apparently thinks he can build his army around them."

Hays stood and turned toward the door, saying, "Let's see if he gives us enough of that rope tomorrow."

The next evening, Hays and Flores and a dozen men from the nearby fort sheltered behind mesquite trees, and downed logs, littered along the Texas side of the Rio Grande. The deep ruts cut in the banks on both sides of the river revealed to Hayes Cordova's likeliest route. The sun had dipped below the horizon a little while earlier and only the red and orange hues reflecting off the clouds provided light. Hays hoped the wagon would come before the twilight was gone.

Hays grinned as two long wagons rolled down to the river on the Mexican side. The gods of luck were smiling down on him. As the wagons lurched into the river, along the ford, several mounted men rode on the flanks, warily watching the northern shore line. Apparently, Cordova thought he was taking few chances. Hays bit down on his own laughter.

"The traitor will figure out real quick how wrong he is," he thought.

As the first wagon rolled up the shallow embankment, Hays pulled his revolver from the holster and glanced back at the soldiers. Each had his rifle ready for whatever action would unfold. The mules pulling the second wagon climbed onto the river bank on the Texas side and it was time, Hays reckoned. With his pistol pointed toward the wagons, he stepped out from behind the mesquite tree. He shouted, "You're under arrest!"

He intended to tell the Mexicans not to reach for their guns, but before those words could leave his lips, the nearest horseman grabbed a pistol from his belt. He hammered the flintlock back and pointed it in Hays' direction. Instinctively, Hays ducked while lining up his shot. He sighted down the barrel and squeezed the trigger. Both pistols went off at the same time. The .36 caliber ball struck the horseman, whose pistol kicked in his hands as it discharged. The musket ball slapped harmlessly into the wet mud a few feet in front of the Ranger.

The riders, accompanying the wagons, were all armed. Next to the second wagon, two of the horsemen bolted forward, reins in one hand, and a pistol in the other. The last of the daylight still reflected off the evening clouds, as Hays saw the riders racing toward him. He aimed at the nearest and pulled the trigger in haste. The bullet sailed harmlessly over the rider, as he charged. Hays fired again, and this time, struck him in the torso. The rider slid off the animal, landing with a bone-jarring crash. The second rider barreled down on Hays. Only ten yards separated the two men. Hays started moving to the side, as one of the soldiers stepped up next to him, rifle already at his shoulder. The butternut clad rifleman fired, striking the rider in the head, knocking him off the back of the horse.

A few more shots echoed as the last of the light fled the western sky. Of the six horsemen, all had been dismounted by Hays' men. Two were dead. Two more were injured badly. Of the last two, one had been shot in the leg while the other had lost his seat when his horse had been startled by the gunfire. Several soldiers hauled the wagon drivers from their perches atop the wagons and forced them at gunpoint next to the other survivors.

As the soldiers secured the prisoners, Hays and Flores clambered onto the wagons and loosened the tarps. They tossed them back, revealing several long crates full of muskets and ammunition. They also found in the saddlebags tied to one of the horses, a few thousand dollars in gold. Flores smiled at Hays. "I told you, my Ranger friend. Cordova's guns and gold!"

Hays returned the smile. "I love it when a plan comes together."

The weapons and gold secured, the two men returned to the prisoners. Flores looked at each of the prisoners, finally bringing his eyes to rest on the lone uninjured man. "Captain Hays, may I introduce you to his honor, Vincente Cordova."

Hays looked down at the dejected prisoner. "Vincente Cordova, you're under arrest for treason."

Chapter 16

The smell of breakfast wafted across the room where Henrietta cooked on an iron stove. Will had hired the former slave to cook and clean around the house. He inhaled deeply, enjoying the aroma of bacon cooking on a skillet. It was just one more reason he was happy Travis' former slave, Joe was doing well for himself. Like several former slaves, Joe held a contract to transport supplies for the army between Texas' port cities and the Alamo. Will was a little fuzzy on the details of Henrietta's route to freedom and exactly how she and Joe had married, but he was happy for both of them, as they made a new home for themselves in San Antonio.

The smell of eggs had nothing to do with his happiness, he told himself as she set a plateful of eggs and bacon in front of him. "*No, nothing at all to do with it.*"

He dug into his plate and returned to reading an article in the *Telegraph and Texas Register*. He was pleased as he read the Texas Supreme Court had denied

Vincente Cordova's final plea in the drama which played out over the previous six months, since his capture with Mexican guns and gold. To date, his was the only trial in Texas for the crime of treason. Will had followed the trial when it had been held in San Antonio earlier in the year.

He recalled how most Anglo-owned newspapers had denounced the Crockett administration's decision to allow the trial to proceed in the Bexar district court. Laredo was within the Bexar district, so the decision to hold it in San Antonio was proper. But even many within Congress worried that San Antonio, with its majority Tejano population wouldn't find Cordova guilty. The fears were groundless. The jury consisted of some of San Antonio's more prominent Tejano families as well as several wealthy Americans. While Cordova's trial for treason lasted more than a week, the jury took less than an hour to convict him. When Will found out Jose Salinas, the mayor of San Antonio, had handpicked the jury pool, he was disquieted. On one hand, the evidence was damning, but Will didn't like the idea of tampering with a jury, even when the result should have been a forgone conclusion.

As he finished reading the article, Will was irritated over the method Salinas had used to avoid the risk of an acquittal from the town's largely Hispanic population. He looked at his plate, where he saw he had been moving his eggs around. He let out a loud breath, realizing sometimes it was necessary to break an egg in order to make an omelet.

Charlie, who was sitting across the table, asked, "Pa, what's the matter?"

Will looked up from the plate. "Nothing, son. Just reading the paper."

As the boy went back to polishing off a plate of biscuits and gravy, Will marveled at how much he had grown in the two years since he had brought his son home. The boy's red hair matched nearly exactly his own, but the dusting of freckles on his face showed how much Charlie enjoyed playing outside.

Pushing both the plate and newspaper aside, Will asked, "Will you be ready to start back to school next week?"

Charlie shook his head. "No, sir. I ain't got any paper or pens yet. Friar Jesus said we're going to need lots of both."

Will smiled but said, "Ain't? You mean, you don't have any paper." He smiled as he corrected the boy. "Let's help Henrietta with the dishes and you and me will go find your supplies."

Charlie grinned slyly at his father. "You mean, you and I?"

The boy left the table to retrieve his list as Will decided to finish breakfast. He pulled the plate towards him and then wiped the plate clean. As he sopped up the last of the bacon grease with a biscuit he thought about how much had changed in Texas since the transference. What would Texas look like to Charlie as an adult? Already, the country he now called home looked very little like the economic basket case he had known in a history which survived only in his memories.

As he recalled, in 1838 in the world in which he remembered, the frontier was afire with raid and counterraid between the various Ranger companies and the Comanche. The population was still feeling the economic effects of the Runaway scrape, which had been a result of the fall of the Alamo and the Mexican army's march eastward, which had only ended following Houston's victory at San Jacinto. But those were just memories of a world gone forever. Now, Texas had a strong monetary policy, and a working currency backed by more than simple "good faith." The Comanche had been forced north of the Red River. The twin stabilizers of peace with the Comanche and a stable currency, had led to a wave of settlers.

While immigration remained steady from the Southern states, including slaves, Will noticed there had been an increase in immigration from the Northern states and Europe because of Texas' increased stability.

As he heard Charlie's footsteps returning, Will hoped the changes he was helping to make would lead to a better future. He handed his plate back to Henrietta and as she took it, he renewed a vow, he would continue doing whatever was within his power to end the blight of slavery. He grabbed his uniform jacket and met Charlie at the door.

A little while later, the two found themselves in one of several general stores on Alameda Street. They gave a sheet of paper to the clerk behind the counter and he collected the lengthy list. After tabulating the cost, the clerk said, "The bill comes out to four dollars and fifty cents."

From his jacket's inside pocket, Will retrieved a leather wallet and fished a white and green bill from it. The clerk examined the bank note. Across the top, it read, "Commodities Certificate of the Republic of Texas. Five Dollars."

"Seeing more of these showing up every day, sir," the clerk said. "Haven't had any problems trading them for supplies from the coast, either."

"That's music to my ears. I'd hate to think about what business would be like if we had to rely only on pesos or US silver."

The clerk had wrapped the supplies in brown paper, and handed the package over. "May it never be again."

Will and Charlie left the store and walked down the street toward San Antonio's main plaza. New storefronts ran along both sides of the road. Charlie gasped as he saw a sign on one such store. "Bexar Confectionary Delights"

The boy squealed, "Pa, can we go inside?"

Will stopped, while the boy tugged on his hand. The last time he had been in a candy store had been several years earlier, long before the transfer into Travis' body. He recalled the memory like it was yesterday. He and a girl he had been dating had finished their date on Galveston's Strand. Along the street ran a gamut of touristy stores. But Will's favorite was a candy shop on the corner of the Strand and 24th Street, where they served the best vanilla and chocolate floats on the island.

Charlie's tugging brought him back to the present and he let his son drag him into the candy shop. The countertop was covered with assorted glass jars full of rock candy. An older man behind the counter said, in a thick brogue, "How can I help you fine gentlemen on this wonderful summer's day?"

Charlie's enthusiasm was infectious as he went down the counter, picking a few pieces of candy from one jar and more from another. When they had filled a paper bag full, Will said, "Let's not run this fine establishment out of business."

When the bill was tabulated, Will wasn't worried about the candy shop going out of business, as he handed over another five dollar note. He was tempted to grumble about the cost until the delicious sweetness hit his taste buds. As he and Charlie walked slowly back to the house, the candy gradually dissolved in his mouth. What had started out as a fun reminder of good memories, by the time they arrived back home, left Will missing all the conveniences the transference had stolen. As he sat at his work desk, he tried to push away the thoughts about the conveniences which he would never again experience. Eventually he succeeded, as he worked through a pile of correspondence, ignoring the small bag of candy on the desk.

Fall of 1838 felt a lot like the summer of the same, as Will sat across from President Crockett. The door and windows were open, letting the languid breeze feebly stir the papers on the table in Crockett's office.

"As my latest report shows, David, Ben is doing exactly what he set out to do. He's peeled ten companies away from Rusk's militia and has been training them to the new army standards."

Crockett wiped a bead of sweat from his brow and asked, "How many men are we talking about, Buck?"

"Around six hundred or so. It's all infantry, and most of these companies are located in or around our towns. One of the companies is located in San Antonio, and two more are located here, in Harrisburg and Houston. Ben's thinking is that these guard companies can be mobilized quicker than militia that's spread over hundreds of square miles."

"That makes sense. Any luck getting more carbines from Harpers Ferry yet?"

Will shook his head, "Not much. But our gunsmith we've been using here to repair and replace parts has actually been able to make a few dozen carbines. If we use the money Congress approved for the purchase of rifles to fund his expansion, it may fill the gap nicely. Plus, it plays to our own needs if we can develop our own manufacturing base."

Crockett looked surprised. "Damned if the thought had ever crossed my mind, Buck. By all means, use the money and give our gunsmith the contract."

As a hot gust of wind sent a few sheets of paper floating to the floor, Will retrieved them and asked, "What's the latest on our request to replace our three schooners? My most recent reports say the *Invincible* and *Brutus* are still seaworthy, but the *Liberty* has been laid up in New Orleans, and isn't worth repairing."

Crockett spread his hands, as though they reflected the emptiness of the treasury. "I agree. In principal, Congress is with you on this. I know this begs credence, but even Robert Potter has agreed with you about the need to purchase new steam powered schooners from the United States. The challenge is, it's going to cost us upwards of three hundred sixty thousand dollars. As the budget situation now stands, it will probably take us three years to fully upgrade the navy. But with any luck, by the summer of 1840, we'll have our new fleet."

Before Will could ask his next question, Crockett found an envelope he had been searching for on the cluttered table. He said, "Here it is. Been looking for that. I know what you're about to ask. I was able to get Congress to agree to expand the army, too. But it's going to take time. For the current budget year, they have agreed to expand the cavalry to three troops."

He handed the envelope to Will, who opened it and pulled out two shoulder boards, with embroidered golden oak-leafs denoting the rank of major. "Give those to Juan Seguin, Buck. He's definitely earned them."

Will whistled appreciatively as he read the letter accompanying the insignia. "Forty-eight men per cavalry troop, and three troops. That should make defending the Nueces region a lot easier."

"It should. You'll get your ninth and tenth infantry

companies over the next two years. And an extra battery of artillery by 1840."

Will did the math in his head, "Aside from the Rangers, That'll give us right at a thousand soldiers." Another thought crossed his mind, "What's that going to do to the budget?"

Crockett's laughter was tinged with bitterness. "Nothing good, that's for sure. Michel nearly choked when Congress agreed to the expansion."

Will wondered how Michel Menard managed to keep paying the Republic's bills, but the wily former Québécois seemed to balance the receipts and outlays like a master magician.

Like a medium reading minds, Crockett said, "If it hadn't been for you and Erasmo cooking up your commodities scheme, I fear we'd been passing along chits we had no intention of paying. But if if not for the Commodities Bureau, the land bank and the cotton-backs circulating throughout the country, we'd be in worse shape than we are."

As the day wore on, Will provided Crockett detailed numbers for the president to use in the next annual budget. The sun peeked through the westward facing window when Crockett threw a quill pen across the table. "Tarnation, Buck, I don't see how you do it. If I see one more one or zero today, I'm going to bite its head off."

As Will collected the pen from the end of the table, Crockett stood and stretched. "Enough of this. Liza and Becky have been cooking up a meal and I know at least one of them would be sorely disappointed if you didn't stay for dinner."

A warmth spread across Will's face at the idea of seeing Becky again.

After a lively dinner of pork and beans with the Crocketts, Will found himself sitting on the porch, next to Becky, as the last light from the western sky disappeared. The silence stretched on, until he broke it. "I'm really looking forward to the Christmas party next year, Miss Rebecca. I'd dearly love to have the first dance with you again."

"*Damn! Damn! Damn!*" Will thought, as he remembered how he managed to step on her toes throughout the dance.

Will thought he saw a shadow of a smile play across her face. "That is too kind of you. I think we know each other better than to be calling each other 'General' and 'Miss.' Please call me Becky, Will." She paused, recalling the tribulation her feet were subjected to at that party the previous year. "I think I would be perfectly happy to sit with you while the peacocks flap their wings across the dance floor."

While he was uncertain if he saw a smile cross her lips, his own split his face, as he placed his hand hesitantly and gently on hers, ready to retreat if she gave any hint at displeasure. His fingers tingled and sent goosebumps up his hand, when Becky responded by placing her other hand over his. She leaned against him and whispered, "I'm glad Pa came to Texas, and gladder still that Ma followed. I don't want you to think I'm a forward girl by letting you take my hand, but I'm really glad you stayed for dinner, because I enjoy your company."

Will left his hand covering hers, her breathy words sending waves of pleasure along his skin. He hadn't felt this way since college, and Becky's closeness felt good. He tilted his head, until it rested against hers. "I'm really glad you came out here, too, Becky." He turned and planted a kiss on her cheek. What had begun in his heart on the dance floor of the Christmas party last year came to completion as he sat next to the slender young woman. He whispered, "Will you be my girl, Becky?"

She turned and despite the lack of light, Will saw her smile was writ large across her face. "Will, I'd do anything but dance with you."

Behind them, the sound of the door squeaked, and a voice said, "Now, that's a pretty sight, wouldn't you say, Liza?"

Another softer voice replied, "Enough to melt my heart, David."

Within a second several inches materialized between Will and Becky as they turned and saw Crockett and his wife standing in the doorway. Will leapt to his feet, "Ah, David. We didn't see you there."

Chuckling, Crockett said, "I'd rather figured that, Buck. Is there something you need to tell me and Becky's mother?"

Blushing furiously under the gaze of the elder Crocketts, Will stammered, "Well, um, I'd consider it a real honor if, I, ah, could call upon your daughter, sir."

Crockett's chuckle slid into a belly laugh as the noise echoed into the night. "Oh, that's rich. It's always David this or David that. But now it's *sir*. Buck, you beat all. Of course, you can call on my Becky, if she's a mind to have you."

Will glanced back at Becky as she playfully slapped her father's arm. "Oh, Pa, don't raise a ruckus. It's bad enough when the neighbors raise a din, we don't need to compete with them. And, of course Will can call on me. I'd not let anyone else kiss me on the cheek like that with you and ma in the next room."

28th October 1838

Dearest Will,

I received your letter from 1st of the month, and was mighty glad to get it. I wish that they would hurry up and finish the move of the government to the new city of Austin. I was poor sorry to hear of Mr. Austin's ship sinking when he was returning from Washington. Pa said he was a good man. It was only fitting the town should be named in his honor. Once we move, then I will be so much closer to you. Pa is always complaining about some congressman or senator, it is very funny. All of them are congresscritter this or that. You can scarce imagine how the town of Houston is growing, it has fair bumped up against Harrisburg, as to make one think both towns are but one. When we moved in with Pa, there were only a few other houses nearby. But now our nearest neighbor, we can hear when they're having a row, and they fight all the time. Ma and me went shopping last week, and there are new stores with the latest fashion. I saw a pretty, pink dress all the way from Paris in one of the stores. It's a caution! When you write me to me again, be sure to tell me what the ladies in San Antonio are wearing. I will wait eagerly for your next letter.

Affectionately yours,

Becky

30th of November 1838

My dearest Becky,

Every letter I receive from you causes me to want to jump on my horse and ride to Harrisburg straightaway to see you. I was dismayed when I read about the sinking of the *Brutus* with all hands in that terrible storm. Stephen Austin faithfully served Texas as minister to the U. States. I have been told the surveyors are done surveying the new city, and within a year, the government will move there. Of course, the president may conspire to keep me in the field, lest he lose his girl to the wiles of a frontier officer. It is funny, Texas is independent of the U. States, and yet we celebrate Thanksgiving, just like our friends and family back east. As such, I received an invitation to a Thanksgiving celebration held by Juan Seguin's sister and brother-in-law. The ladies were dressed in reds, and blues and yellows. When they twirled in their men's arms, the dresses flared up, like spinning parasols. Charlie told me the dresses looked like spindle tops.

Had I realized how much paperwork a general goes through I think I may have decided to become a simple cavalryman, with nothing to worry about. I will be taking Sid and Juan with me on a tour of our forts along the Rio Grande next month, and from there, we will travel to Galveston to inspect our forts there, and when I do, I will make sure to come by Harrisburg to call upon you.

Until then, I remain most affectionately yours,

Will

Chapter 17

He folded up the latest edition of the *Telegraph and Texas Register*, scowling as he pushed it to the side of the table. Henrietta set a steaming plate of grits and honey on the table in front of Will. There was seldom a day that passed by in which he wasn't grateful to have Henrietta taking care of him and Charlie. As he scooped up a spoonful of grits, his scowl faded as he savored the taste.

"Yes, she is a far better cook than I will ever be," he thought.

"Eat 'em up, Gen'ral. You ain't gonna sit in my kitchen all Saturday." Henrietta's smile was infectious. Charlie was devouring a plate of biscuits and gravy, one of his favorite meals. A school textbook was set next to his plate, where he would pause between bites to turn a page. The only thing missing, in Will's opinion was Becky. His planned trip down to the coast was coming up soon, and part of him wanted nothing more than to scrap it all and go immediately to her and ask her to marry him.

Whenever his thoughts went to her, as they frequently did these days, it always made him long for Becky. So he tried setting the thought aside, as he heard Henrietta humming a tune behind him, as she began cleaning up a couple of pans. If there was a good place in Texas to be a former slave, San Antonio was probably it. While the influx of immigration was changing the demographics of the town, it was still majority Hispanic. In some respects, Tejano views on race were no less complicated than those held by the immigrants from the United States, but overall, they tended to treat freed blacks better than their white counterparts. It was true, rich Tejanos were nearly as likely to own slaves as their wealthy white neighbors. Erasmo Seguin was a case in point. Despite that, San Antonio, Will decided, was a better place to be a freedman than any other town in the Republic.

Will had plans to change that, for the better, he hoped. The entire institution of slavery rankled him, and he was determined to find a way to rid the Republic of this scourge. He just needed to figure out ways to diminish it and unwind Texas' involvement from the horrid institution.

That thought brought him back to the article he had read in the newspaper. Defaults on farms had been climbing over the past year. According to the *Telegraph* nearly one of every ten farmers who bought land from the land bank over the past two years were in default or foreclosure. The article blamed the failure on spillover from the ongoing financial crisis in the United States and also pointed out the rate of foreclosures was still below the foreclosure rate back east.

As Charlie finished eating his breakfast, he asked, "Anything wrong, Pa?"

Will thought, *"Between slavery and farm foreclosures, take your pick."*

Instead he said, "Set your schoolwork aside for a moment, Son, and read this article." He unfolded the newspaper and slid it across the table, where Charlie studied the article.

After a few minutes, the boy finished reading and Will asked, "What do you think the writer was saying?"

The boy's face grew thoughtful as he considered the question. "It sounds like lots of farmers are struggling to pay back the money the bank gave them when they bought their farms." The boy paused as he processed the information. His thoughtful expression was replaced by a look of confusion. "But, Pa, I don't understand. Both you and Friar Jesus said farmers could pay the land bank in, ah, comedies."

Will briefly smiled at the malapropism. "I think you mean commodities. But yes, you're right. The article doesn't address that, and without knowing what's causing these ranchers and farmers to default on their loan payments when they can pay with their farm produce, it doesn't tell the whole story. What do you think one of the reasons could be they aren't able to make their loan payments?"

After a lengthy pause, Charlie ventured a guess,

"Maybe they're trying to grow crops where the land can't support them, or maybe they're lazy."

"I doubt very many of them are lazy," Will said, "The average farmer is very hardworking. From what I have read, some of the farmers are losing their farms because they established them too far from water sources or the ground was poorly suited for the crops they tried to grow, and some small number just didn't understand the harsh demands some parts of Texas make on a farmer."

Charlie's curiosity led to more questions. "Pa, why aren't we farmers? Didn't Uncle Davy give you a lot of land?"

A small smile crossed Will's face, as he imagined Crockett's response to being called, 'Uncle Davy.' He dismissed the image and replied, "Most of the time, Charlie, I enjoy my job in the army. I doubt very seriously I'd make a very good farmer. Why? Do you want to become a farmer when you grow up?"

The boy tossed his head in an exaggerated manner. "No sir, Pa. I wanna be a soldier, like you, when I grow up. If I can't be a soldier, then I wanna be a politician, like Uncle Davy!" He tumbled out of his chair in a fit of giggles.

The boy's antics made Will laugh. But Charlie's words got him to thinking. The land grant he had received for service to the Republic totaled more than six thousand acres. The land was in East Texas, along the Trinity River. It was supposed to be very good farmland, but it was undeveloped and lying fallow. An idea began to circulate in his mind. Maybe it was time to do something about that.

The following day, Will and Charlie were walking home from the Methodist service. The congregation was not yet able to afford to build a church building, so they rented the dining room of a cantina near the main plaza, where they held service every Sunday morning. As they walked down the hard-packed dirt street, Will spotted one of his former soldiers walking past, toward the cantina.

Will stopped and turned, "Corporal Wynters, have you forgotten your manners after only six months out of the army?" Will's broad smile belied his stern voice.

The former soldier, walking with a cane, turned, and looked Will over. As recognition dawned, he said, "Sorry, General, sir. Didn't recognize you in your Sunday best. Onlyest time I seen you, you was in uniform."

Will asked after the former soldier's wellbeing and discovered he was working at the very cantina from which they just came. "Been here for a few months now, sir. It helps to put a roof over my head."

Curious about how the former infantryman was adjusting to civilian life, he and Charlie returned to the cantina, where the Methodist circuit rider and the cantina's owner had just finished moving the tables back into place. As Will and Charlie took a seat, the former corporal came over and said, "It'll be a few minutes before the cook gets the kitchen open. While you're waiting, can I get anything for you, General?"

Will pointed to one of the empty chairs at the table. "Sit a spell, Corporal. What did you do following your discharge from the army, before you found this job?

Wynters sat and rested his cane against the table. "I was laid up in the hospital for several weeks. After that arrow struck the bone in the leg, I was afeared of ever walking again, but the Doc, he got me well again and after that, I couldn't walk good any more so, I was given my land grant and mustered out. I found this here job a few weeks later, and been here ever since."

An idea which had been forming since the previous day resurfaced in Will's mind and he asked, "Have you redeemed your land voucher yet?"

Wynters shook his head, "No. What the hell am I going to do with the four thousand acres that the government gave me? I can't farm with this bum leg, any more. Hell, I can't even stay on a horse for more than a little bit at a time these days."

Will said, "Have you considered leasing your land to farmers?"

Wynters shook his head, "No. why would farmers lease land from me? They can get it cheap enough from the land office." Intrigued at the question, he asked, "What are you getting at, General?"

Will laid out his thoughts, "Now, Corporal Wynters, right now, who's making all the money growing cash crops in Texas?"

The former corporal grumbled. "It's those damned plantation owners, with their slaves, growing and selling cotton. But it takes a lot of money to buy the slaves and all that equipment. It takes money to make money. And I ain't got any."

Will acknowledged Corporal Wynters' position. "That may be true, but you do have the land. What if you were to divide the land into, say, forty-acre tracts and lease it out to other farmers. I could provide you both the seed, and money for some of the equipment, and pay to get some cabins built. These tenants wouldn't have to worry about making loan repayments. All they have to do is provide their labor."

Wynters scratched his chin as he tried to work out how the scenario would work.

Taking his thoughts from the previous day, Will said, "Well, Corporal, one way it could work is a tenant would lease the land from you, I would loan the tenant the supplies for the crops, the tenant would own everything he produces, but would pay you rent and repay the loan from me."

Wynters shook his head. "I don't know, General. I knew some folks back east who were tenant farmers. The landlord kept half the crops. Those poor men were only one step about a nigger. I don't know about it."

Between his own memories and stories he'd recently heard from soldiers, Will didn't think much of the tenant farming which was becoming more common in the South. "I don't think I could do something like that to a tenant, Corporal. I think it would demoralize a man to work like that. What I want to do is provide men who are struggling with the ownership of land the ability to work a tract of it, and profit from their own labor. Even at eight or nine cents for a pound for cotton, I think between the rent and cost of the seed and materials, any farmer working with us, would still have more than half the value left."

Wynters' eyes lit as he saw the possibilities. "It do seem too good to be true, General, but if you can put together something like this, hell, I'd be happy to use my land grant for something like that."

The day before Will was scheduled to leave to tour the forts along the Rio Grande, Juan Seguin found him working in his office in the Alamo. After settling himself in a chair across the table from him, the Tejano said, "What is this I hear about you plotting to start a plantation? I can't fathom you'd be willing to buy and sell slaves. This doesn't sound like you at all."

Will was startled by the accusation. "Major, I would never deal in slaves." Apparently, word had leaked about Will's conversation with Wynters and as rumors tend to, it had been twisted. Will explained the idea of tenant farming of cash crops to him. "What I was thinking of doing, is form a corporation which would provide the tenants the necessary equipment and seed, in a competitive loan. The land would be leased to the tenant farmer at competitive rates. The idea is the tenant's income won't be arbitrarily compromised by a landlord or a banker taking most of the tenant's crop."

The Tejano officer nodded, "I think I see where you're going with this. I know a few men who work land near my father's hacienda who might be interested in this. The land they own is too small to ranch and too poor to grow cotton. What you're proposing might work well for them. But," he paused for a long moment, "I wonder, why create a tenant system?"

Will said, "It's an inexpensive way to connect the land and the farmer. My hope is that everyone wins. The owner of the grant gets paid for the leasing of the land. I get a return on my investment for the loans and the farmer gets most of the sale of the crop."

"That's true, to a point, but everyone's risk is high. If there aren't enough farmers to lease the land, the landlord has too little return on the investment of his land. If the tenants are not able to do well, then you, as the lender, run the risk of losing your investment."

Will hadn't thought of it in that way. "Do you have a better idea, Juan?"

The other officer nodded. "Maybe. My father is the expert here, but have you considered a single corporation handling everything? Imagine for a moment, a corporation owns the land, hires the farmers and provides the means of production, like seed, shelter, and equipment."

"Wouldn't that put all of the risk on the corporation?"

Seguin nodded. "Yes, but it also puts all of the control in the hands of the corporation. Let me explain, the corporation owns the land, and hires men to work the land and pays them a wage and in turn, sells the crops. The corporation schedules the farmers' production in a way that is most efficient, rather than each farmer being responsible for their own little patch of ground."

Intrigued, Will said, "This could work. If we hire a worker and later find he isn't pulling his weight, he gets replaced by someone who will."

Seguin thoughtfully added, "We could compete well against the plantation owners. These 'gentlemen' farmers bring their slaves with them to farm the land, and they have to force them to work with the overseer and the whip. I could find you a hundred men between the Nueces and the Rio Grande that would work hard for steady pay."

Before the new year of 1839 was far along, the idea of the farming corporation had gone from concept to reality. The first step Will and his business partners took was to acquire the necessary land. He, Juan Seguin, Corporal Wynters and several more veterans took their grants, and with the aid of the Texas Land Office, consolidated all the grants into a single tract along the Trinity River, totaling 26,000 acres in Liberty County. Each of the men transferred their portion of the tract to the Corporation in exchange for shares of stock. In addition to the land, Will and several other investors, including Juan and Erasmo Seguin, contributed $15,000 in cash as seed capital for the business. Thus, was born the Gulf Farms Corporation.

Will was still feeling the effects of the stagecoach ride from San Antonio to Austin and the subsequent ferry ride across the Colorado river as he settled into his hotel room for the night. The building was so new that the smell of cut pine was heavy in the room. He had opened the window to lessen the smell and to let in the cool night breeze. The mattress ticking was stuffed with hay, which the proprietor swore was changed after each customer.

As he lay in the narrow bed, staring at the dark ceiling, Will couldn't get Becky from his mind. He hadn't felt like this about a woman since college. He recalled the last time he had seen Ashley; it was a few days after graduating from University of Houston and he had just received his deployment orders from the 36th Infantry Division's 144th Infantry Regiment. He had taken her to her favorite restaurant near campus and after dinner broke the news to her. "It's only nine months, Ash," he had told her.

The way she had stared back at him, as though he were not even there, made him feel there was more wrong than simply the order to deploy. She'd known of his prior service before college and his two days each month played hell with their dating life. This shouldn't have been a surprise to her, he remembered thinking.

When she pursed her lips and bit back a sigh, his heart crept into his throat. But the words she spoke cut to the quick. "Nine months or nine years, Will. It doesn't matter." Will's heart felt squeezed in a vice as she spoke. "Now's as good a time as any to tell you. I can't do this anymore. When we started dating I thought I felt something, and God knows, I gave it more than a year of my life. But I realize now it's not love."

There was a too long pause as she looked at him. "Don't look at me that way, Will. Would you rather get a 'Dear John' letter a few months from now? I can see you think I'm a bitch, but this is better for both of us."

As his eyes followed the lines on the whitewashed boards on the ceiling, he was amused how his brain worked. He hadn't thought of Ashley since before the transference. Now, having thought of her, he couldn't stop himself from making a comparison between her and Becky. They were as physically different as could be. Ashley had been short, with the muscled build of the cheerleader she had been, while Becky took her height from her father. She was also willowy thin. Ashley had always worn makeup and she was good at accentuating her cheeks and full lips. Will had never seen Becky wearing makeup. It's not that a little face powder wasn't socially acceptable. It was. But as a girl raised in the backwoods of Tennessee, it was neither affordable nor available. Now, as the daughter of the president of the Republic of Texas, she behaved as though wearing face powder would be pretentious.

That lack of pretension was one of the things which had drawn Will to Crockett's daughter. To Will, part of his attraction to Becky was because she acted as though what she looked like didn't matter at all. That she obviously liked him didn't hurt his ego either.

As he closed his eyes and ignored the crunching sound of the hay shifting beneath him, he hoped his trip to the capital would be successful.

The next morning, Will noticed the paint on the walls of the president's small office was barely dry. The glass-paned windows were raised, letting the early spring air into the new office. Will fidgeted while he waited for Crockett to finish addressing a letter. "Damned if one day, I'll find myself a clerk to do this part. There are parts of this job that are drier than a Baptist's liquor cabinet, Buck."

After he dusted sand across the letter and placed it in a pile of other correspondence under which was placed a wooden shingle with the word "out" stenciled on it, Crockett said, "What has gotten you out of San Antonio, Buck? Did you hear tell that we got the whole government relocated to Austin town and now, having hung our shingle out here, are now open for business? Or maybe you just got yourself a hankering for Becky's fine cooking. She learned it from the master, my Liza."

Crockett's banter, as always, put Will at ease. "Well, Mr. President ..."

"Hell's bells, Buck, that damn door is closed and ain't nobody to hear you call me David than the two of us. That 'Mr. President' talk is for the honor of the office. Betwixt the two of us, it's David and Buck. Right, Buck?" Crockett said, with a rather toothy grin.

Will smiled in return. "Well, David, it actually is about Becky's cooking."

"Well, just come around the home this evening, and I'm sure she and Liza will have fixed up some good vittles. Is it just the cooking that brought you to Austin?"

"Pretty much, David. Actually, I came by to see if I could talk you until letting me take her back to San Antonio, and cook for me regular like," Will said.

Crockett's eyebrows edged up a bit, "Are you aiming to ask Becky to be your cook or your wife, Buck?"

Will's eyes crinkled at the corners, as he dug a tiny box out of his jacket pocket, "The latter, sir." He opened the box revealing a small gold ring, with a dark green stone fixed in the setting.

Crockett whistled as he picked up the box, "That's a mighty fine bloodstone you found there, Buck. Becky's going to love it. So, I figure you are looking for her Pa's permission to marry?"

"Marriage or Cooking, either is fine by me, David," Will replied with a twinkle in his eye.

Crockett laughed, "I doubt Liza or Becky would let me across the threshold if I said no. That's to the marriage. You're on your own about the cooking though."

Will stood and shook hands with his soon-to-be father-in-law and said, "I'd best go find Becky. I can't wait to tell her."

A few days later, back in San Antonio, Will sat at the dinner table, as Henrietta cleaned off the supper dishes. Will's proposal to Becky was going to make a huge change around the household and he owed it to the boy to explain things.

"Son, I suppose you know why I went up to Austin

this past week."

Charlie shrugged, "I guess you went to see Miss Becky. I think you're sweet on her, Pa."

"I can't pull the wool over your eyes, son. Yes. I'm definitely sweet on her."

"Are you going to ask her to marry you?"

Will's face colored at the question. "Well, Charlie, I actually already asked her when I was in Austin. I hope you don't mind?"

The boy closed the book he had been reading, and gently sighed. "No, I don't guess so. You're gone a lot, so having someone beside Henrietta around will be nice."

Will didn't think Charlie meant anything negative by the comment, even so, it bothered him that his son saw how much his job demanded of him, and how often his duties as a soldier took him away from his responsibility as a father. Now, with marriage on the horizon, he couldn't help wondering if Becky would eventually come to the same conclusion. He hoped not. He liked the way she made him feel when she was close and the last thing he wanted was to ever repeat the same mistakes William B. Travis had made in the years before Will's transference.

Will tousled the boy's red hair and said, "Thanks, Son. We'll make it work."

Chapter 18

The lone Texas Ranger nudged his horse up Congress Avenue in the new town of Austin. The establishment of the government here the previous year led to a flood of construction, although most of it was for administrative buildings to house the growing government. The Ranger passed by a clapboard structure, on front of which there was a sign proclaiming to all who passed by the building housed the Republic's War Department. He continued around the large Capitol Square, where masons and carpenters were building a capitol building. The structure he was looking for was across the street from Capitol Square. He guided his horse to a hitching post in front of a modest building where a sign announced it belonged to the Commodities Bureau.

The youthful Ranger climbed down from his mount and secured the reins to the hitching post and stepped up to the door. It opened as he reached for the knob. A soldier stood in the door frame, eying him. After a moment, the rifleman stepped aside, and allowed him the enter. His feet had barely crossed the threshold before the door was closed and locked behind him. A clerk, with thick spectacles, rose when he saw the Ranger. "I'll be right back, sir."

The narrow lobby was devoid of furnishings, other than the clerk's desk and a hardback chair, which the soldier had settled back into as he looked out the window by the door. Only a flag hung on the spartan wall. The horizontal blue field, which stretched for a third of the flag's length, held a white star in its center. Two vertical stripes, a white and red, extended from the blue field. It was adopted by the army in the months following the Battle of the Nueces, and called the *Fannin Flag* in honor of Colonel James Fannin, the highest ranking Texian to die during the Revolution. A couple of years later, Congress had formally adopted it as the national flag.

The Ranger was staring at it when a door against the back wall opened and an older Tejano gentleman walked through. "Captain Hays, I'm glad you were able to get here as quickly as you did."

The Ranger shook the other man's hand. "Señor Seguin, it is my pleasure, sir. I confess, General Travis was short on details about why my services were needed here."

"Come on back. I'll show you."

As Hays followed the elder Seguin into the rear of the building, he saw a large printing press in one corner of the room and several large tables shoved together in the center. Seguin led him to the nearest table, on which were several stacks of commodities certificates.

Seguin said, "This is where we print the certificates which are backed by the basket of commodities, Captain." He indicated to a sheet of bills, which were denominated in ten dollars. There were twenty bills in the sheet.

Seguin pulled the sheet over to them and passed it to Hays. "Feel the paper."

Hays ran his fingers over it. It was heavy, and the engraving plates had indented the image of an Indian maiden on one half of the paper and on the other half, a river steamer. Seguin said, "It's made from a cotton blend. We get it from a paper manufacturer in Philadelphia. I've been assured the blend of this particular paper is unique to our certificates."

Hays set the sheet of uncut currency back on the table. "It does have a particular feel to it. Never noticed it when I collected my pay before, but I can see how it feels different than normal paper."

Seguin said, "Now, look at these certificates." He slid a small stack over to the Ranger. Hays picked up a couple of bills and ran his fingers along the indentions, which felt different. He set one of the bills next to one on the sheet and leaned in, closely studying them. At first inspection, the two looked identical, but as he took time to look more closely, he noticed the level of detail on each certificate on the sheet of currency. The individual bill lacked some of the finer details. And after rubbing his fingers on it, he thought the paper's weave felt different from that of the currency sheet.

When he mentioned the differences to Seguin, he replied, "Exactly, Captain. The quality of the cotton paper is high. If I had to hazard a guess, I wouldn't be surprised to find the paper used to make these counterfeit bills came from some bank that prints its own currency, like in the United States or Mexico."

Hays nodded in agreement. "How many of these fake certificates have been found?"

Seguin pointed to the stack on the table. "I fear those bills just scratch the surface. We've audited the bills the treasury has received from tax payments and those received by the Land Office's bank and have found more than ten thousand dollars in bogus certificates. It's just a guess, Captain, but I fear as much as ten percent of the certificates in circulation could be counterfeits. If this gets out before we find the source and close it, it could destroy the people's faith in the Commodities Certificates."

Hays grimaced at the thought. "I suppose that's why General Travis ordered me to come here."

Seguin nodded, "I realize this doesn't really fall under the function of the Texas Rangers, but General Travis said you have a sharp mind and that if someone could figure out who is bringing the forgeries into Texas, it would be you."

The Ranger smiled ruefully. "I got lucky breaking up Cordova's little rebellion, sir. I'll give this a go, and hope I have some luck. Do we have any idea where these counterfeit certificates are entering the country?"

Seguin pulled a small ledger from across the table

and referred to the opened page. "Almost half the forgeries which we have discovered have come from the Galveston area. And nearly all of the rest, one can make a reasoned argument, could have flowed through the port on the way to where they were detected."

After studying the book's entries, Hays slammed it shut and said, "Well, Señor Seguin, it looks like I'm going to Galveston."

A week later, the coastal cutter sliced through the water of Galveston Bay. Jack Hays watched the docks of Galveston come into focus as the small single-masted ship approached one of the docks, which jutted into the channel separating Galveston from Pelican Island, along the leeward side of the island. Several schooners and other merchant ships were either at dock or were riding at anchor in the channel. As Hays understood it, the town was already larger than San Antonio.

As the cutter was secured to one of the docks, Hays' eyes were drawn to a warship, anchored northeast of the town. He recognized it from the woodcut, which had been on the front page of one of the newspapers. It was the *TRS Nueces*, recently constructed in the Annapolis shipyards. She was the second of three steam-powered warships to be purchased between 1838 and 1840. Her sister ship, the *Crockett* was currently at sea, patrolling off the gulf coast of the Republic. As Hays recalled from the article he read, the *Nueces* was finishing up her outfitting and training of her crew.

The young Ranger officer found lodgings at one of the hotels in town and immediately went to work. There was scant doubt in his mind, Galveston was either a point of entry for the counterfeits or they were printed in town.

Lucien Thibodaux clenched a cigar tightly in his mouth as he swept the dust from below the printing press in the small office out of which he ran his advertising business, when the door opened, and a breeze caused the dust bunnies to fly before his broom. He swore under his breath as he looked up and saw a young man, in his early or mid-twenties come up and lean on the counter, which separated the press from the front of the building. Thibodaux eyed the young man. What did he want? Maybe leaflets advertising the newest saloon. Maybe something different. Then his eyes fell to the newcomer's waist where he saw the holster and the revolver.

Thibodaux came to the counter, took his cigar, and placed it between his fingers and asked, "How can I help you, young sir?"

"Captain Jack Hays, Texas Rangers. I've got a mind to look at your printing press, sir." A stack of neatly cut business cards on the countertop announced the proprietor. "Ah, Mr. Thibodaux."

It took everything within him to keep his nervousness from creeping into his voice. "It's not much to look at, Captain. But there it is." Thibodaux turned and pointed to the press.

"Mind if I take a closer look?"

Thibodaux shrugged and gestured to the low, swinging door, "Help yourself."

He watched the Ranger walk around the press several times, lift the print plates, and go over to the wall to examine the brass letters Thibodaux used in the design of his advertisements. Despite his nervous apprehension, he tried to keep his voice steady when he asked, "Perhaps there's something in particular you're looking for?"

After a pause which stretched out to an eternity as far as Thibodaux was concerned, the Ranger shook his head. "No, sir. I don't think you have what I'm looking for." With no reason to stay, the Ranger left.

After he clamped down on his cigar again, it took the better part of a half hour for Thibodaux's heartbeat to return to normal after the Ranger had departed. There was no doubt in his mind the Ranger was looking for proof of counterfeiting. He drew a ragged breath as he thanked the blessed Virgin he had decided against running any counterfeit currency on his own press.

Part of him considered shutting up shop then and there and finding the next boat back to New Orleans. But the risks of returning to Louisiana were high. He had taken a large fee from a group of Spanish speaking investors to come to Galveston. They would not take kindly to him abandoning the press or breaking the chain bringing in the fake commodities certificates.

"Still," he thought, *"the timing is bad."*

The next shipment of certificates was due later that night. If he stayed clear, his *investors* might decide he had cold feet and their reaction was unpredictable. He shuddered at the choices he faced. Finally, as he thought about how much he was being paid, he swallowed hard. *"There is nothing to be done. I shall collect my fee. A few more such as the last one, and maybe I can find somewhere other than New Orleans to retire to."*

He took a lantern from a shelf and locked the door to the office and decided a satisfying meal was in order, oysters on the half shell would help to steady his nerves and he knew just the oyster bar.

"Easiest choice I'm faced with today," he thought as his legs carried him toward the docks. There is only one oyster bar in town.

The sun had retired in the western sky when he stepped out of the bar, pleased his steps were steady and sure. He'd managed to find the right ratio of beer to food. Even so, as he stepped off the wooden sidewalk the risk he was running caused him to get nervous. He fumbled in his jacket and retrieved a cigar. Once it was lit, he puffed on it, as he made his way toward the other side of the island, passing by the hotel in which Captain Hays was staying.

Hays leaned his chair back, on two legs, resting his head against the wall of the hotel's porch, where he was balancing a tobacco pouch in one hand and rolling paper in the other, when the pungent smell of burning tobacco caught his attention. It hadn't been that long before when he last smelled that particular blend of tobacco. He let the paper fall to the ground as he cinched the pouch. He watched, bemused as the owner of the last printing press he had looked at earlier in the afternoon, hurried by, a cigar in his mouth and a lantern swinging by his side.

His own cigarette forgotten, and curiosity piqued, Hays let the chair's front legs fall to the floor as he stood up and descended the hotel's steps and settled into a gait matching that of his prey, as he followed him toward the ocean side of the island. Between the red glow of the cigar's tip and its pungent, burning smell, the Ranger allowed some distance to separate him from his quarry. Thibodaux's sure and steady steps moved

straight as an arrow in flight until they arrived at the
end of the street where it terminated against the sand
dunes. In the distance, he heard the ocean lapping
against the seashore.

He watched Thibodaux slide down one of the sand
dunes on the beach and hurry over to the water's edge.
Hays crawled onto the sand dune and inched forward
until he looked over the lip. Thibodaux had lit the
lantern and was swinging it in front of him, as he looked
out into the gulf.

At less than half a mile distance, as Hays judged it,
he saw a light appear offshore. The moon overhead,
was adequate to let him see Thibodaux on the shore,
but the ship in the gulf was invisible except for the light
which flashed some sort of signal to the ersatz printer.
This was getting interesting, Hays thought. A bit later a
longboat surged out of the murky darkness and slid
onto the shore with a soft crunching noise. Several men
leapt from the boat. The first, with a rope, secured the
boat to the shore. Two others stood on either side with
their muskets at the ready.

Hays thought, "*Yes, it's getting more and more
interesting.*"

A small lockbox was hefted over the side into the
waiting arms of one of the sailors, who deposited it at
Thibodaux's feet. A small bag was also handed over,
which Thibodaux made disappear into his jacket pocket.

The exchange was over, and the sailors pushed the
longboat back into the surf, and climbed back in as they
shipped oars and pulled toward the waiting ship.
Thibodaux hefted the strongbox onto his shoulder and
turned toward the sand dune. Hays ducked below the
lip and hurried down the other side, until he reached
the dirt road running along the gulf side of the island.

He found a cross street and hurried down it, just before Thibodaux crested the dune and started back toward his office on the other side of the island.

As he hurried along, back toward the center of town, Hays was convinced he'd found his man. Thibodaux's hurried behavior was plenty suspicious, but the transaction under the moon on the beach with a mysterious crew clinched the matter. He had gone no more than few hundred yards when he saw several shadowy figures moving with purpose down the center of a cross street. His hand flew to his holster and he drew up at the intersection as out of the gloom, a small group of armed men in blue uniforms emerged. As they approached Hays' position, he saw each of them carried a carbine. It was a patrol of Marines from the island's small naval garrison.

A gray-haired NCO, with three stripes on his sleeves, saw Hays and raised his hand as the men following him spread out in the road, forming a semicircle behind him. Hays thought it best to quickly defuse any potential situation, "Captain Jack Hays, Texas Rangers. Who do I have the pleasure of meeting on this fine spring evening?"

The graying sergeant spit a stream of tobacco juice onto the street, a few feet short of Hays, "If you say it is, Captain. I'm Sergeant Williams and these are my men. We saw some lights offshore and were coming out here to take a gander at it."

Hays said, "You can save yourself a trip, Sergeant. I think it may have been smugglers or more likely counterfeiters. The men who came ashore have already returned to the ship. A couple a hundred yards behind me is a man I'd be happier than a hog in mud if you'd help me capture. He's hard to miss. He's carrying a strongbox."

Hays led the marines to a vantage point near the intersection, where they waited until Thibodaux trudged by. The heavy weight of the strongbox slowed his pace. After he had passed by, Hays waved for the Marines to follow him and they trailed behind the oblivious Thibodaux.

No sooner had the Louisianan entered his printing office, locked the door behind him, and lowered the window shades then Hays drew his pistol and stepped onto the porch. With the marines right behind him, he kicked in the door. The lock shattered the wooden door frame, and with the weight of several marines at his back, Hays practically flew through the door. Like a deer caught in the glare of a lantern, Thibodaux stood next to the printing press. The lockbox rested on the floor, where he had set it. A couple of boards had been moved, revealing a hidden space under the building.

With a vicious grin, Hays pointed his pistol at the smuggler. "Move and you're a dead man!"

Thibodaux stood, frozen in place. Hays called out, "Get the strongbox and cover him."

Two marines dashed by Hays and knocked the counterfeiter to the ground, hard. One retrieved the small metal strongbox while the other leveled his carbine at the cowering Thibodaux.

The strongbox was secured with a padlock. "If you'll tell me where the key is, I'll make these men go easier on you," Hays said to Thibodaux.

The sergeant took something from his pocket and as he fiddled with the lock, said, "Never mind him, Captain. We'll get in and see what he's got."

A moment later, the padlock clicked open. "How in the hell?" Hays asked.

Smiling malevolently, the sergeant said, "Let's just say I had a misspent youth, Captain."

When opened, the lockbox revealed hundreds of commodities certificates. Hays picked up one on the top and it felt just like the earlier counterfeit bills he had handled in Austin. He put the bill back in the lockbox, "Alright, Sergeant. Close it back up. If any of those go missing, I'll personally see to it, you'll find yourself transferred to the furthest fort on the Red River."

Closing the box, the Sergeant said, "Hell no, Captain, sir. I'd rather die at sea than live that close to the Comanche."

Hays own smile matched the sergeant's earlier malevolence. "Now that you mention it, I do believe they'd find your silver locks quite the pretty trophy. I'd hate to tempt you. Why don't I take the lockbox and let you and your boys take this rapscallion to the nearest jail?"

The sergeant laughed. "Have it your way, Captain. You want my boys to take good care of him?"

As Hays hauled the strongbox onto his shoulder, he said, "That's up to you. As far as I'm concerned, he's either a spy or a traitor."

The waves lapped at the schooner's hull, as Captain Hays climbed onboard the ship. He scrambled over the gunwale as Captain Thompson greeted him by the pilot's ladder. With a perfunctory nod, he said, "Welcome aboard, Captain Hays." He promptly turned away and ordered the ship to weigh anchor.

As the sun edged above the eastern horizon, smoke billowed into the sky from the stubby smokestack, as the paddlewheel fixed to the side of the ship churned the water of the bay, propelling the ship forward from her anchorage. Hays stayed near the ship's railing as she made her way through the narrow Bolivar Roads and entered the Gulf of Mexico.

Despite the sooty smoke which curled into the early morning sky, Hays had no problem seeing all around the ship, as she cut though the water. The ship's captain had been provided with the information the marines had obtained from Thibodaux. Hays hoped it was enough to locate the ship which had brought the counterfeit certificates to Galveston. A lookout was stationed atop the main mast, where he could scan the sea with a powerful spyglass.

There was part of Hays who would have been happy to return to Austin, with Thibodaux in tow and consider the matter closed. Given how the movement of the deck made his stomach lurch, the largest part of his mind was thinking along those lines. But during the interrogation, which Sergeant Williams had referred to as *intensive*, the counterfeiter had been completely broken, and now the Texas Navy was in possession of what Hays hoped was enough information to find the ship.

As the sun slowly rose over the eastern sea, the lookout shouted, "Ship ahead! One point to port."

Hays unsteadily moved from his position along the starboard railing and crossed over to the port side. Sure enough he saw another ship, still a few miles ahead, but closer to the Texas coastline. As he watched the ship in the distance, it appeared it was maintaining a steady eastern direction. A commotion broke out behind him and he turned as a blue-jacketed Marine drummer began beating the ship to quarters. Sailors and marines rushed about. To Hays it seemed like total chaos, but in less time than he would have imagined, the gun ports had been opened and the heavy guns run out. The sails were unfurled and added the strength of the southerly blowing wind to the thumping, mechanical power generated by the steam engine below deck.

Slowly the *Nueces* closed the distance with the fleeing ship, until less than half a mile separated the two vessels. Captain Thompson gave an order and the sound of a warning shot echoed across the open water. Moments later, an iron ball from the schooner's bow chaser, splashed harmlessly into the briny water of the Gulf of Mexico, more than a hundred yards to the starboard side of the fleeing ship.

Seconds later, from the stern of the vessel a United States flag was raised. Hays glanced over to Captain Thompson, who spit over the rail and said, "Ignore that, boys. Let's put a shot across her bow." When he saw Hays' raised eyebrows, he clarified, "'Tis a false flag, Captain. I'll bet all the prize money in the world she's been doing the Mexicans' business, no matter who might actually own her."

A moment later the second bow chaser fired. This time, the shot landed less than a hundred yards ahead of the other vessel. As the two crews hastened to reload their guns, the flag on the other ship slipped from the stern. The sails were reefed, and the ship slowed. The *Marigold* waited for the boarding party.

Hays accompanied a Marine lieutenant and his squad of men across the short distance which now separated the two ships. As the little boat bobbed in the water, he desperately wished he had taken Thibodaux back to Austin. But in less than five minutes, a rope ladder was lowered down the side and the boarders clambered up the *Marigold's* side.

As the ship's captain protested, several Marines barreled around him and secured the ship's wheel. The marine lieutenant said, "Button it up. We're turning this tub around and returning to Galveston."

As the *Marigold's* captain blustered and threatened the young officer, the other Marines watched closely as the ship's crew raised sail and turned back toward the port. The Lieutenant soon tired of being berated by the impotent captain and had him thrown into the ship's hold. Hays took the opportunity to rummage through the captain's cabin where he found the log, which detailed the ship's previous port was Vera Cruz. He also found a large lockbox, the key for which he forcefully removed from the unhappy captain. The contents of the lockbox were a veritable treasure trove of information. He found the ship's manifest showing a lockbox with 'miscellaneous cargo' had been marked as delivered. He also found a large bag, full of silver Mexican pesos. But the pièce de résistance was a new letter of marque issued by the Mexican government to the *Marigold's* captain, Jason Barstow.

Once the two ships returned to Galveston, the news of the Mexican government's use of the *Marigold* became news across the Republic. The issuance of the Letter of Marque to a United States flagged ship was denounced by the United States' chargé d'affaires Alcée Louis la Branche. Despite the ship's United States Registration, it was quickly decided between the use of the *Marigold* to transport counterfeit currency, and the issuance of a Letter of Marque, the owners' rights were forfeited.

Several weeks later, when Hays had returned to Austin and made his report to Señor Seguin, in person, he said, "I appreciate the reward, sir. But please, the next time you need to send someone to sea, why don't you just send me the other way. I'd rather be fighting Comanche out west than ever step foot on a ship again."

Fall had arrived in San Antonio by October of 1839, and a cool breeze lifted the flag flying high above the Alamo chapel. The interior was festively lit up with several hundred candles. Supplies, which normally were stacked around the chapel, were crowded into its transepts, as the space from the nave to the chancel had been cleared. Now it was crowded with chairs, benches, and the occasional pew, which were arranged in rows. They were filling up with officers from the army and their wives as well as many of San Antonio's most prominent citizens. Even a few politicians had made their way south from Austin for the happy occasion.

When entering the chapel, it was impossible to miss the building's origin as a Catholic church, as those who entered the building passed by the carved statues of St. Francis and St. Dominic, one of which was missing his head, having been damaged during General Cos' use of the Alamo in the early days of the Revolution. The soaring arches which again supported a roof over the attendees, were carved in the classic Spanish style common among the aging frontier missions, many of which still conducted Catholic mass.

The chapel, along with the entire Alamo mission belonged to the Republic, and its stout walls now reinforced, protected Texas' interest in the southern parts of the Republic. But this day, the chapel served a far different purpose, hosting the marriage between the commanding general of the Texas army and the daughter of the Republic's president. Will was happy to have found a Methodist minister who was agreeable to conduct the wedding ceremony inside the old walls of the chapel.

Will stood with the minister in the chancel. He wore the same dark-brown dress uniform he had worn when he first started courting Rebecca Crockett at the Christmas party nearly two years before. To his left, his best man, Juan Seguin was dressed in his own cavalry dress uniform. Rather than the long frock coat, it was an elaborately embroidered double-breasted shell jacket. Beside Seguin, stood Charlie Travis. The eleven-year-old stood proudly next to the two soldiers, wearing a black jacket and white shirt, with a cravat. As Will leaned forward and smiled at his son, the boy proudly smiled back, feeling grown up, wearing the expensive suit.

The room grew silent as the heavy chapel doors swung opened, and Will watched Rebecca Crockett, enter on her father's arm, as they walked down the aisle. She was dressed in a cerulean gown, which made her eyes look like a cloudless sky at sunset. Everyone stood until she arrived at the altar, where she stepped next to Will. David came around, facing the two lovers and set Rebecca's hand into Will's. He leaned in, whispering, "William, in marriage, you can be happy, or you can be right. Maybe it's why I spent too much time away." He paused for a moment, and Will thought he saw a little moisture in Crockett's eye. "The daughter of my blood, who I love so deeply I give to the son of my spirit. May you together make a happy life. Else, I know where to find you," he said, looking at Will, as his lips curled into a happy smile.

The remainder of the ceremony passed by quickly for Will. Most of it was a blur, and he remembered very little except for the part where he said, "I do," and the minister pronouncing them man and wife, and then kissing Becky's sweet lips. It wasn't their first kiss, but by Will's estimation, it was their sweetest. As the kiss lingered, several officers whistled and coughed. There were certain proprieties to which fashionable members of society adhered, and lengthy kisses in public, even at a wedding, were frowned upon. Will couldn't have cared less. As the first lingering kiss as man and wife ended, Will saw most of the officers were standing, applauding them. He smiled back at them, proprieties be damned.

Blushing at the attention, Becky took Will's arm and they hurried down the aisle and out the chapel doors. As well-wishers filed out, Will turned around, still holding tightly to her hand, and looked up at the tall fortress-like walls of the Alamo Chapel and marveled at the turn of events which had led him to this moment. A little more than three years before, he woke up in the body of a man he knew of as a martyr to Texas liberty, and now a scarce three years later, he commanded the army of the Republic. He had watched David Crockett become its first elected president, and now, he had married the beautiful daughter of one of his best friends.

He couldn't help but think, *"I wanted nothing more than to forget the Alamo when I arrived."* He looked over at Becky, who radiantly smiled back at him, *"Now I want to remember the Alamo."*

Chapter 19

As Will and Becky settled into married life, despite the fact Will's scheduled didn't give him time to take an extended honeymoon with his new bride, he was surprised to discover the idea of a honeymoon was something for which Becky saw no need.

"Will, why do we need to get away somewhere and spend a bunch of money, just to make a baby? We can do that right here in San Antonio."

Smiling crookedly at her, he couldn't argue with his wife, so they stayed in town and he spent more time at home in the weeks following their marriage.

As a particularly nasty cold front caused most of the folks in San Antonio to seek warmth indoors, Will was sitting at his work-desk at home, plodding through the mound of paperwork required to run even a small army. Becky and Henrietta were sitting in rocking chairs near the hearth and Charlie was sitting at the dinner table, with a textbook open. The eleven-year-old was transcribing Latin from the textbook onto a sheet of paper. As Will set his own pen down, he glanced over at the boy, who was biting his lip as he transcribed the text.

"Friar Jesus is a good teacher," Will thought.

Many of the wealthy Tejanos, as well as the town's growing merchant class sent their children to the school attached to the San Fernando parish. As far as Will was concerned, there was no better option which wouldn't require sending Charlie away to a boarding school back east.

Will was dismissive of the idea. Some of the wealthier plantation owners in East Texas who could afford to, sent their children back east to attend boarding schools. It wasn't an option as far as Will was concerned. He hadn't decided if the twenty-first century working-class values which he grew up with or the fact it was the rich plantation owners sending their kids to boarding schools, but Will was happy for Charlie to attend the small, private academy.

As he listened to Charlie's pen scratch across the paper, Will opened an envelope he recently received from Don Garza, president of the Gulf Farms Corporation. Most of the letter was split between the results of the 1839 harvest and developmental plans for 1840. Toward the end, Garza disclosed plans to build a school in West Liberty, where the corporation's offices were located. Nearly all the farmland under development by the corporation was located within a short distance from the town, and Garza speculated a school would allow him to attract more farmers, allowing the corporation to expand.

Will chuckled to himself. Part of him found it amusing Garza's obvious intent was driven by the financial bottom line. To the president, the school was an investment in the future of the corporation. As he thought about Garza's actions, he realized the principle of providing an education to the children in Texas would similarly act as an investment in the Republic's future. With that thought firmly in his mind, Will lifted his pen and began writing a letter to Crockett.

The day's session of the Senate had concluded only moments before and Lorenzo de Zavala was exhausted from dealing with the twenty men who comprised that august body. As the Republic's vice president, he had the misfortune, as he thought of it, to preside over the senate. Their constant squabbles and pettiness were wearing him down. He exited the capitol building, which was still surrounded with scaffolding, as the builders worked to put the finishing touches on the structure. He cursed David Crockett under his breath for asking him to serve as his vice president. He heard a noise behind him and turned. *"Of course."*

David Crockett was following him down the dirt path, which winded down the hill on top of which perched the capitol building. Zavala stopped and waited for the president to catch up. "Speak of the devil and see if he doesn't turn up."

Crockett smiled at the comment and slapped Zavala

on the back. "It's good to see you singing my praises, Lorenzo."

As the two of them crossed the street, Zavala saw a small rock in the road and kicked at it. "To what do I owe the pleasure of your company, David?"

As they entered the smallish building which currently housed the Texas Department of State, as well as both of their own offices, Crockett led him into the cramped temporary office of the president. Crockett settled into his own chair and with a crafty smile, said, "I doubt you'll find this particularly pleasurable. I've got a problem and I need you to solve it for me."

As Zavala moved a stack of books from a small chair opposite of Crockett's own, he said, "What sort of problem, David?"

Crockett waved a letter in front of him. "The problem with competent people is they tend to make more work for lazeabouts like me. I got a letter from Buck Travis and damned if he hasn't presented me with a humdinger of a problem I was ignorant about until he wrote to me."

Crockett handed the offending piece of correspondence to Zavala, who took his time to read the letter a couple of times. Finally, he said, "Public education's actually a pretty good idea, David. We've been so busy trying to hold the Republic together that we haven't given much thought to what comes next. But General Travis is right. An investment in education is commitment to the future of the republic. But we're as poor as church mice."

Crockett conceded the point. "While it's true the Republic may be as poor as Job's turkey, at least we've got a pot to piss in."

Zavala looked askance, "Nearly every dollar we collect or borrow goes to pay for our army and navy, where are we going to find the money to start our educational system?"

Crockett pointed out the window, "Lorenzo, we have a hundred ninety million acres of land in the Republic."

Zavala's eyes followed his finger. As he glanced out the window, he said, "But most of that land isn't worth damn all today, David. How do you propose to make a go of public education?"

"That's a fair assessment of our predicament, but much of our land is rich in timber and there are places where there are deposits of coal and other minerals. Hell, we already have a growing timber industry and I hear tell that north of Santa Fe there are silver and gold deposits on land we won in our treaty with Mexico."

Zavala grumbled. "A treaty their current government doesn't recognize."

Crockett ignored the comment. "I allow, we've got too many taxes to make me comfortable, but thinking about our country's future I've been considering the possibility of adding a mineral tax for things like coal, iron, silver and anything else that can be mined. That revenue would be used exclusively for educating Texas' children."

Zavala weighed Crockett's idea. "It has some merit, *if* we can enforce on Mexico the Rio Grande as the border of Texas. Right now, the folks who are currently running things down there, won't even give us the time of day."

Crockett shrugged, "We'll deal with that as the situation demands. Do you think we can make a go of this?"

"Maybe. Do we delegate the collection of any mineral tax revenue to our counties?"

"Hell, no. They're having a difficult enough time just managing to get the district courts, which the constitution puts on their shoulders, to run. No. But maybe in a few years. Let's talk about the present. Right now, where in Texas is education happening, Lorenzo?"

Zavala thought about it. "Mostly in private schools. I know Juan Seguin swears by the San Fernando Parish school in Bexar. Most of the Seguin kids attend there. So does General Travis' son, if memory serves me correctly. San Felipe has a Methodist run school and there's another Catholic parish school in Nacogdoches. Are you hinting we should work with these existing schools?"

Crockett nodded. "Possibly. What do you think the courts would say?"

Zavala chuckled. "As long as the money isn't used for sectarian purposes, like religious instruction, I think they'd allow it."

Crockett said, "That was my thought too. I got no truck with the Republic funding any church, but so long as the money is only for basic education, it could work, at least until our cities and counties get well enough organized to help carry the load."

Zavala laughed. "You have no idea, David. I'm sure that my fellow Catholics in Congress would love to see more Catholic schools started, and our Baptist, Methodist and Presbyterian members would jump at the chance to see their own schools bolstered. Getting them to agree on that, is the easy part."

Crockett smiled back slyly, "And the hard part is selling them on another tax. And that, my dear Lorenzo is where you come in, my exalted vice president. I need you to push it through Congress."

Zavala groaned and let his head fall into his hands.

John Wharton resisted the urge to heave a sigh. The room in which he sat was cold, despite the closed window. A Franklin stove in the corner gave off scant heat. He glanced out the frosted panes and saw the dry docks of the Philadelphia Navy Yard below. He desperately wanted to be back in Texas, where he belonged. He wondered for what seemed the hundredth time how he found himself here.

He had campaigned for Sam Houston during the election four years earlier. When Crockett had won the election, Wharton won a seat in the House of Representatives, where he'd intended to serve in the government until the next presidential election, but when Stephen Austin drowned in the storm in which the *Brutus* was lost back in 1838, he was as surprised as anyone, when Crockett had appointed him to the post of Minister Plenipotentiary to the United States.

Despite his best efforts, that sigh finally escaped his lips. He would have been hard pressed to think of a city he detested more than Washington D.C., but now sitting in Philadelphia, he had found a winner. Were it not for a letter from both President Crockett and General Travis, he would have returned to his brother's family in Houston for Christmas. Now, it looked like he would have to spend the season alone in Philadelphia. The mousy little assistant to the assistant to the assistant to the Secretary of War glanced over at him and asked, "Is there anything wrong, Minister Wharton?"

Wharton's thoughts were drawn back to the present as he dryly replied, "Nothing a little warmth wouldn't fix, Mr. Jones."

At that moment, the door opened and a portly man, dressed in an expensive, heavy, woolen jacket entered the room, accompanied by a Naval Lieutenant and a cold gust of wind from the frigid hallway. As they settled around the table in the center of the room, Wharton took the opportunity to speak first. "Mr. Ericsson, it is a pleasure to meet with you in person. Even as far away as the Republic of Texas, we have heard of your contributions and inventions in the field of steam propulsion." Having exhausted his own limited knowledge of Ericsson's inventions, he concluded, "More to the point, your inventions have captured the attention of our president and War Department. Thank you for agreeing to this meeting."

The mousy man, Mr. Jones, to his left piped up.

"Minister Wharton, the United States has, since before your revolution, looked favorably on the people of Texas. Let me speak candidly, sir. Your government's recent purchases in our shipyards has been very favorably received and is the reason, Secretary Poinsett arranged this meeting."

Before the loquacious Jones could continue, John Ericsson interjected. "I'm pleased to hear my inventions have reached the ears of the government of Texas, but what does that have to do with me? I'm not sure how my inventions can help a few wild frontiersmen beyond the edge of civilization."

Not for the first time since accepting the prestigious post as minister to the United States did Wharton curse the wildly inaccurate novels making their way around the United States about Texas. James French's novel about the then Colonel Crockett sprang to his mind, but he set the unproductive thought aside as he said, "Civilization is making its way across the American continent, Mr. Ericsson, and that's why I am grateful to Secretary Poinsett and Mr. Jones here for arranging this meeting. I have been sent by my government to seek a contract with you to build a ship. We understand you have developed a steamship powered by screws from inside the ship rather than side paddlewheels."

Ericsson's eyes lit up at the news and a smile creased his face for the first time since entering the room. "Yes. I have been trying to get these ... gentlemen to build my ship designs." As he finished, he pointed to the naval officer.

The naval lieutenant raised his hand, as though picking up a familiar discussion, "As we have said, repeatedly, Mr. Ericsson, your design requires more testing before the department of the navy commits two hundred thousand dollars from our appropriations budget to build this design."

Before Ericsson could retort, Jones said, "And that's where Mr. Wharton comes in, Mr. Ericsson."

Picking up the cue, Wharton nodded. "Yes, that's exactly right, sir. The government of Texas will appropriate in the 1841 budget the necessary two hundred thousand dollars for a frigate based upon your latest designs." With that, he pulled from an envelope several sheets of paper on which had been drawn the proposed ship's specifications, including the draft of the ship and the number of guns required. As he skimmed the details, he smiled as he realized someone back in Texas had taken into account Galveston Bay's shallow ship channel.

Ericsson studied the drawings for a moment, "Ah, someone out there has been paying attention. You've included a forty-two-pound swivel mounted bow chaser. I've been working on a gun design as well as the mount that I think would benefit any ship."

Jones, who evidently had become bored with the technical aspects of the design, chimed in. "If we're all in agreement, the government of the United States will lease to the Republic of Texas one of our dry docks here in Philadelphia, where Mr. Ericsson will be chief engineer, designing and building a frigate for your government, Mr. Wharton."

The meeting broke up, but Wharton was forced to take up residence in the dirty, northern city, as contracts were drafted, and initial payment was received. He followed progress closely as Ericsson began designing the frigate. The following February, he received notice from Austin his role was concluded, when it arrived accompanied by Captain James Boylan. Boylan, one of the republic's naval captains, had been dispatched to oversee the continued development of Texas' largest single expense, and to provide periodic updates until its scheduled completion.

Boylan's arrival brought with it a summons for Wharton to return to Austin. And less than a month later he found himself in Austin, where the recent resignation of Crockett's original Secretary of State, Thomas Ward, created a vacancy, which the president had offered to Wharton.

He received regular updates from Boylan and met regularly with President Crockett, passing along the latest information. During one such meeting, they were to be joined by General Travis, who was running late. They were meeting in the newly constructed presidential mansion. Wharton, a native of Virginia, was dismissive of calling the eight room house a mansion. Even so, Wharton was surprised Crockett, as a native of Tennessee, had not chosen a more Southern Plantation style for the building which would be home to Texas' future heads of state. Despite his preference for the plantation style, Wharton couldn't deny the Spanish hacienda design of the home had a certain warmth and charm to it.

He was taking a sip of Tennessee whiskey proffered by the president, when General Travis finally arrived in the small salon Crockett used as his home office. As he took a lingering sip of the president's excellent whiskey, Wharton found he harbored a degree of jealousy toward General Travis, who even at thirty-one, seemed to lead a charmed life. He had read the reports from the battles at the Rio Grande and the Nueces and knew that had those fights gone differently, then Travis and a lot of other men would have died, and Texas, as a republic, would have been stillborn. He decided there was no point arguing with success, and Travis' reforms over the past few years had given the Republic a small but highly effective army.

Once the officer was settled into a chair with a glass of the president's whiskey, Wharton said, "The latest reports from Philadelphia are promising. Captain Boylan believes Ericsson will have the ship ready to launch early next year. He's contracting the forty-two-pounder long gun to a foundry in England, which has an excellent reputation for naval artillery. As you've read in his reports, it's evident the captain anticipates steaming into Galveston Bay before the first breath of spring next year."

The general set his whiskey glass down on the mahogany table and said, "If Mexico attempts to do anything against us by sea next year, we'll lock down the gulf so completely, their trade will die on the vine."

After seeing the detailed design of the new ship, it was hard for Wharton to disagree. Travis fished a sheet from his jacket and set it on the table. "David, in order to field the new frigate as well as our schooners, we're going to need to expand our navy. I've put pen to paper for next year's budget, we're going to need six hundred sailors and three hundred marines."

Wharton watched the president throw back the remainder of his whiskey, swallowing it in a single gulp. As he slammed the empty glass on the table, he said, "Buck, one of these days, I'm going to make you give this damned budget to congress. Those polecats are going to raise a stink when they see these numbers."

The hotel room was crowded and despite the open window, cigar smoke swirled above their heads. Henry Clay looked around the room, aware that some of the nation's most powerful men were there with him. Sitting on a chair nearest the window was Daniel Webster. George Evans, Maine's leading Whig congressman, leaned against the wall and John Crittenden, Clay's fellow senator from Kentucky sat on the bed. The other men looked to Clay, waiting for him to explain why they were sitting in a hotel room in Harrisburg, Pennsylvania as the Whig National Convention got underway a few blocks away.

The most powerful man in America, at least as Clay thought of him, was not there. Until a little more than a year before, Clay would have bet the most powerful man in the United States would be one of the four men in this room, but around that time he received a mysterious letter, addressed from *a friend in Texas*. At first, he ignored the anonymous writer, as he thought he had no time for some frontier Nostradamus. But after Mexico's declaration of War against France, he came back to the letters and found that very prediction. Granted, France's little pastry war with Mexico was hardly of significance to the United States, but the letter's writer was certainly prescient.

It was soon apparent Clay and the mysterious writer shared a common interest, neither wished to add Texas as the fourteenth slave state to the Union. When the mysterious writer predicted the beating the Whigs would take in the election of 1838, Clay dreaded any further correspondence, but the following missive took a different tact. Gone were predictions, in their place was a call to action. Clay and the other party leaders had been intending to move early in choosing the Whig candidate for the presidential election of 1840, but based upon the letters, Clay adjusted course and convinced other key politicians to let the dust of their defeats from 1838 settle and wait until the spring of 1840 to hold the convention.

The other call to action the mysterious oracle had advised was a pact with Daniel Webster. It was for that reason Clay had called these other men to meet with him this day. He cleared his throat and said, "Thank you for joining me this afternoon. I fear if we do not join together, we'll either get stuck with a former general or a current general. Neither Scott nor Harrison have the vision to lead our country out of the crisis created by the economic folly foisted on us by Jackson and his plantation aristocrats."

Webster laughed. "And I presume that you alone are the one to lead us into the promised land, Henry?"

Clay smiled back. "Hardly that, Dan. I'd happily follow you like the children of Israel followed Moses across the Red Sea. But the truth is old fuss-and-feathers Scott will contest the convention against Harrison just out of spite."

Webster shook his head, "Give General Scott his due, Henry, he's got more than enough arrogance to think he'd be the best president. But point taken. What are you proposing?"

Clay smiled conspiratorially. "It's simple. Over the next few days we each work to build as much support we can get in the convention hall, at the generals' expense. After the first ballot, whichever of us has the least support, he will throw it behind the other. One of us will be president."

Webster smiled coyly at his fellow senator, "And what of the loser?"

"The nation expects a unity ticket, Dan. A Northerner and a Southerner. I think we can claim that mantle."

Webster conceded the point. "True enough. What about you, Henry? If the wind blows my way, will you be *my* vice president?"

Chapter 20

The stagecoach jostled over the uneven road, as the steel rimmed wheels seemed to find every chuckhole on the road between Austin and Houston. Will had been skeptical of the Houston-Austin Overland Stagecoach Company's advertisement to deliver passengers in just two days between the two growing towns.

As the coach found another chuckhole, Will amended his thought, *"At least not without jostling a passenger's teeth loose."*

As he looked over at his son, who was attempting to read one of the pulp novels featuring Nimrod Wildfire, he was pleased with how the previous four years had progressed. The twelve-year-old Charlie was doing well in school and had adjusted to having Becky as a step-mother. As his mind wandered, he thought about how much the army had developed. While still small, at little more than a thousand men, it could stand toe to toe with any like number of soldiers in the world.

As he thought of the breech loading carbines every

soldier carried, he amended his thought, *"They can more than hold their own."*

While the steam frigate was more than a year away from delivery, the three steam schooners were an equalizing force against any aggression by sea from Mexico.

Rather than a shrine, into which the world of his memories had turned the Alamo, now it was the central command for the army. In four short years, the fort had been expanded, allowing for more troops to be comfortably garrisoned there as well as for the command structure to function out of the facility. With two forts on the Rio Grande, Texas controlled the Rio Grande Valley from the mouth of the river and snaking northwest to where the Camino Real intersected the river, 340 miles upriver.

As he thought of the reason for his and Charlie's trip east, Will was especially proud of the success of the Gulf Farms Corporation. He felt he played a simple role of investor and made no claim to be the brains of the operation. Don Garza's sharp business acumen was the driving energy behind the success of the business. Nevertheless, Will felt pride at contributing more than just money and land. Garza and the other investors had agreed to his suggested pay structure. Cotton farming was a labor-intensive process, even for the corporation, and during both the planting and picking seasons it was necessary to add the wives and older children to the labor pool. While it had required more than a little arm twisting and even a bit of shouting, in the end, Will had shamed the other investors into agreeing to pay the farmers' wives and their children for their labor. While each farmer kept about half of the income generated by his children, the other half was escrowed until the child was sixteen. The wives kept all their pay. It was radical for the frontier, but the whole concept of a corporation competing against traditional plantations was radical.

Philosophically, Will would have loved to have kept child labor from the corporation's cotton fields, but when he had floated the idea at a board meeting, the blank stares he received from the other board members told him the idea wasn't ready yet. Every small farmstead the wagon rolled by reinforced that reality. On nearly every farm, every available family member was needed to make a go of it on the frontier. He had learned a long time ago to pick his battles. The corporation's farm would need more automation before changing their rules on child labor, and more automation was likely years' away. But there were other changes which could be made, and that's why he was allowing his body to be jounced about the coach, as it rolled eastward.

His thoughts were interrupted when Charlie said, "Pa, what are those wires for?" The boy pointed out the window to several copper wires, strung between two rickety wooden posts.

Will looked out the window and smiled when he saw the wiring hanging between the posts. "Those are telegraph wires."

"What're those?" Charlie asked.

"The end of each of those wires is a telegraph machine. It's a device that sends an electronic signal along those wires. They can send signals back and forth over long distances."

Will recalled his own surprise when President Crockett sent for him the year after the Revolution had ended, while the government was still in Harrisburg.

"If I recall, three years ago your Uncle Davy received a letter from the inventor of the telegraph offering its use to Texas. Your Uncle Davy asked me what I thought, and I told him that if Mr. Morse wanted to let us use the device we'd be foolish to pass on it."

His son grew thoughtful as he watched the rickety poles slide by the window. "How fast can they send a message, Pa?"

"Almost instantly. We actually tested these telegraph devices around the Alamo and ran some wiring between the fort and the main plaza in San Antonio. Mr. Morse and several of his men paid us a visit as we set the system up. At first the system worked poorly. The further the signal traveled the weaker it became. It took Mr. Morse more than a year to figure out how to keep the signal strong enough to travel long distances. Last year was the first time we were able to successfully send a message between the main plaza and the Alamo and back again."

His book forgotten, Charlie asked, "Does that have something to do with those papers on your desk about the Across Texas thing?"

Will nodded, "Yes. A few dozen of us, along with

some investor friends of Mr. Morse chartered a company called the 'Across-Texas Telegraph Company' last year."

His next question caught Will off guard, "Pa, are we rich? You're on the board of that Farm company and you also own part of those wires. I'd think it takes a lot of money to do that."

Will suppressed a smile, as he thought about how best to answer a simple question which had a complex answer. "There are certainly people that we know who are richer than we are, Charlie. But the truth of the matter is that as the General of the army, I am paid well. When we founded Gulf Farms, I put the land I received for my serving in the army and used it to get part ownership. Between the land and some savings, I was able to buy a part of Gulf Farms. Now, when the opportunity to buy into Mr. Morse's invention came around, I took more savings as well as something called dividend payments that I received from Gulf Farms to buy stock in the telegraph company. I don't think we're rich, but I hope these investments will make money."

It was an incomplete answer. Texas had based the military pay scale on one being used by the United States in 1836. A brigadier general earned more than three hundred dollars each month. In an era in which the average clerk made twenty dollars, he knew he was doing much better than nearly everyone else. Even though Texas was about as far removed from the financial markets of New York and London, Will also wasn't afraid to make his own opportunities. He hoped his investments would multiply with time. If he and the other investors could stay the course while Samuel Morse perfected his telegraph machine, Will knew just how profitable it could become. On that note, Will thought a little discretion was in order.

"As you can see, they're just now running copper wiring between Houston and Washington-on-the-Brazos. It's all still rather secret, Charlie. Both Mr. Morse and President Crockett are holding off reporting this to our newspapers. So, just like those reports you see me reading in the evenings that are secret, this one is like that, too."

The stagecoach rolled to a stop in front of a two-story, wood and stone tavern in Houston. As Will stepped out and stretched it felt as though every bone in his body creaked and protested the abuse the previous forty-eight hours had inflicted on it. As advertised, he and Charlie had travelled from Austin to Houston in two days. As he crossed the street to the tavern, Will thought there was an air of pretention among the town's developers. The street was mostly dirt, the part which wasn't dirt was mud. But to cross from one side to the other was ninety-two feet from sidewalk to sidewalk.

Will secured a room for the evening at the tavern. The coach to West Liberty would not leave until early the next morning. After cleaning the grime of the previous two days' travel, he and Charlie were about to head down to the tavern's taproom for dinner when there was a knock at the door.

Perplexed by the sound, as the decision to stay here had been made when they had alighted from the coach, Will wondered who was knocking. As he opened the door, a short, portly man stood in the doorway offering his hand. "Merrill Taylor, at your service, General Travis." The heavyset man spoke with a clipped English accent. Will looked him over, and there was something inviting about his smile, as though he were genuinely happy to be there. "May I come in? I represent banking interests in London, sir."

Hardly what he was expecting, Will opened the door and allowed the Englishman entry. As he settled into the lone, wooden backed chair, Mr. Taylor sighed painfully. "I do miss the comforts of England, General. Truthfully, while I have the utmost admiration for the fortitude and élan in which you Texians excel, I fear I would not last two weeks in this hardy land. But suffice to say, it seems to agree with you and your family." He nodded briefly in Charlie's direction, where the boy sat on the bed, studiously pretending to read his novel about Nimrod Wildfire.

Will acknowledged the comment with a nod of his own but thought it best to let the other man divulge the reason for the visit.

"I'm sure you're curious as to what could motivate one such as myself to surrender my comforts and hie to this godforsaken place. I have been commissioned by several investors who have taken an interest in your investments, especially the, ah, Gulf Farms Corporation."

Will cocked an eyebrow and asked, "What about my investments has caught your factors' attention, Mr. Taylor?

"As I understand it, this year alone, Gulf Farms is projected to produce more cotton than the next five largest suppliers of cotton in Texas. You and your partners' success is of special interest in that it has been done in defiance of the American South's particular institution."

Will grimaced at his words. "Everything seems to come down to slavery, doesn't it?"

Taylor's normally jovial face was solemn. "That, I regret to say, is as true a statement as can be made, General Travis. My factors were impressed by your impassioned stance during your own republic's constitutional convention against the American South's economic interests."

Will laughed bitterly. "That's the irony, Mr. Taylor, I actually favor the South's economic interest. Where I differ is that I know slavery will be the ruin of their interests, but they're too mired in the weeds of their system to realize they've made a pact with the devil."

Taylor said, "Indeed. Your candor deserves the same on my part, sir. The men I represent have been impressed with the way your farming corporation stands on the cusp of changing the way in which cotton is farmed. You are industrializing the process. In England, the textile industry is growing by leaps and bounds. New mills are sprouting up from Liverpool to Bristol and everywhere in between. But their growth, until now, has come from cotton grown almost exclusively from slave labor, in your neighbor's southern states."

Will's ears perked up. "Are you proposing that your investors wish to invest in Gulf Farms?"

Taylor tilted his head and pursed his lips before answering. "Not exactly. For reasons that are entirely their own, my factors wish to remain anonymous. Let's say there are other interests at work in England heavily invested in their own Mexican adventure, and my factors desire anonymity. What they propose is a personal loan facilitated by the Lloyds Bank of London, my present employer, to you directly.

Several thoughts stampeded through Will's mind as he digested the news. "Just how, uh, invested do your factors intend to be, Mr. Taylor?"

Taylor leaned in, conspiratorially, and said, "One quarter of a million pounds, General."

Will collapsed on to the bed in shock, where he sat next to Charlie, who had given up any pretense at reading and was staring, slack-jawed at the Englishman. Will strangled out, "Just who in the hell are these benefactors of yours, Mr. Taylor?"

Taylor smiled, leaned back in the rickety chair and said, "The generosity in the terms of the loan is only exceeded by their strict requirement for anonymity. I would not be giving anything away to say among their number are several of my country's leading abolitionists as well as several well-connected politicians."

Will's thoughts tracked to Texas' repeated efforts to obtain recognition from the British government and said, "This wouldn't hasten Britain's recognition of Texas, would it?"

Taylor shrugged apologetically, "I'm afraid I don't travel in those circles, General Travis. If I could hazard a guess, Her Majesty's government will do nothing to jeopardize the sizable investments her people have made in Mexico. But an independent Texas, which eschews the United States, may eventually find herself with many more friends. You may even view the loan as an informal means by important men to test such waters." He paused, letting the words sink in before concluding, "I have overstepped my bounds, General. Let this remain between two gentlemen, if you please."

While Will and Charlie traveled in a small coach from Houston to West Liberty, Will spent much of the time considering how to make use of the loan, having accepted the generous terms. He contemplated buying more shares of Gulf Farms, or perhaps a railroad.

"Really," he thought, *"the possibilities are nearly endless."*

As the coach arrived in West Liberty, the only thing he had decided about the loan is no matter which choice he made, eventually he would discover whatever strings the *investors* had attached to the loan.

The members of the board of the Gulf Farms

Corporation met in Don Garza's study. He had built in the Spanish style, a beautiful hacienda, with twenty rooms. The study was spacious and held a large table in the middle. Will enjoyed the soft, leather upholstery on the sturdy chair as he looked around the room. He acknowledged Erasmo Seguin with a nod and a smile. The elder Seguin sat at the head of the table, where his position as chairman of the board entitled him to sit. To his right sat Don Garza, who was president and chief executive officer. To the elder Seguin's left, the chair was empty. Juan Seguin was a member of the board in his own right, but his duties in San Antonio prevented him from attending this meeting. In his vest pocket, Will held Juan's proxy vote. On either side of the table were Clayton Wynters, the former corporal and another invalid veteran, Nathan Hood, and John Bowles, the twenty-four-year-old son of the elderly Chief Bowles of the Cherokee. As the Cherokee Land Corporation had expanded its holdings, they had made a sizable investment in Gulf Farms. As a result, the board had been expanded to include a designee from the Cherokee Land Corporation.

Rounding out the Board, at the foot of the table was Charlotte Allen, the wife of Augustus Allen, one of the founders of the town of Houston. Since Allen had invested in the corporation, his wife had acted on his behalf. Everyone else on the board considered the arrangement odd, but since she had a much better head for business than her husband, and had proven to be a woman of strong convictions, no one took issue with the arrangement.

After Don Garza finished providing the members of the board with a detailed account of the previous year's activity and the regular business was concluded, Clayton Wynter stood and said, "As each of you have been provided correspondence about this, I don't want to belabor the issue, but we have had more than a dozen of our best workmen leave our employment over the last year to make a go of their own farms. Their chief complaint was that they don't own their own land, nor will their families have anything when they become too old to work."

Erasmo Seguin asked, "Isn't it the responsibility of their children to care for them in their old age? That has been the tradition in my family as I'm sure it has been with yours, Mr. Wynters."

Wynters shrugged, "My Pa died when I was young, and my mother's remarriage was an ... unhappy time for me. I can't speak for others, but I wouldn't waste the board's time if these men's' concerns were unfounded."

Will set back, watching the back and forth discussion between the elder Seguin and the former soldier. The two men had very different perspectives. As they sat glaring unhappily at each other, Will chimed in. "My friends. In very real ways, you are both right, but Clayton has a valid point. It is with every expectation that a man can come to work here for us and spend his best years working here. We derive the benefit of his labor, and in exchange, we pay him a fair wage. Hopefully both the worker and the company are well served by this arrangement. But it raises a question of what happens when his body can no longer meet the rigors the work requires?"

He paused and smiled warmly at Seguin before continuing, "Not all of us will have the good fortune which God has blessed you with, Erasmo. I know your three children and my own son plays with your grandchildren, and I have learned that should you ever stop working long enough to retire to your hacienda to enjoy life, your true wealth isn't in your land or your many businesses, but in your family. They will honor you and look after you, in the unlikely event you should require it. But Clayton is also right. We must find something that addresses this need our employees have. I believe our employees' situation demands something that gives them a long-term sense of ownership and security."

Seguin nodded and smiled at the compliment. "General, there are times I believe your diplomacy is wasted serving in the army. But what would you have us do about these men who leave?"

Will stood and took from a satchel a set of papers for each board member. "I'm glad you asked. There are two things we should do sooner rather than later. On the first page, you'll see an outline of the first proposal. I think we'd all agree that, apart from our employees, our greatest asset is our land. But it isn't easily divisible. Our stock is how we represent the value of our company. My first proposal is we set aside a portion of our stock, which can be used to reward our hardworking employees for each year of service. When they retire, they can sell their shares to other employees, back to corporation or to whomever they wish. This will reward those employees who have many years of service and it also provides them the means to become better off. Farming is demanding work, and with us holding both the tools of production as well as the land, at the moment all of our employees have nothing for themselves, other than their wage. Giving each of them ownership in our company gives them another reason to stay with for us."

As the board members read the details of the proposal, Will launched into the second item. "On the third page, I have outlined another means to retain good workers. It can work in tandem with the first proposal or it could stand on its own merits. As Mr. Wynters has pointed out, not all our men are married, and have no family to care for them when they are too old to work. What I propose is that we create a separate company expressly for the purpose for providing our workers with a pension when they are too old to work, or for the widows of the men who die while working for us."

As Will finished, silence descended upon the room, as everyone digested Will's proposals. Erasmo Seguin was the first to speak. "General Travis, I can see how we could reward our employees with stock. We control the process for determining how many shares exist and how many could be created in any given year. It's not to my own credit I have never thought of this before, as it has real merit. Your second idea perplexes me, though. How would you go about setting up a pension plan for a company? I have only heard of governments setting up pensions for war widows and old soldiers, and these have always been paid for with public moneys."

Will said, "I have in my mind a couple of different ways this can be done. The first is the simplest. Each employee can be given the opportunity to set aside from each month's pay a certain amount of his wage. That amount is set aside and deposited into an account with this holding company. We'll call this his pension account. We, as the employer, could encourage the employee's participation by making an equal contribution into his pension account. This holding company, with contributions from the employees, invests the money into a bucket of investments. For instance, there are many corporations in the United States which sell their stock. This holding company pools the employees' money together and buys such stocks as makes sense to own. Once the employee retires, he could then could take his money from his pension account and use it to live on."

Will looked around the room, and saw each member of the board looking back at him.

"*Good,*" he thought.

He still had their attention. It was about to get more complicated. "The weakness of this system is that there are no guarantees the employee's account would be enough for his widow to live on. The second part of the pension plan addresses this. Each employee could be given something called an annuity. The value of the annuity would be derived from his own contributions, plus our contributions as the employer, the value accrued over his years of service and the ability of the holding company to manage the stocks in the investment pool.

Don Garza said, "Isn't that part of what an insurance company does?"

Will nodded, "At its core, yes. Let me use an example to illustrate my point. Clayton, if I may, I'll use you. He's thirty years old now and let's say, he works for another twenty-five years. Speaking hypothetically, maybe he makes a hundred dollars each month. Every month he invests five dollars into his annuity and we match that five dollars. Over the next twenty-five years, three thousand dollars is contributed to his annuity. The insurance company will maintain what's called an actuarial table. This examines many factors which determines how long a man in Clayton's condition will tarry on this mortal coil. For the purpose of this example, our hypothetical Wynters lingers on another fifteen years, arising to meet his maker at three score and ten years."

Wynters muttered, "From your lips to God's years, General." Everyone around the table laughed.

Will smiled at the former soldier before continuing, "Mr. Hypothetical Wynters' three thousand dollars has been invested by the holding company over the entire time and now has grown to more than four thousand dollars. It pays him a monthly payment of twenty dollars until he dies. It matters not if he lives another thirty years or five. The payments are guaranteed until he dies."

Wynters said, "What if I'm married, what will that do for my wife?"

Will nodded, "I'm glad you caught that, Clayton. That's one example of what you can do. If you're married, you would probably opt for what we might call a joint survivor annuity. Simply put, it pays until both you and your wife have fled this life for glory. Because of a greater probability your wife will outlive you, the payments are somewhat less than if it were just for your own lifetime."

Will watched as the information he provided sank in. Slowly around the room the light dawned in each board member's eyes. Garza said, "I see. This could be done in several different ways. An annuity pays out to the worker or his wife until both have died, while a pension creates an account which could pass on to the worker's estate."

Will said, "Yes, that's correct."

The board discussed the merits of Will's proposal throughout the day. When they adjourned for the day, they had passed a resolution to set up Texas' first insurance company, Republic Annuity and Insurance Company of Texas. Additionally, they agreed to set aside fifty thousand dollars in the next year's budget to fund it.

Chapter 21

The day after leaving West Liberty, Will and Charlie arrived at the Trinity Gun Works. Will sat across from John Berry, who was the master gunsmith and owner of the works. Berry and his sons had been awarded the army contract to maintain and repair the Patterson Colt revolvers and the Halls Carbines three years before. What began as a modest contract, the work of which was done between custom rifles projects, now accounted for nearly all the production of the Trinity Gun Works. Since awarding the contract in 1837, five hundred pistols and three thousand carbines had been purchased for use by both the army and the national guard, all of which had cycled through the repair shop. In keeping with the terms of licensing with the Patterson Arms Manufacturing, Berry was limited to building replacement parts for the pistol. A similar arrangement with the United States Armory and Arsenal at Harpers Ferry allowed Berry to manufacture replacement parts for the carbine.

The fact was, the gun works could build both the pistol and carbine from scratch. Only the licensing contracts prohibited it. Which was why Will was sitting across from John Berry. Next to him sat his son, Andy Berry. They sat in a small office, off the side of large smithy. Berry turned to his son and nodded. "Go ahead, and show the General."

The younger Berry pulled out several detailed drawings and spread them out on the table. "General Travis, I confess these drawings you gave us last year sent me to bed on more than one evening as frustrated as I have ever been. Other days, they might as well have taken me to my reward at the pearly gates of Heaven."

As the elder Berry glowered at his son's choice of expression, the younger man ignored it and said, "It wasn't until I got a chance to talk to the Rangers who have been using the Patterson Revolver that I began to understand what your designs were hinting at. Your man, Captain Hays swears his pistol, chambered in .36 caliber, just doesn't pack enough of a punch when fired. The easiest part was designing a larger caliber for the pistol. The hard part was everything else. Watching your Rangers reload their revolvers was a sight to behold. Reloading the current model requires they break open the gun and remove the spent cylinder and then replace it with a fresh one. And that assumes they don't drop the barrel or cylinder in the process."

This wasn't news to Will. He'd been getting an earful from both Juan Seguin and Jack Hays over the gun's many limitations. "I'm aware of the Patterson's limitations, Mr. Berry. I realize my drawings leave much to be desired. I'm a soldier, not an artist. But where do things stand with our project?"

The younger Berry ignored the displeasure in Will's voice. "Figuring out the iron top-strap was actually easier than designing a lever that would hold the cylinder in place inside a single frame."

He was about to continue with his explanation when his father growled, "Why don't you show him the gun, instead of talking our ears off."

Blushing from his father's criticism, Andy Berry pulled an oblong box from below his seat and set it on top of the drawings. He cracked open the case, saying, "Let's show you our prototype, General."

Will involuntarily sucked in his breath. He reached into the case and picked up one of the matching pistols, which were nestled on a cushion of red velvet. As he hefted the gun, he guessed it weighed nearly three pounds. As he eyed it, he noticed the frame's iron top-strap gave the gun a much sturdier feel than the Patterson pistol. He slid the pistol's loading lever out of the pistol and removed the cylinder. He looked at the large cylinder and noticed it had been machined to hold six rounds. He easily slid the cylinder and the loading levers back into place. Will smiled as he set the pistol back into the ornately carved box. The Berry family had done it. They had built the next evolution of revolvers for the Republic of Texas. As he admired their handiwork, there was no denying in his own mind, that in another universe, one living only in his mind, the pistol was the very image of the Remington Model 1858 revolver.

"It's a real beauty, Andy, but tell me how does it handle?"

Andy Berry said, "Before we go outside and see, sir, I want to show you something my brother, John, has been working on." He reached under his chair and brought out a cartridge box. Will was very familiar with the ones the infantry carried, but this one was different. He flipped the leather flap open and saw a wooden frame snugly fit in the box's leather sides. Set into the wooden frame were six cylinders, loaded and ready to fire. This would make it easier for cavalry to quickly load the weapon.

Behind the buildings of the gun works was a gun range. The range was surrounded on three sides by earthen embankments. Will set the heavy box on a table and gingerly picked up one of the pistols, and stepped over to a chalky line. He hefted the gun in his hand. He liked the feel of the balance. He held the pistol out, pointing it down range. He lined up the rear and front sights and grinned. The lack of any sights on the Patterson had been a constant complaint.

"*No problem like that here,*" he thought.

A paper target was set up twenty-five yards away and he aimed and fired the six rounds into the target. When the hammer landed on an empty cylinder, he slid the loading lever out and removed the cylinder. He took one of the loaded cylinders from the cartridge box and set it into the frame and slid the lever back into place.

Then he fired the next six rounds as quickly as he could cock the hammer.

When the revolver was empty, he smiled and handed the gun back to Andy Berry. "Damn, man. You can load it on Sunday and fire it all week long."

They retrieved the target from downrange and Will was impressed with the tight grouping of the first six, aimed shots. The second set of six shots had been fired faster, and as such, were spread over the paper. Will couldn't keep the grin from his face. Even firing fast, the last six had all hit the paper.

The younger Berry said, "That's some good shooting, General."

Will nodded, "I presume the barrel here is rifled, like the Patterson?"

Andy nodded. "Yes, sir. What with all the machining tools we've had to purchase or build over the last few years, keeping the Patterson pistols working, creating this one from your drawing, by trial and error wasn't too hard. Despite using the same machining tools, this gun is so radically different from the Patterson, my father and I believe we can patent it without violating any of Sam Colt's existing patents."

Will had set the pistol back in the box when John Berry, the elder, joined Will and Andy at the firing line. In his hands he carried a rifle. As he set the gun on the table next to the pistol box, he said, "I was quite happy leaving the revolver to Andy's devices, and dedicate my efforts to the problems which are inherent with Mr. Hall's breech loader. We all know that too much of the gas is wasted and vented out through the breechblock. Sure, the bullet will travel three or four hundred yards, but by the time it has traveled that far, with a normal charge of gunpowder, It's pretty much spent. On the other hand, if you put enough gunpower in Hall's gun to do the job at those ranges, it stresses the block and has been known to cause failures."

Will shuddered at the thought. "Soldiers don't react pleased when their rifle blows up in their face."

The elder Berry nodded, "I can only imagine, General. After carefully studying your drawings, and a heavy dose of trial and error in the designs, I believe I have found a solution to the problem." He picked the rifle back up and pointed to the gun's breech, "This rifle uses what I call a falling block for the breech."

Berry levered the breech open, dropping the block down, showing Will where the paper cartridge was inserted. "I've got a lubricated paper cartridge here." He slid the rolled-up cartridge into the breech until the paper was snugly seated at the block. "I liked your idea to use the edge of the breechblock, as a blade, slicing off the end of the cartridge. In my testing of Mr. Hall's carbine, that was one thing I didn't like, having to tear the end of the cartridge with my teeth before pouring the powder and shot into the breech." He levered the breech closed, lopping off the end of the paper cartridge, exposing the gunpowder in the barrel to the firing hole. He set a cap on the nipple and handed the gun to Will. "Let's see what you think of this."

Unlike the stubby length of the Halls Carbine, this

prototype was a full-length rifle. The barrel alone was thirty-six inches long. As he stepped back to the firing line, he saw a target had been set up at the end of the range, a hundred yards away. He sighted down the barrel, and liked that the front sight lined up nicely with the rear. He squeezed the trigger and felt the gun recoil into his shoulder. When they retrieved the target, Will saw his shot was just off the bullseye. "Not too bad," he said, "Is it me or are the sights off a smidgen?"

With a twinkle in his eye, the elder Berry said, "I've put over a dozen shots dead in the center of the bull's-eye, General. I don't think the sights are the problem."

Will chuckled as he was about to hand the rifle back to Berry, then noticed a smudge of fouling on his right sleeve from the rifle's discharge. When he asked about it, Barry replied, "We haven't completely stopped gas from escaping from the breech when this rifle is fired. I thought we had the problem licked when we designed the breech to have a metal sleeve in the back of the breech's chamber. The idea is the sleeve would seal the breech when the gun was fired. Unfortunately, it gets fouled after a couple of shots. But even then, the gun remains very accurate and deadly out to a range of five hundred yards."

"Mr. Berry, you've built a fine prototype here." Still holding the rifle, Will levered the breech open and looked at the metal sleeve. Something tickled the back of his mind, recalling something he had read back in college. "You know, sir, I may have an idea about how to seal the block more effectively. Try putting a platinum ring in this metal sleeve. I believe if you can do that, when the gun is fired it will make a seal that is less likely to get fouled. Do that and we can conduct another test."

Platinum's use as a superconductive metal meant there was a small quantity available at the gun works. It took another day for John Berry, the elder, to machine a platinum ring which was fitted into the prototype's breechblock. After a few dozen rounds were fired from the prototype, in which the seal kept gas from escaping, Will and the Berrys were satisfied with the new rifle.

That evening Will and Charlie joined John Berry, his wife, his sons, and their wives, and several of their children around a crowded dinner table. As the meal wound down, the elder Berry stood and cleared his throat until everyone around the table settled down. "I don't have to tell most of you how much it has meant to not just us, but also to the men we employ, that we have been blessed by the contracts the army has given to us. We are doubly blessed to have General Travis and his son join us today and we would be remiss in not showing our appreciation to the general."

As a teetotaler, and a Baptist, John Berry lifted a glass of buttermilk in Will's direction. "To your good health, General Travis."

Never a fan of buttermilk, Will accepted the toast with a nod and a sip in the spirit in which it was given. The Trinity Gun Works was critical to Will's plans for his evolutionary strategies through which he intended to take the army. Berry's gesture came from the heart.

Will stood and lifted his own glass and replied, "Mr. Berry, on behalf of a grateful army, I thank you. If I may, I would like to raise a toast, not just to you and your fine sons, but to the .44 Caliber Trinity Arms Revolver and the .52 caliber rifle."

Cups full of buttermilk clinked across the table and Will chugged the cloying drink down his gullet.

As Will and Charlie returned to San Antonio by way of a stage coach from West Liberty, Will's spirits were buoyed by the positive developments. Even so, he knew several members on the House of Representative Appropriations Committee would scream like bobcats, when they saw the bill for the new weapons. The new 1840 Model Trinity Arms Revolver was going to cost nearly twenty dollars, nearly five dollars more than the revolver they were buying from Colt's factory. The saving grace was the initial order would be limited. The new rifle, which he was thinking about calling the Sabine Rifle, was expensive at thirty-six dollars each. Just to outfit the regular infantry was going to cost nearly $30,000.

Will gazed up at the gray December sky and watched a few scattered snowflakes tumble along the biting northerly wind. He pulled his heavy, woolen greatcoat tighter around his throat as he climbed the stairs to his office above the Alamo's hospital. The office was cold as he lit the lamps. In the corner, the coals from the previous day had grown cold in the Franklin stove. He loaded the stove with coal, grabbed an old copy of the *Telegraph and Texas Register,* and lit it with a match. An editorial by Sam Houston was visible, as the flames licked at the newspaper's corners. Houston had been advocating annexation, again. As the flame spread, eating away at Houston's words, Will slid the rolled-up newspaper under the coals and closed the stove's door.

Will slid into his chair and allowed himself a smile as he enjoyed watching Houston's words eaten by the flames. At least for the next couple of years, Texas was safe from any concerted effort at annexation. Two years remained until the next presidential election and it was too early to know who would follow Crockett. No doubt, Will reasoned, Lorenzo de Zavala would run. As the current vice president, it made perfect sense. But he worried whether the transplanted Mexican would be able to win enough votes. With no crystal ball to gaze into, he set the thought aside and glanced down at his clean desk.

He unrolled a large map, which stretched across the desk's width. The whole of the Republic was spread out before him. Even though Texas claimed the Rio Grande to its headwaters, the reality was the Republic only controlled the lower Rio Grande valley's first three hundred miles or so. Two forts were clearly marked on the map. The nearest was Fort Moses Austin, at Laredo. At long last, he had managed to get a full company of infantry stationed there. But more than fifteen hundred miles of the river, claimed by Texas, and ceded by Santa Anna, remained nominally in Mexican hands. For reasons easily understood, Santa Anna had been deposed when he returned to Mexico having lost Texas. None of the governments in Mexico City, and Will knew there had been a few of them, recognized the treaty. Eventually it was going to cause another war.

As Will looked at the western part of the map, studying where the Rio Grande curved from its northwesterly route to one which was more northerly, he thought, *"If we want to capture the rest of our claimed territory, forget going straight for Santa Fe. That route takes an army too close to the treaty line with the Comanche, and there's five hundred miles with nothing but dirt and sand."*

Will fixed his eyes on El Paso. *"Take El Paso, and cut Santa Fe off from the rest of Mexico."*

Any planned expedition to bring the villages on the north shore of the Rio Grande at El Paso under Texan rule would be a huge undertaking. As he sat, eyeing the distance between San Antonio and El Paso on the map, he recalled his study of Texas history in college, before the transference. A Republic of Texas that now would never be, had made several attempts to conquer the parts of Nuevo Mexico ceded by the treaty between Santa Anna and Sam Houston. All had failed.

In Will's mind, the single biggest reason for their failure was the efforts were amateurish. There was a quote he had heard when he served in Iraq. "Amateurs talk about tactics, but professionals study logistics." His fingers followed an imaginary line between San Antonio and El Paso. To capture the Mexican enclave on the northern side of the river would require several supply depots which meant more men in the quartermaster's corps and more teamsters and civilian contractors hauling supplies along that line. For Will's little army it would take a herculean effort, and stretch their resources, but he was determined to make it so.

He heard a sharp knock at the door, and glanced at the clock on the wall. Right on time. Now was the time to start designing the force he would need. He called out, "Come in."

The door opened, and Captain Jack Hays strode in. The room temperature had climbed until the room was only mildly chilly. The young officer loosened his brown military greatcoat before sitting in the chair opposite Will. "General, I got your order to report here, sir. But I'm a might confused about it. You had me turn my company over to Lieutenant Ross. Am I in trouble?"

Will smiled warmly at the younger man. "No, Captain. Actually, your service earlier in the year in Galveston was exceptional. Major Caldwell has only good things to say about you since then. No, Jack, the reason you've been recalled to the Alamo is that I have a little project for which I need your skills. Before I get into it, take a gander in yonder wooden box against the wall and fetch its contents for me."

Intrigued, Hays went over to the box and brought out a matte green jacket. It was a cotton and wool blend, similar in manufacture to the butternut uniforms worn by the Texas army. "What have we got here, sir?" Hays fingered a stitched black star on the right breast.

Will leaned back, watching Hays hold up the jacket, and said, "Captain, you're looking at the jacket that Company I of the Texas Rangers will be wearing. Oh, and by the way, you're being assigned to Company I, Texas Rangers."

Hays plopped back in the chair as his mouth was agape. After a long moment he found his voice, "But General, there is no company I. Last I heard, congress has only authorized eight companies of Rangers."

Will pulled an envelope from a drawer and handed it over to the captain. It was closed with a wax seal of the Republic. "What's in there is not to be shared with anyone else. Further, what we talk about here is to be kept in the strictest of confidence. Understood?"

After Hays nodded, Will continued, "President Crockett and Secretary of War, Bernard Bee have authorized this special company on the condition the total size of the military remain unchanged until next year's budget. I have instructed each of the other Ranger captains to send me their best four men by the first of January. Additionally, between our infantry, cavalry, and artillery, those sixteen company commanders are also to send me their best four men. The navy and marines will be sending around twenty, as well. That's about a hundred and ten men. Now, Company I won't be keeping all of these men. No, you're going to spend the next couple of months sorting out which of these men you'll keep. I want you to select the best shots, the hardiest fighters, best riders but more importantly, those who can think and act most independently, while still following orders. Once you've sorted the wheat from the chaff, you'll keep around forty men in your company."

Hays whistled appreciatively. "That would be one humdinger of a command, General. But, if I may ask, why?"

Will pointed at the map on the desk. "Captain, while the Comanche have been pushed out of Texas, by and large, we'd be fools to simply give them the benefit of the doubt. Also, Mexico will, no doubt, test us again, if for no other reason than to distract their people from their own government's failures. When that time comes, I want a small force that can ride anywhere, fight anyone and whip everyone."

Hays chuckled at the evocative image before replying. "Hell's bells, General. That's a tall order. How are we going to do that?"

Will's smile slid into a malevolent grin, as he opened another drawer and pulled out the new 1840 .44 caliber Trinity revolver and set it in front of Hays. The captain picked the heavy weapon up and examined it. After cocking the pistol, he slid the loading lever out and watched the cylinder slip out of the frame. "Hot damn, General, you can reload this gun quicker than greased lightning."

"You ain't seen nothing yet, Captain," Will said as he stood and retrieved a rifle, wrapped in a blanket. He unwrapped the weapon and hefted it. "The Trinity Gun Works just started producing this one here. We're going to call it the Model 1841 Sabine Rifle. We've fixed the

295

gas leakage and it is accurate out to five hundred yards. I believe a trained rifleman will be able to fire up to eight aimed rounds a minute. I'll leave it up to your men to prove me right."

Captain Jack Hays, all of twenty-three years of age was giddy as he thought of the firepower which would be at his command with these weapons. "Sign me up, General."

Chapter 22

Will was impressed by how much Galveston had grown in the five years since the founding of the Republic. The ship's pilot who had brought him across from the mainland said there were more than four thousand souls on the island. Judging by the ships' masts alongside the docks, more were arriving weekly. As he'd ridden his horse away from the docks and into the town, he must have heard at least a dozen languages.

As he came to a wide crossroad, a white-painted wooden sign proclaimed he was looking at Broadway. He chuckled as he urged his mount to head to the west. By the time he was past twenty-fifth, or Bath Avenue, he was leaving the city proper behind. It was a far cry from what he remembered, as every time his horse's hoofs struck the dirt, little puffs of dust kicked up, carried along by a cool, southerly-blowing breeze.

"Not an unpleasant day for February," he thought.

He rode along, enjoying the cool breeze, blowing from the gulf. It reminded him of the last time he had been to Galveston. He and President Crockett had toured the two coastal forts, which covered Boliver Roads, the narrow channel between Galveston Island and Bolivar Peninsula. While he wish Congress had chosen a different name for the fort on the eastern tip of Galveston, he was growing used to seeing Fort Travis on the maps and charts of the area. Despite it's name, he couldn't help but be impressed by the development of the fort.

Battery C of the 1st Texas Artillery was garrisoned there, along with Galveston's contingent of Marines. The fort also served duty for the navy as a storage facility for equipment and supplies.

In addition to the two company-sized regular military units, Fort Travis also served as the muster location for General McCulloch's national guard units on the island. When fully manned, including the reserve units, it could hold as many as four hundred men and twenty-four large coastal artillery pieces. As Will came to another cross street, which was in fact a dirt trail, he dismissed thoughts of the fort from his mind as the dirt trail became little more than a meandering foot path, which he followed until he came to another large, white-painted road sign, declaring to any and all who passed it by that he was at the intersection of Avenue P and 33rd Street. As he sat atop his horse, looking down two tracks which could only charitably be called streets, he thought it pretentious to go to such expense labeling cow paths with street posts. But he then recalled in his own time, the entire eastern end of the island was fully developed. The town developers, Mr. McKinney and Mr. Williams motto might as well have been, "Go big or go home."

He reined in his horse as he arrived at his destination. He was outside a large story and a half, white house. Will had been amused when he had read in a newspaper Thomas McKinney had shipped in two pre-fabricated houses from Maine, but now as he stood in front of one of them, it was clear prefabricated housing in 1840s meant something entirely different than in 2008. There must have been nearly a thousand homes built on the island over the past few years, but without a doubt, this was one of the nicest.

A man appeared from around the side of the house. His skin was as dark as ebony, and he walked with a pronounced limp using a walking stick. When he saw Will, still sitting on his horse, he hobbled over and after bobbing his head, in what must have passed for a bow, asked, "You be Gen'ral Travis, sir?"

As he dismounted, Will swallowed the bile which rose in his throat and handed the reins to the slave. "Yes, I am. Mr. Williams is expecting me."

Will sighed unhappily, as he followed the slave. He felt angrier at that moment than he had felt five years earlier, as slavery had continued to expand its tendrils across the Republic. While things were better than in the history he knew, because no master was required to seek permission from the government to free a slave, he wouldn't be satisfied until the whole horrid practice was consigned to the ash heap of history.

He stuffed aside his misgivings, as he followed the elderly slave up the stairs, where he expected another slave to hold the door open. But when the door flew open, he saw a young, tow-haired boy standing, with his eyes wide and his mouth slightly agape, staring at him. As Will made as if to enter, the boy grinned and stepped aside, while hollering, "Pa, General Travis is here!"

As Will followed the lad into a large sitting room, at the front of the house, he was struck by the number of shelves, lined with books, which ringed the room. A large, wooden desk was at one end of the room and two men sat there. From their looks, Will guessed his arrival had interrupted a conversation. Samuel Williams stood as Will followed the boy. "General Travis, it is indeed a pleasure to meet you."

Will strode up and took Williams' outstretched hand and shook it. "It is I who am indebted to you and Mr. McKinney for agreeing to meet with me."

Will sat down in front of the desk, in the chair offered to him. As he was about to speak, he noticed the boy was hanging back, toward the door. Samuel Williams said, "General, if you'll indulge my son, Austin for a moment, he has positively been bouncing off the walls when he found out who our visitor would be. I believe he has a question for you."

As the boy approached Will's chair, he asked, "General, sir, is it true that you and President Crockett whipped Santa Anna's army single-handedly. My friend, Josh, he said it was just you swinging your sword and President Crockett swinging his rifle at the Mexicans until they retreated in fear."

Will hid his laughter in a realistic sounding cough until he could respond. "Ah, Austin, I'm afraid your friend, Josh has been telling tales out of school. The truth is far less glamorous. The president and I were only two of more than six hundred men who defeated the Mexican army that day. Had it only been the two of us, well, let's just say you and your friend might have been having your conversation in Spanish."

Williams pulled a pocket watch from his waist coat and said, "It's time to stop bothering the General, Austin. Close the door on your way out."

As Williams shooed the boy out and closed the door, he said, "General, I confess my surprise at receiving your letter requesting a meeting between me, my partner and yourself. I'm afraid, your arrival interrupted our speculation as to why you wish to meet with us."

Will allowed a moment of suspense to build as he watched the two men. Williams was dressed in a fine, but ruffled jacket. His waistcoat and pants were black, but his shirt was white. His prematurely graying hair appeared to defy familiarity with a comb and Will would have been forgiven for thinking the merchant cum banker was not concerned with his presentation. In appearance, McKinney was William's opposite. His black hair was slicked down, as though no hair would dare be out of place. His Jacket and pants were dark blue, tailored from expensive wools, and he wore his clothing in a careful manner.

The suspense was enough, Will gaged as he said,

"The Banco de Commercia y Agricultura."

As he spoke, Will carefully watched their expressions. Dapper McKinney spoke first. "Had it not been for what came from it, that particular enterprise would have been more trouble than it was worth, General. The only thing keeping that carcass of an idea alive is it holds more than one-hundred-fifty thousand dollars in government bonds. Had it not been for that, Sam and I would have dissolved it."

Williams nodded his agreement. "We started with some grand ideas before the revolution, but our other commercial interests, here in Galveston and on the mainland, have actually turned out better for us, than a bank that Jacksonian politics has soured our fellow Texians on. If I may, what is your interest in it?"

Will weighed how much to share with the two men regarding the sizable loan he had received from the mysterious Merrill Taylor. Better to reveal a little to test the waters.

He leaned in and without realizing he had done so, spoke in a hushed tone, "What I am about to share with you, I share in the strictest of confidences, gentlemen." Will waited until both had acknowledged him with their assent. "As you may be aware, I own a sizable stake in the Gulf Farms Corporation in West Liberty. Recently, I have received a sizable personal investment which I intend to use to make an additional purchase of stock in the company. Because of several factors, I wish to have the money invested through a bank and have the bank hold any additional stock. I worry what some politicians might say if they were to learn the general of the army was a money grubbing mercantilist. Personally, I don't think they like the competition."

Williams laughed. "No fear of that here, General. The grubbier the money the better. But, how much of your loan are you interested in passing though such a bank?"

As Will looked between the two men, he decided to reveal his hand slowly. He said, "What is the current value of your bank, gentlemen. Before I talk about numbers, knowing the solvency of the financial institution would be helpful to me."

Both Williams and McKinney were silent for a moment, as Will watched the two men trade looks of concern. Will added, "As I mentioned, this conversation is held in the strictest of confidence, nothing you share with me will leave this room."

Eventually, McKinney said, "While it's been a few months since either of us have worked on the commercial bank's books, as I last recall, the bank's assets are one-hundred-fifty thousand dollars in Texas bonds. Our liabilities are the debt instruments from other banks totaling more than one-hundred-sixty-five thousand dollars."

Williams nodded and added, "Nearly all of the bank's liabilities were added during the revolution, when we acted as its officers and used our lines of credit to outfit ships for the navy back in '36 as well as to secure gunpowder and other munitions."

Will nodded sagaciously as he listened to the men.

This was information he had obtained over the previous month. He frowned, as though taking in the information. Then he said, "I'm concerned as things now stand, your bank lacks the solvency to act for my interests, but let me ask, what would it cost to buy your interests in the bank, gentlemen?" There, he had done it. He asked the question which had brought him to Galveston.

Both men rocked back in their chairs, absorbing the new development. This wasn't what they had expected to hear. McKinney was the first to break the silence. "I might be of a mind to part with my interest in the bank. Austin is now the nation's capital and there is a lot of growth going on there. I have a league of land near there and my instincts tell me there's a future to be had ranching in the hill country to the west now that the Comanche are no longer a threat. It might be a good time to not have my interests divided, provided the right set of circumstances presented itself."

Williams smiled at his partner, "I'm probably more optimistic than Thomas is. I have no interest in selling my ownership in the bank. I'd like to think its future could be bright."

Will was pleased at what he was hearing. "For a company with liabilities at least fifteen thousand more than assets, what would you consider to be a fair price for your part in the bank, Mr. McKinney?"

After a long, thoughtful pause, McKinney said, "I would consider my half of the enterprise worth twenty-five thousand dollars, provided you assume my portion of the liabilities."

"My ass," Will thought.

Over the past few years, Will had learned more about business than he could have imagined before the transference had happened. He saw McKinney's bluff and decided to call it.

"Mr. McKinney, I thought Sam was the optimist," Will said, indicating toward Williams. "I'm not sure how a company with fifteen thousand dollars in liabilities in excess of its assets could possibly be worth twenty-five thousand between both of you, let alone yourself. I readily concede the two of you have expended your effort and expense during the revolution and such a sacrifice merits recompense. Now correct me if I am wrong, but aren't some of those liabilities held by the bank actually debt instruments to the two of you?"

McKinney shrugged and said, "A debt is a debt, regardless of who it is to, General. You asked me what I thought it was worth. We obviously have different ideas, but it would be churlish of me to not consider a reasonable offer."

Will decided if McKinney could demand the moon, he would low-ball his own offer. "I'm prepared to offer the fair price of ten thousand dollars to you for your share of the bank."

McKinney wore a studied frown as he considered Wil's offer. "That would hardly compensate me for the past five years' worth of effort. Given my contribution to the war effort, my half of the business can scarcely be worth less than twenty-five thousand dollars, but as I am eager to see to new opportunities in Austin, I would accept an offer of twenty thousand."

A thin smile creased Will's face as he said, "I happily acknowledge your significant contribution to our recent revolution, Mr. McKinney. Where it not for the powder and balls that you and Mr. Williams shipped to Texas, our victory on the Rio Grande and the Nueces might not have been possible."

At the less than subtle reminder of Will's own contribution to the revolution, Williams gave a knowing smile at McKinney before saying, "Tom, why don't you accept the general's offer? Everyone in the room knows that as it stands today, the stock's nearly worthless."

McKinney glowered at his partner and then relented. "Fine, I accept your offer, General. Ten thousand dollars it is. Somehow, I strongly suspect, you're getting a much better deal than that which is apparent." He reached out his hand and Will took it, sealing the deal.

Will gave his best impression of a Teddy Roosevelt smile and said, "Mr. Williams, it looks to me like we're now business partners. Would you do the honors of drafting the document for Mr. McKinney's stock sale?"

Williams agreed. "I'll have the contract ready tomorrow afternoon, if that's acceptable to you both?"

After another round of handshakes, McKinney took his leave and left with a spring in his step, as Will imagined the other man mentally spending his money on anything of value between Galveston and Austin. He caught the thought, and reminded himself that neither McKinney nor Williams were spendthrifts. Both men had robust business acumen and he would do well to remember that.

After McKinney's departure, Williams asked Will to join him and his family for lunch. Will recognized the repeated looks Sam traded with his wife, Sarah, as it was the same look Will traded with Becky. Williams' family was young, there were four children, all below the age of twelve. Organized chaos was the word which came to Will's mind, as he saw Williams' three sons clowning around and being silly. The tired smile of an apology from Sarah was one Will recognized from his own childhood, having frequently seen it on his own mother's face.

With lunch behind them, Sam Williams and Will were alone in the room and the other man asked, "General, after reading about Señor Garza's success with the Gulf Farms Corporation, my own sources have told me you are an instrumental member of the board. After watching you and Tom haggle over the bank, I'm inclined to think my sources were right. What are your plans here?"

Will said, "Sam, my friends call me Buck. Don't discount Señor Garza's own business skills. Much of the growth and success of the corporation belong to him. Let's talk about the bank. My goal is to add an infusion of capital into the bank, and as mentioned earlier, make a sizable capital and land acquisition loan or stock buy to Gulf Farms."

Intrigued, Williams asked, "Just how much of a capital infusion do you have in mind, ah, Buck?"

Will stared at Williams, thinking about how much he would be able to trust his new partner. His thoughts drifted back to the old slave he had seen earlier, and he asked, "A question for you, Sam. I noticed when I arrived, you have a slave working for you. I had heard you were a Rhode Island man. I'm curious about how you found yourself owning a slave."

Williams raised a curious eyebrow. "That's an odd question, General. Nevertheless, the short answer is that after my wife and I married, I guess it's been thirteen years ago now, our family grew as nature has a way of doing, and my wife wanted help around the house. Around that time, I found Billy, who you saw out there. He was for sale by his master, who had let him get grievously injured in a farming accident. If I recall correctly, I paid around a hundred dollars. You haven't seen her, but we also have another slave, Chastity. I guess it was after Austin was born. One of our neighbors had this young slave woman who was barren. We inquired about it and bought her."

Williams paused as he looked quizzically at Will. "I have heard, General, you have particularly strong views on slavery. It has been twenty-five years since I left Rhode Island. I've been in Texas now for nearly twenty of them. My view on that particular institution has evolved, living as I have, among my Southern born wife and neighbors. There is something you should consider, General. I may not be a savior for Chastity or Billy. No matter how bad you may consider their plight as slaves under my roof, consider how much worse their lot would be if they had to toil away in the cotton fields all day."

Will tried to reconcile the image of the loving husband and father, against the image of a slave owner. "Be that as it may, Sam, I imagine their lot would be considerably better if they were free."

Will was surprised by Williams' response. "Would it, General? I wonder. If Chastity had her freedom, who would protect her? She is unable to have children. I'd like to think she'd find a husband to care for her and provide for her, like I do my Sarah. But do you really think it likely? You saw Billy. He's an old man now. Hell, General, he was born during the American Revolution. I think the reason he was injured was that he was getting past his prime to work in the fields. Rather than admit to his own mistake, his former owner cut his losses and sold him. I really do understand your position, but if I manumitted him, where would he go, what would he do?"

Will was bewildered by William's logic. "If they were free, they could freely remain and work for you for a wage."

Williams nodded, "Perhaps. But two things to consider, General. First, is that if they were free they wouldn't have to. The second is that if they are free, my obligation to care for them also is over. As ugly as it may seem to you, General, to me, cutting them loose runs the risk of being just as bad."

Will shook his head. "I respectfully disagree, Sam. I believe the black race has the capacity to be just as capable as we are, if they are given the same opportunities as we have. Ultimately we owe it to them to not hold them back in chains."

Williams considered Will's words before thoughtfully responding, "May your vision of the world come true before the lion and the lamb lie down next to each other, General. It would be a better world than the one in which we live. I admit, Texas would be a better place if every child born here were born free and we were to let slavery die of old age.

Will found what he had been hoping for, in Williams. To Will there were a mess of contradictions in his newfound business partner. He was a New England born man who made peace with slavery, yet saw his role as much protector as master. He was a man who was demonstrative in his love to his wife and children and was a hardnosed man of commerce. And as Will was discovering, he seemed a man who saw a better future would come by changing the present.

Will said, "Sam, I know we see the world through different eyes, but, by God, man, I do believe I can work with you."

Williams smiled sheepishly. "I have to admit, I thought you'd storm off when you asked about slaves."

"If I limit my dealings with men who see the world exactly as I do, it would be a very lonely place," Will replied.

Williams drew up the agreement which would govern their arrangement for managing the bank's operation. Will had him include a provision in which both men could add capital to the bank, in exchange for new shares.

As he read the details of the agreement, Will said, "As we breathe new life into this bank, it's important to me that we not extend loans to plantations or to accept slaves as collateral."

Williams conceded the point and noted it in the contract.

As the afternoon grew late, Will said, "There are a couple of more points, partner. First, I want you to run the day to day operations of the bank. It serves my interests to be a silent partner."

Williams said, "That suits my interests just fine, General. What's the other point?"

"If you're in agreement, I would like for our first act to be the issuance of bank stock to me for the value of the loan, which would provide the bank's seed capital?"

"You've played your cards close to the vest, General, up until now," Williams said, "that was something I had meant to ask, just how much capital do you bring to the table?"

Will's face lit up as he took out the letter of credit from the Lloyds Bank and set it before Williams, "At current exchange rate, around one million dollars in US specie."

Williams' jaw dropped, and a smile slowly spread across his face. "I do believe that this is the beginning of a beautiful partnership."

Chapter 23

As he stepped down from the stagecoach, Will brushed off some of the dust from his uniform. The trip from San Antonio to Austin still took the better part of two days, but the grade of the road was noticeably smoother, and the coach found fewer chuckholes than before. That wasn't the only surprise he'd noticed as the stagecoach rolled along the prairie between the two towns. As the coach had forded the Guadeloupe River, he had looked out the window and saw a surveying team. It appeared to Will, they were surveying the right-of-way for railroad tracks.

Will recalled an article from the *Telegraph and Texas Register* a few years earlier in which the writer had written about a railroad company, chartered by Congress in 1836, but it had never taken off, squandering its investors' money before closing its doors a few months later. A second one had received a charter in 1838. Will was passingly familiar with it, as Don Garza, the president of Gulf Farms Corporation, had heavily invested the company's money into the railroad. By the beginning of 1841, a few months earlier, it opened a short, thirty-mile line between Anahuac and West Liberty. Garza had confided the project nearly floundered when they began construction of the bridge over the Trinity River. Their first design had to be scrapped, and they were forced to bring in engineers from New York to design and lead the construction of the bridge. The project finished six months behind schedule and several thousands of dollars over budget. But it allowed the corporation to transport their cotton by rail to the port at Anahuac.

Will wondered who was behind the enterprise between San Antonio and Austin. Between his own personal financial dealings and the heavy demands on his time as military commander, Will was only able to follow a fraction of the financial schemes working their way through the economy of the Republic.

As he left the stagecoach office, he ran into Ben McCulloch. "General Travis, just the man I had hoped to find."

Will shook hands with his counterpart, who commanded the militia's reserve, as neither of them were in uniform. "When did you get into town, Ben?"

"Yesterday. Took the coach from Houston. I had been visiting the Trinity Gun Works. Damnation, Buck, but they have one hell of an operation, you know."

Will nodded perceptively. "They should. We've thrown enough money their way, as of late. What do you think of their new model rifle?

313

"I ain't never seen it's like. That rifle beats all. Why, a good marksman could knock the chip off old Santa Anna's shoulder at five hundred yards with it. Mr. Berry told me they have completed a few hundred rifles, but less than a hundred are ready for delivery. There's a bit of a challenge to getting enough of the platinum for the sealing rings. Those that are ready will ship to the Alamo within the week. They're also running behind on the Trinity pistol design and expect to ship around fifty at the same time," McCulloch said.

Will awoke the next morning, the lumpy mattress hadn't made for the best rest, but it was better than the cold, hard ground. He looked over to his side, where normally he would find Becky still sleeping.

"*As much time as I spend traveling, you'd think I'd get used to her absence*," he thought.

But she was well along in her pregnancy, and he loathed being away from her as frequently as circumstances required. This time was different, in one respect. With less than eighteen months until the next election cycle, Crockett was determined to secure the boundary between Texas and Mexico as agreed upon in the Treaty of Bexar, before his term of office ended.

Will rolled out of bed, and began getting dressed. This morning's meeting would set the military's agenda for the next couple of years. Even so, it was hard to set thoughts of his wife aside as he crossed the road to the Capitol building, arriving just in time for the meeting. As he entered the Capitol, the scaffolding which had surrounded it over the last couple of years was gone.

The chambers for both houses of Congress had been finished and all of the executive and legislative offices were also completed.

Crockett's office was finished, the white plastered walls would have looked drab and uninteresting except for the various mementos which hid much of the plastering. His own desk was shoved to the side, and a trundle table took up most of one side of the office, where a large map of Texas was spread out. Within a few minutes of Will's arrival, he and the president were joined by Vice President Zavala and Secretary of War, Bernard Bee and lastly, a tardy Ben McCulloch.

As McCulloch took up station at one end of the table, Crockett growled, "Now that we're all here, let's stop wasting daylight, gentlemen. As all of you are aware, all of my efforts to get Mexico to recognize Texas' independence and ratify the Treaty of Bexar have come to naught. They simply do not see what is plainly staring them in the face."

Bee added, "Having been to Mexico twice in the last few years at the president's request, it's worse than that, in my opinion. The lack of stability in their government has made them overly sensitive in their international relations. In my opinion, the only reason they haven't tried to invade us again is that they are bogged down trying to wrestle the Republic of the Yucatan back into their fold."

Zavala said, "Let's not forget, gentlemen, the Mexican government, whether it is being led by Santa Anna, or Bustamante, is proud. The French humiliated them a few years ago at Vera Cruz and because the Mexican government perceives it is much stronger than either us or the Yucatan, they have the power to simply refuse to treat with us. I think, they believe once their internal fortunes change and the central government has fewer domestic challenges they intend to completely repudiate the treaty and invade again, as Bernard has stated."

Crockett leaned against the table and shook his head. "Were they asleep when we defeated the Comanche, Lorenzo?"

With a shrug, Zavala said, "What happens a thousand miles from their capital is unfortunately of little concern to the Centralists controlling the Mexican government today, David. It's unlikely they made the connection."

With an air of resignation, Crockett said, "That leads us up to the present. I have received reports from an agent in El Paso that folks thereabouts are scared of the Apache and apparently are asking Texas to provide protection against the Mescalero Apache. It appears that the Comanches' retreat north of the Red River may have emboldened the Indians in Nuevo Mexico to increase their raids against their traditional enemies. The Mexican central government either can't or won't make any effort to keep the people of El Paso safe from the Indians."

Will was perplexed. This didn't match his own source of information from the region in question. McCulloch beat him to the question when he asked, "Mr.

President, I was under the impression the Apaches are further west than El Paso del Norte. How reliable are these sources?"

Crockett smiled sardonically. "This is to remain betwixt the five of us, gentlemen, but the accuracy of these reports would make me as nervous as a cat in a roomful of rocking chairs, if it were not for one tiny detail."

The three politicians in the room traded knowing glances. Will knew a false flag when he saw it. He cocked an upraised eyebrow at Crockett, waiting for him to continue. "This communication serves us chiefly by conveying to other countries who would care to see, we are acting in the interests of those Mexican settlers who live in the land ceded to us by the treaty of Bexar, to protect them. The fact that we're also enforcing the treaty's border is just a happy coincidence."

As the president had been speaking, Will was studying the large map spread out before them. "You're unusually quiet, Buck. What are your thoughts?"

Still looking at the map, Will gestured toward it. "It's a long way from here to El Paso, David. Near enough six hundred miles from the Alamo, if I recall correctly. If we decide to send a force of cavalry out there, we're going to need at least thirty days to travel the distance. If we add infantry into the mix, then add another fifteen days to that." Crockett's proposal was one Will had been thinking about quite a bit lately and he hated to burst the president's enthusiasm, but he had no choice. "At this time, we lack the ability to support a force necessary to hold the town north of the Rio Grande at El Paso del Norte if the Mexican government decides to contest our claim."

Deflated, Crockett said, "Sometimes Buck, I wish you'd do what a lot of these fine politicians in Austin do, and tell me what I want to hear, instead of the truth. If we can't do it today, then what's it going to take to hold El Paso for Texas?"

"It depends on a lot of different variables, David," Will said as he was trying to think through the president's long-term goals, "What's the purpose of holding El Paso? Is it a jumping off point for a future campaign to take control of Santa Fe and Albuquerque?"

It was an open secret among the political and military leaders of Texas Crockett was determined to secure the borders guaranteed by Treaty of Bexar before the end of his six-year term the following year. "Yes. I know it don't exactly count to my credit, Buck, but I will do everything within my power to give the next president the gift of a republic, secure within her own borders."

The president's words validated a scenario Will had been discussing with Sid Johnston for the past few months. When Will spoke, he relied heavily on the earlier conversation. "We were blessed with good luck and rapidly evolving tactics to win our earlier fights with Mexico and the Comanche. The problem is that amateurs spend their time talking about tactics. Professionals study logistics. In order to bring El Paso under our flag, we're going to need to turn our focus to supporting an army, six hundred miles from our nearest town. To do that, we're going to need to set up a line of supply depots between San Antonio and El Paso."

He leaned over the map and with a pencil, marked a spot on the map about seventy-five miles northwest of the Alamo, "We can set the first supply depot and fort here along the Guadeloupe River."

As he moved the pencil over the map, and traced westward he stopped and marked the map a second time. "About a hundred miles west of the first fort, we'll set up a second supply depot here." The spot on the map was devoid of rivers or other notable markers. "We'll want to verify a decent water source, but assuming reliable, year-round water, we'll put the second stop there."

Will tossed the pencil on the map and waved his hand over the empty space on the map, "As you can see, we don't know enough about the lay of the land that far to the west. We'll need at least two more supply depots to the west, but we need to send out a scouting company to reconnoiter the area and find a route by which we can send our force. That's going to require more time." He pointed to the last few hundred miles east of El Paso. "You're looking at some of the most desolate land in Texas. If we choose a northerly route, the places we can establish depots are going to be few and far between. And if we choose a route near the Rio Grande, then it puts our supply line too close to Mexico. If they find and cut it, our army is cut off."

Crockett grimaced as he looked at the two penciled in depots on the map. The line stretched less than two hundred of the six hundred miles. "That's a passel of assumptions between here and yonder, Buck. I need to know two things. What's it going to take to get to El Paso and can you get there this year?"

All the men in the room stared at Will as he studied the map. After longer than he would have liked, Will said, "To pull this off, we're going to need to expand our quartermaster's department, a lot. Presently, Major Wyatt, our infantry battalion's executive officer, plays the role of quartermaster, with a dozen or so men acting as his quartermaster's corps. We're going to need to split it off and establish a new unit whose sole purpose is to supply an army in the field. Additionally, we're going to need to hire quite a few contractors to haul supplies between the Alamo and these depots. I'd suggest a company-sized unit, maybe sixty men, to staff the quartermaster's corps and a big enough budget to hire as many waggoneers as needed to do the job. We should plan on four depot forts between here and El Paso. At a minimum, we're going to need to station a platoon at each fort, so that's two more infantry companies."

Crockett was mentally tallying the cost and as Will spoke, his face grew long. "That's a lot of money, Buck."

Will conceded the point. "True, but I'm not finished. Before we send a force to secure El Paso, we're going to need to add another company of cavalry, at a minimum. Additionally, we're going to need to rearrange our

Ranger companies on the Red River frontier, so we can shift three Ranger companies to be part of that force. But fortunately, that should not impact our budget, David."

The president grumbled, "Is there anything else?"

Will chuckled mirthlessly. "I want to include another company. As we're all aware, I have had Captain Hays working with his special Rangers. They're going to be the vanguard of this operation, when they're finished with their training."

Will paused to catch his breath before continuing, "To summarize, if we're going to do this, let's do it right. We'll have eight companies of mounted troops. Four regular cavalry, and four Ranger companies. That'll total three hundred and forty men. Add to it, two hundred men to protect the supply depots and another hundred contractors to haul supplies."

Crockett finally smiled, "It appears you've been thinking about this for a while, Buck."

"Congress keeps you up at night. This is the kind of thing which keeps me up," Will said with a weary smile.

Zavala said, "It looks to me, David, like we're going to have to grow the army if we want to pull this off."

Crockett looked over at Will, "Is there anything else we should consider?"

Will hated to deliver unwelcome news, but he had just detailed the easy part. "Unfortunately, getting to El Paso is just the first part. A few hundred mounted troops may not be enough to pacify Santa Fe and Albuquerque. While my information is a few years old, as I understand it, the governor of Nuevo Mexico has several hundred regulars and more than a thousand militia. As far from Mexico City as they are, it wouldn't surprise me if he's been operating his own little kingdom these days and I doubt he would willingly give up the taxes he collects from the Santa Fe Trail trade. To crack that nut, I think we should use a battalion of infantry, Seguin's regular cavalry and a battery of field artillery."

Crockett looked up from the map with concern in his eyes, "We're going to need more men."

Will produced a neatly folded sheet of paper from his vest pocket and gave it to the president. "Yes, sir. To bring all of this together, we're going to need a total of four more infantry companies, and another of cavalry. It would be a good idea if we can talk congress into another artillery battery as well."

Crockett studied the prepared numbers on the page and asked, "How long will this take you, Buck?"

Will leaned against the table and thought about it. "I think we can start by sending a company of infantry to the first of the depot locations within the next couple of weeks. We have a couple of dozen engineers in the army, and I'd like for them to go along with the infantry and lay out the road between the Alamo and the first depot. I'll prepare orders for Colonel Caldwell as soon as I return to San Antonio. He's going to need a couple of months' time to reorganize Rangers along the Red River and to send his three companies down to us. Also, I believe Captain Hays' men need at least another month's training before they'll be ready. Juan is going to need two months to recruit and train another company of cavalry, too."

McCulloch spoke up. "General, if I may, why don't we mobilize one of our cavalry companies from our reserves? We've got six companies of cavalry which are equipped to the same standards as our regulars. If you give them two months' training, you'll save both time and money and won't need to recruit a new company from scratch."

Will agreed and asked McColloch to select and mobilize the unit. Then he turned to Crockett and said, "Liberating El Paso will primarily be a mounted operation. I've decided Juan will command the cavalry campaign. Before I head back to San Antonio, I'll draft a request for his promotion to Lt. Colonel. I'll leave it to you to push it through Congress."

Crockett walked over to the lone window in his office and looked outside. From the Capitol's second floor, he could see Congress Avenue running straight as an arrow to the south, where it ended on the north bank of the Colorado River. His eyes looked beyond the town's checkerboard pattern, past the languidly flowing river, to the rolling prairie beyond. Will and the others in the room watched him as minutes ticked by. After an interminable amount of time, Crockett turned back to the men in the room, and said, "When I think about what we're about to do, gentlemen, I am in awe at the risks we're taking. If we fail, I fear the forces of annexation will triumph in next year's election. I know

I'm putting a heap of responsibility on your, Buck, but if there is one man I trust to make Texas secure within our borders, it's you."

With that, Crockett opened one of the drawers in his desk and pulled out a glass bottle, full of an amber colored liquor, and then produced five glasses from the same drawer.

As he poured the liquor into the glasses, he said, "It's only fitting, with so much at stake, that we raise high a glass to our success."

He raised his own glass before the others and said, "To our continued success!"

The glasses clinked. Zavala chimed in, "To Santa Fe!"

After the liquor burned his throat, Will upended the glass and slammed it on the desk. "To Texas!"

Epilogue

The cameraman leaned away from the television camera which rested on a heavy-duty tripod, and pointed toward Douglas Earl King, counting down the seconds until the show was live. As the technician's fingers reached zero, King heard audio in his earpiece, as introductory music played. A producer stood at a small table behind the camera, where he watched the introduction play on a monitor.

The flag of the Republic of Texas briskly waved on the screen. A gargantuan diamond spun from the bottom of the screen and the words, Happy 175th anniversary scrolled from above, until they were superimposed over the spinning diamond, which was in front of the rippling flag. The producer heard the national anthem playing in his ear, as the scene on the monitor faded, replaced by a sweeping panoramic view of a prairiescape. Villages zoomed into focus before slipping away, as the helicopter which was filming the vista flew overhead.

As the last notes of the anthem sounded, the screen was filled with a gleaming skyscraper, standing five hundred feet above the green prairie. Atop the building two flags waved in the lively wind. One was the lone star flag, the other was a blue and red flag, with a gold Comanche warrior emblazoned in the center.

The image in the monitor faded, as the light over the camera flashed red. Each of the men in the spacious room heard the announcer's voice in their earpieces. "Retrospectives in History is Texas Cable News' special one hundred seventy fifth anniversary series, that looks back at significant milestones since the founding of the Republic of Texas in March of 1836. This evening's show is brought to you by the good folks at First Comanche National Credit Corporation and the Texas National Chapter of Habitat for Humanity, restoring homes and hopes across the Republic for the past thirty years."

The producer watched Douglas Earl King appear on the monitor, as the camera in the room centered on the special news anchor. He was sitting on a tall, highbacked chair, his feet rested on a metal bar several inches above the floor.

The anchor looked directly into the camera and with a characteristically folksy charm said, "Welcome to this evening's presentation of TCN's one hundred seventy fifth anniversary retrospective. Tonight's guest is Elijah Walker, Chairman-emeritus of one of Texas' oldest continuously chartered corporations, First Comanche National Credit Corporation. Elijah, thank you for joining us this evening."

As King announced his guest, the camera panned out, allowing the viewers to see an older gentleman, with dark complexion. His high cheekbones belied his Amerindian derivation. His once raven hair had long given way to silver. It was cut short, and sharply parted down the middle.

The older man nodded and smiled at the camera. "Thank you for having me on your show this evening, Douglas Earl. It is a real pleasure to represent one of the views of Texas' first peoples and share it with your viewers."

The camera panned out and framed both men in the center of the screen. Beyond the two, a floor to ceiling window ran the entire length of the large executive suite, providing a stunning view of the prairie forty floors below.

King smoothed his tie and flashed a smile perfected by thousands of dollars of orthodontics. "Last week, we visited with Jason Ross, of the Cherokee Land Corporation. Do you take exception to any of his statements regarding the Cherokee's early contributions to our nation?"

With a grandfatherly twinkle in his eye, Walker crossed his legs before replying. "No, of course not. In the early days of the republic, obviously we all know that the Comanche and Cherokee took very different paths to adding the ingredients of our cultures into the melting pot that defines Texas today. But allow me to remind your viewers that neither were the Cherokee native to Texas. They arrived around the same time as the white man. We Comanche were here before hem or your own ancestors."

Douglas Earl King's folksy charm hid a highly skilled touch at asking questions designed to elicit controversial reactions from his guests, and the old Comanche, veteran of many boardroom battles, was no stranger to subtle biting questions, riposted and put the anchor in his place.

With a placid smile, King moved the interview along. "Tell me, Elijah, in your opinion, what was the greatest challenge your ancestors faced in the early days of the republic."

Walker's eyes grew thoughtful, as he considered the question. "I think the first mistake my ancestors made was to underestimate the resolve of the early Texas settlers. Back in the first half of the nineteenth century my people were nomadic. In those days, we followed the buffalo and fought with anyone who approached the land we claimed. If I had to pick a point at which things started to change, it was a few months after Texas won independence. My people were afraid that if we didn't try to stop the encroachment of the white settlers, we would be driven from the land. So, more than five hundred Comanche warriors rode out of the Comancheria and attached a settlement, Fort Parker.

"Among my people, we have never forgotten the response by General Travis. In your current history books, it gets downplayed, but the response by Travis was disproportionate. He tore through our land with his invading army, determined to force us to the peace table, no matter the cost to my people."

King leaned in, "You said the first mistake the Comanche made was underestimating the resolve of the early settlers. A first mistake implies a second. Please elaborate."

Walker smiled in the same grandfatherly way as earlier. "I believe it was Euripides who said that those who the gods would destroy they first make mad. It was utter folly to attack San Antonio. It's hard to think about it now, with the city having several million people, but even back in the earliest days of the republic were there still a few thousand people living there, and most of the Texas army was there, too. My ancestors rode right into General Travis' trap. The next twenty years were very hard on my people. Exiled off the plains south of here, we were forced to make our home here on the Red River."

King plastered an inquisitive smile on his telegenic face. "I recall learning how hard life was for the Comanche in the years following the Comanche war. What do you consider to be the turning point for the Comanche's fortunes?"

Walker's eyes swept around the opulently decorated executive suite before focusing on the camera. "Ask any ten of us and you'll get eleven answers. I'll tell you my own thoughts, Douglas Earl. But keep in mind, I have my own biases. I think things started turning around when President Seguin offered to pay for what was then the panhandle of the Indian territory. You can be forgiven for wondering how an event that nearly caused a civil war between the northern and southern bands of the Comanche could be a turning point, but the decision by a handful of tribal leaders to take the money from the land sale and use it to found the First Comanche National Credit Corporation in 1858 was really genius.

At the time, poverty was a serious problem. The buffalo herds were fewer in number and there was growing pressure to our north from the northern plains tribes. Something had to change. My ancestors used no-interest loans from the corporation to found the first permanent Comanche towns on the banks of the Red River. Time, I think, has proven them right."

The camera panned toward the floor to ceiling window, showing the viewer a picturesque view of the prairie in the distance. When King spoke, the camera refocused on the anchor. "How long did it take for rapprochement between the northern and southern bands?

Walker leaned back on the stool, and thought for a moment. "It must have been twenty years. Down here on the Red River, our towns were growing, and the railroads had connected them with other cities in Texas and back east. But our northern brethren clung bitterly to our old ways. I think it was their defeat at the hands of the United State cavalry in 1878 that ended their nomadic ways.

"Here in Texas we talk about the flood of immigrants that came to the Republic during the middle of the 19th century, but Douglas Earl, that flood was but a trickle compared to the number of white Europeans racing across the Great Plains in the United States. My own great-grandfather went to Austin, after our northern tribesmen were defeated by the US troops and lobbied for Congress to set aside reservations on the Texas side of the border. I wonder if that reservation saved them from extermination. That was a dark time in the relationship between the Yankee government in Washington and the native tribes across the Great Plains."

King nodded, as if remembering the events himself. "Truly a terrible time, Elijah. Tell me, how much aid did the first Comanche National Credit Corporation provide to the northern bands of the Comanche after that?"

Walker's eyes drifted toward an elegantly engraved map, on a panel of one of the walls. It showed a few counties, square in shape, that were formed around the towns of the southern Comanche. Between those counties and the northern bands were a row of counties formed out of the land bought by the Seguin administration. Largely populated by the descendants of people who fled the disastrous liberal revolutions of the 19th century, they separated the Comanche dominated counties along the Red River from the counties carved from the old Northern reservation.

Walker drawled, "Quite a bit. The land that the Seguin administration set aside was small and arid. The FCNCC bought land around the reservation that was more suitable for farmland and towns and helped our northern kinsmen build several towns and develop some ranches and farms."

King placed a hand gently on the former chairman's arm and confided, "Our one hundred seventy fifth anniversary series has celebrated that which makes us Texans. That which unites us, but Elijah, if I may, what are the differences that separate the Southern bands from the Northern bands of the Comanche?"

The producer, standing behind the table, watched in the monitor as Walker look askance at Douglas Earl. This was not on the script. The producer swore under his breath as the cameraman quietly chuckled. "Douglas Earl has gone off the reservation again."

As though he had heard the cameraman's soft words, Walker's eyes crinkled as his lips hinted a smile. "Well, Douglas Earl, while none of us like focusing on our differences, I believe your own cable channel recently finished a series of programs on, what was it called? Blights across the Republic, if I recall correctly, where TCN chose to focus on the endemic poverty that persists in some pockets of the Northern bands. I wish TCN had taken the time to showcase how many in our Northern bands have done well, and have escaped from poverty that is the legacy of the reservation system in North America."

For the briefest of moments King looked like he had bitten down on a lemon, but he flashed his charming smile at the camera and then looked back at his guest. "Crime and poverty does seem to be pervasive in those counties inhabited by the Northern band, Elijah. Many of our viewers are curious about your bands managed to avoid a similar fate."

Walker uncrossed his legs, and leaned forward, lightly touching King's arm, as he replied with a folksy drawl, "Why, we adapted to the White man's ways. Had we not, would you be interviewing me in a half-billion dollar high-rise office building on the banks of the Red River?" He didn't allow King time to respond. "First Comanche National Credit Corporation is one of the largest financial companies in the western hemisphere. It is one of the five largest closely held corporations in Texas, worth more than fifteen billion dollars in assets. To get to that point, every Southern Comanche who could pull together a few friends and a halfway decent business idea tried their hands at the White man's commerce. Most of it funded by the FCNCC."

Walker slid off the tall stool and walked over to an old black and white photograph hanging on a marble wall. The camera followed him, and zoomed in to show a Comanche, with his hair braided back, hawking silver jewelry on the dockside in Kyoto. In the background were several sailing ships with tall masts. The old Comanche turned back to King. "My great-grandfather and a few other young bucks set up shop in Meiji Japan around 1870, selling Comanche jewelry and trinkets. It may have been glossed over in the standard Texas history books, but it's no exaggeration to say that in the last few decades of the nineteenth century, wherever you found the flag of Texas commerce flying, you'd find a Comanche hawking our wares too."

He returned to the stool and as he sat he said, "I don't really understand why the same entrepreneurial spirt hasn't been as pronounced among the Northern bands. Even so, I would like to remind your viewers, no other financial institution has made as large a commitment to the Northern bands as FCNCC. I'd like to think the First Comanche National Credit Corporation is the lender of choice there."

King had recovered his telegenic charm by that time. "Thank you, Elijah. We have time for one final question on this evening's show. Given that our series focuses on a retrospective of the past one hundred seventy-five years, what would you say is one of the proudest moments for the Comanche as part of the mosaic of the people of Texas?

"One moment to define our relationship with the rest of Texas? That's a tall order, Douglas Earl." Walker drawled, "Naturally, we're proud of the Comanche regiment that served during the dark days of the War of Liberation. Knowing that our people made a substantial contribution to the freeing of the slaves is something we'll always be proud of. I'm mindful that as the world prepares to commemorate the centennial of the Great War, Texas' role has always been controversial, especially as we never ratified, let alone even participated in the Treat of Oslo. But that aside, if you study any significant battle between Texas and the Ottoman Empire, like the battle of Riyadh or the Siege of Baghdad, among the very first soldiers across the trench lines were the Comanche.

Behind the camera, the technician started counting down the end of the segment. King gazed into the camera, conveying the reassuring gravitas he was known for and said, "Thank you, Chairman-emeritus Elijah Walker. That is all the time we have this evening. Join us next week for the exclusive interview with Colton Crockett, the sixth great-grandson of the first president of the Republic of Texas, David Crockett, as he takes us through the battlefields of the War of Liberation. This is Douglas Earl King, reporting from Comanche City."

Stay tuned for the continued adventures of the Lone Star Reloaded Series, book 3 in the Q1 of 2018.

Thank you for reading

If you enjoyed reading Comanche Moon Falling Please help support the author by leaving a review where you purchased the book. For announcements, promotions, special offers, you can sign up for updates from Drew McGunn at:

https://drewmcgunn.wixsite.com/website

About the Author

Drew McGunn lives on the Texas gulf coast with his wonderfully supportive wife. He started writing in high school and after college worked the nine-to-five grind for many years, while the stories in his head rattled around, begging to be released.

After one too many video games, Drew awoke from his desire for one more turn, and returned to his love of the printed word. His love of history led him to study his roots, and as a sixth generation Texan, he decided to write about the founding of Texas as a Republic. There were many terrific books about early Texas, but hardly any about alternate histories of the great state. With that in mind, he wrote his debut novel "Forget the Alamo!" as a reimagining of the first days of the Republic. Comanche Moon Falling is a continuation of the series.

When he's not writing or otherwise putting food on the table, Drew enjoys traveling to historic places, or reading other engaging novels from up and coming authors.

Made in the USA
San Bernardino, CA
23 January 2020